THE START

OF
THE

E
N
D

OF
IT

ALL

Other books by Carol Emshwiller

Carmen Dog

Joy in Our Cause

Verging on the Pertinent

THE START OF THE END OF IT ALL

6/3/91

to Marcia,

Carol Emshwiller

SHORT FICTION

CAROL EMSHWILLER

Mercury House, Incorporated
San Francisco

This is a work of fiction. Names, characters, places, and incidents either are the product of the author's imagination or are used fictitiously. Any resemblance to actual events, locales, or persons, living or dead, is entirely coincidental.

Published in somewhat different form in Great Britain by The Women's Press Ltd, 1990. Grateful acknowledgment is made to these publications: *Universe 11, Omni, The Little Magazine, Twilight Zone, Ice River, Fantasy and Science Fiction, Orbit 6, Orbit 7, Cavalier, Dangerous Visions,* and *Strange Plasma.*

Published in the United States by
Mercury House
San Francisco, California

Printed on acid-free paper
Manufactured in the United States of America

Library of Congress Cataloging-in-Publication Data
Emshwiller, Carol.
    The start of the end of it all : short fiction / Carol Emshwiller.
      p.   cm.
    ISBN 1–56279–001–3 : $17.95. — ISBN 1–56279–002–1 (pbk.) : $10.95
    I. Title
PS3555.M54S74   1991
813'.54 — dc20   90–49563
                                                                      CIP

To Eve, Susan, and Peter

Contents

/ / /

THE START
OF THE END
OF IT ALL
/ / /

First the distant sound of laughter. I thought it was laughter. Kind of chuckling . . . choking maybe . . . or spasms of some sort. Can't explain it. Scary laughter coming closer. Then they came in in a scary way, pale, with shiny raincoats and fogged glasses, sat down, and waited out the storm here. Asked only for warm water to sip. Crossed their legs with refined grace and watched late-night TV. They spoke of not wanting to end up in a museum . . . neither them, nor their talismans, nor their flags, their dripping flags. They looked so vulnerable and sad . . . chuckling, choking sad that I lost all fear of them. They left in the morning, most of them. All but three left. Klimp, their regional director, and two others stayed.

"It is important and salutary to speak of incomprehensible things," they said, and so we did till dawn. They also said that their love for this planet, "this splendid planet," knows no bounds and that they could take over with just a tiny smidgen of violence, especially as we had been softening up the people ourselves as though in preparation for them. I believed them. I saw their love for this place in their eyes.

"But am I"—and I asked them this directly—"am I, a woman, and a woman of, should I say, a certain age, am I really to be included in the master plan?" They implied, yes, chuckling (choking), but then everyone has always tried to give me that impression (former husband especially) and it never was true

1

before. It's nice, though, that they said they couldn't do it without me and others like me.

What they also say is, "As sun to earth, so kitchen is to house, and so house is to the rest of the world. Politics," they say, "begins at home, and most especially in the kitchen, place of warmth, chemistry, and changes, means toward ends. Grandiose plans cooked up here. A house," they say, "hardly need be more than a kitchen and a few good chairs." Where they come from that's the way it is. And I agree that, if somebody wanted to take over the earth, it's true: they could do worse than to do it from the kitchen.

They also say that it will be necessary to let the world lie fallow and recoup for fifteen years. That's about step number three of their plan.

"But first," they say (step number one), "it will be necessary to get rid of the cats."

/ / /

Klimp! His kind did not, absolutely not, descend from apelike creatures, but from higher beings. Sky folk. We can't understand that, he said. Their sex organs are, he told me, pure and unconnected to excretory organs in any way. Body hair in different patterns. None, and this is significant, under the arms, and, actually, what's on their head really isn't hair either. Just looks like it. They're a manifestation in living form of a kind of purity not to be achieved by any of us except by artificial means. They also say that, because of what they are, they will do a lot better with this world than we do. Klimp promises me that and I believe him. They're simply crazy about this world. "It's a treasure," Klimp keeps saying.

I ask, "How much time is there, actually, till doomsday, or whatever you call it?"

No special name, though Restoration Day or (even better) Resurrection Day might serve. No special time either. ("Might take a lifetime. Might not.") They live like that but without confusion.

/ / /

But first, as they say, it is necessary to get rid of the cats, though I am trying to see both sides: (a) Klimp's and his friends' and (b) trying to come to terms with three hyperactive cats that I've had since the divorce. The white one is throwing up on the rug. Turns out to be a rubber band and a long piece of string.

/ / /

Of the three, Klimp is clearly mine. He likes to pass his cool hands . . . his always-cold hands through my hair, but if I try to sit on his lap to confirm our relationship, he can't bear that. We've known each other almost two weeks now, shuffled along in the park (I name the trees), the shady side of streets, examined the different kinds of grasses. (I never noticed how many kinds there were.) He looks all right from every angle but one, and he always wears his raincoat so we don't have any trouble.

"I accept," I say, when he asks me a few days later, anthropomorphizing as usual, and tired of falling in love with TV stars and newsmen or the equivalent. I put on my old wedding ring and start, then, to keep a record of the takeover, kitchen by kitchen by kitchen . . .

Klimp says, "Let's get in bed and see what happens."

Something does, but I won't say what.

I haven't seen any of them, even Klimp, totally naked, though a couple of times I saw him wearing nothing but a teacup.

(They read our sex manuals before beginning their takeover.)

But willing servants (women are) of almost anything that looks or feels like male or has a raspy voice, regardless of the real sex whatever that may be, or if sex at all. And sometimes one has to make do (we older women do, anyway) with the peculiar, the alien or the partly alien, the egocentric, the disgruntled, the dissipated . . . But also, and especially, willing servants of things that can fly, or things, rather, that may have descended from things that could fly once or things that could almost fly (though lots of things can *almost* fly). But I heard some woman say that someone told her that one had been seen actually vibrating himself into the sky, arched back, hands in pockets . . . had also, this person said, been seen throwing money off the Ambassador Bridge. The ultimate subversion.

Also I heard they may have already infiltrated the mayonnaise company. A great deal of harm can be done simply by loosening all the jar lids. Is this without violence! And when one of them comes up behind you on the street, grabs your arm with long, strong thumb and forefinger, quietly asking for money, and your watch, and promising not to hurt you . . . especially not to hurt you, then you give them. Afterward I hear they sometimes crumple the bills into their big, white pipes and smoke them on the spot. They flush the watches down toilets. This last I've seen myself.

But is all this without violence! Klimp takes the time to explain it to me. We're using the same word with two somewhat different meanings, as happens with people from different places. But then there's never any need to justify the already righteous. Sure of his own kindnesses, as look at him right now, Klimp, kiss to earlobe and one finger drawing tickly circles in the palm of my hand. He sees, he says, the Eastern Seaboard as it could be were it the kind of perfection that it should be. He says it will be splendid and these are means toward that end.

Random pats, now, in the region of the belly button. (His pats. My belly button.) Asks me if I ever saw a cat fly. It's important. "Not exactly," I say, "but I saw one fall six stories once and not get hurt, if that counts."

As we sit here, the white cat eats a twenty-dollar bill.

/ / /

I was divorced, as I mentioned. We were, all of us women who are in this thing with them, all divorced. DIVORCE. A tearing word. I was divorced in the abdomen and in the chest. In those days I sometimes telephoned just to hear "Hello." I was divorced at and against sunsets, hills, fall leaves, and, later on in the spring, I was divorced from spring. But now, suddenly, I have not failed everything. None of us has failed. And we want nothing for ourselves. Never have. We want to do what's best for the planet.

Sometimes lately, when the afternoon is perfect . . . a pale, humid day, the kind they like the most . . . cool . . . white sky . . . and Klimp or one of the others (it's hard to tell them apart sometimes, though Klimp usually wears the largest cap . . . yellow plastic cap) . . . when the one I think is Klimp is on the lawn chair figuring how to get rid of all the bees by too much spraying of fruit trees or how best to distribute guns to the quick-tempered or some such problem, then I think that life has turned perfect already, though they keep telling me that comes later . . . but perfect right now, at least as far as I'm concerned. I like it with the takeover only half begun. Doing the job, it's been said, is half the fun. To me it's all the fun. And I especially like the importance of the kitchen for things other than mere food. Yesterday, for instance, I destroyed (at the self-cleaning setting) a bushel of important medical records plus several reference works and dictionaries, also textbooks, and a bin of brand-new maps. When I see Klimp, then, on the lawn, or all three sometimes, and all three gauzy, pale blue flags unfurled, and they're chuckling, and whispering, and choking together, I feel as though the kitchen itself, by its several motors, will take off into the air . . . hum itself into the sunset, riding smoothly on a warm updraft, all its engines turned to low. I want to tell them how I feel. "Perfect," I say. "Everything's perfect except for these three things: wet sand tracked into the vestibule, stepping on the tails of cats, and please don't look at me with such a steady, fishlike gaze, because when you do, I can't read the recipes you gave me for things that make people feel good, rot the brain, and cost a lot."

But I shouldn't have reminded them of the cats. They are saying again that I have to choose between the cats or them. They say their talismans are getting lost under the furniture, that some of their wafers have been found chewed on and spat out. They say I don't realize the politics of the situation and I suppose I don't. I never did pay much attention to politics. "You have to realize everything is political," they say, "even cats."

I'm thinking perhaps I'll take them to the state park outside of town. They'll do all right. Cats do. Get rid of them in some nice place I'd like to be in myself, by a river, near some hills . . . Leave them with full stomachs. Be up there and back by evening. Klimp will be pleased.

/ / /

But look what's coming true now! Dead cats . . . drowned cats washed up on the beaches. I saw the pictures on the news. Great flocks of cats, as though they had been caught at sea in a storm, or as though they had flown too far from shore and fallen into the ocean from exhaustion. Perhaps I understand even less about politics than I thought.

I decide to please my cats with a big dish of fresh fish. (Klimp is out tonight turning up amplifiers in order to impair hearing, while the others are out pulling the hands off clocks.)

The house has a sort of air space above the attic. If the little vent were removed, a cat could live up there quite comfortably, climbing up and down by way of the roof of the garage and a tree near it. A cat could be fed secretly outside and might not be recognized as one who lived here. It isn't that I don't dedicate myself to Klimp and the others. I do, but, as for the cats, I also dedicate myself to them.

/ / /

Klimp and the others come back at dawn, flags furled, tired but happy. "Job's well done," they say. I fill the bathtub, boil water for them to dip their wafers in. They chuckle, pat me. (They're so demonstrative. Not at all like my husband used to be.) They move their hands in cryptic signals, or perhaps it's nervousness. They blink at each other. They even blink at me. I'm thinking this is pure joy. Must never end. And now I have the cats and them also. I love. I love. Luff . . . loove . . . loofe . . . they can't pronounce it, but they use the word all the time. Sometimes I wonder exactly what they mean by it, it comes so easily to their lips.

At least I know what *I* mean by "love," and I know I've gone from having nothing and nobody (I had the cats, of course, but I have people now) to having all the best things in life: love, and a kind of family, and meaningful work to do . . . world-shaking work . . . All of us useless women, now part of a vast international kitchen network and I'm wondering if we can go even further. Get to be sort of a world-watching crew while the earth lies fallow. "Listen, what about us in all this?" I ask, my arm across Klimp's barrel chest. "We're no harm. We're all over childbearing age. What about if we watch over things for you during the time the earth rests up?"

He answers, "Is as does. Does as is." (If he really loves me, he'll do it.)

"Listen, we could see to it that no smart ape would start leveling out hills."

"What we need," he says, "are a lot of little, warm, wet places." He tells me he's glad the cats are no longer here. He says, "I know you love ('luff') me now," and wants me to eat a big pink wafer. I try to get out of it politely. Who knows what's in it? And the ones *they* always eat are white. But what has made me worthy of this honor, just that the cats are no longer in view?

"All right," I say, "but just one tiny bite." Tastes dry and chalky and sweet . . . too sweet. Klimp . . . but I see it's not Klimp this time . . . one of the others . . . urges another bite. "Where's Klimp?"

"I also love ('luff') you," he says and, "Time to find lots of little dark, wet places. We told you already."

I'm wondering what sort of misunderstanding is happening right now.

/ / /

I have a vision of a skyful of minnows . . . silver schools of minnows . . . the buzz of air . . . the tinkling . . . the glitter . . . *my* minnows flashing by. Why not? And then more and more, until the sky is bursting with them and I can't tell any more which are mine. Somewhere a group of thirty-six . . . no, lots more than that . . . eighty-four . . . I'm not sure. One hundred and eight? Yes, my group among the others. They, my own, swim back to me, then swirl up and away. Forever. And forever mine. Why not?

I wake to the sounds of sheep. I have a backyard full of them. Ewes, it turns out. They are contented. As I am. I watch the setting moon, eat the oranges and onions Klimp brings me, sip mint tea, feel slightly nauseous, get a call from a friend. Seems she's had sheep for a couple of weeks now. Took her cats up to the state park just as I'd thought of doing and had sheep the next day, though she wishes now she had put those cats in the attic as I've done, but she's wondering will I get away with it? She wants me to come over, secretly if I can. She says it's important. But there's a lot of work to be done here. Klimp is talking, even now, about important projects such as opening the wild animal cages at the zoo and the best way to drop water into mailboxes and how about digging potholes in the roads? How about handing out free cartons of cigarettes? He hangs up the phone for me and brings me another onion. I don't need any other friends.

She calls me again a few days later. She says she thinks she's pregnant, but we both know that can't be true. I say to see a doctor. It's probably a tumor. She says they don't want her to, that they drove her car away somewhere. She thinks they pushed it off the pier along with a lot of others. I say I thought they were doing just the opposite. Switching road signs and such to get people to drive around wasting gas. Anyway, she says, they won't let her out of the house. Well, I can't be bothered with the delusions of every old lady around. I have enough troubles of my own and I haven't been feeling so well lately either, tired all the time and a little sick. Irritable. Too irritable to talk to her.

The ewes in the backyard are all obviously pregnant. They swell up fast. The bitch dog next door seems pregnant, too, which is funny because I thought she was a spay. It makes you stop and think. I wonder, what if I wanted to go out? And is my old car still in the garage? They've been watching me all the time lately. I can't even go to the bathroom without one of them listening outside the door. I haven't been able to feed the cats. I used to hate it when they killed birds, but now I hope there are some winter birds around. I think I will put up a bird feeder. I think spring is coming. I've lost track, but I'm sure we're well into March now. Klimp says, "I luff, I luff," and wants to rub my

back, but I won't let him . . . not any more . . . or not right now.
Why won't they all three go out at the same time as they used to?
What's wrong with me lately? Can't sleep . . . itch all over . . .
angry at nothing . . . They're not so bad, Klimp and the others.
Actually better than most. Always squeeze the toothpaste from
the bottom, leave the toilet seat down . . . they don't cut their
toenails and leave them in little piles on the night table, use their
own towels usually, listen to me when I talk. Why be so angry?

I must try harder. I will tell Klimp that he can rub my back
later. I'll apologize for being angry and I'll try to do it in a nice
way. Then I'll go into the bedroom, shut the door, brace it with a
chair and be really alone for a while. Lie down and relax. I know
I'll miss cooking up some important concoctions, but I've
missed a lot of things lately.

/ / /

Next thing I know I wake up and it's dark outside. I have a
terrible stomach ache as if a lot of gas is rolling around inside. I
feel strange. I have to get out of here.

I can hear one of them moving outside my door. I hear him
brush against it . . . a chitinous scraping. "Let me in. I loofe you."
Then there's that kind of giggle. He can't help it, I know, but it's
getting on my nerves. "Is as does," he says. "Now you see that." I
put on my sneakers and grab my old sweatshirt.

"Just a minute, dear" — I try to say it sweetly — "I just woke up.
I'll let you in in a minute. I need a cup of tea. I'd love it if you'd
get one for me." (I really do need one, but I'm not going to wait
around for it.) I open the window and step out on the garage
roof, cross to the tree, and climb down. Not hard. I'm a chubby
old woman, but I'm in pretty good shape. The cats follow me. All
three.

As I trot by, I see all the ewes in the backyard lying down and
panting. God! I have to get out of here. I run, holding my
stomach. I know of an empty lot with an old Norway spruce tree
that comes down to the ground all around. I think I can make
that. I see cats all around me, more than just my own. Maybe six
or eight. Maybe more. Hard to see because, and thank God,

Klimp has broken all the streetlights. I cross vacant lots, tear through brambles, finally crawl under the spruce branches and lie down panting . . . panting. It feels right to pant. I saw my cat do that under similar circumstances.

I have them. I give birth to them, the little silvery ones squeaking . . . sparkling. I'll surprise Klimp with eighty-four . . . ninety-six . . . one hundred and eight? Look what we did together! But it wasn't Klimp and I. Suddenly I realize it. It was Klimp and that other. Through me. And all those ewes . . . fourteen ewes and one bitch dog times eighty-four or one hundred and eight. That's well over a thousand of them that I know about already.

My little ones cough and flutter, try to swim into the air, but only raise themselves an inch or so . . . hardly that. They smell of fish. They slither over one another as though looking for a stream. They are covered with a shiny, clear kind of slime. Do I love them or hate them?

So that's the way it is. As with us humans, it takes two, only I wasn't one of them. I might just as well have been a bitch or a ewe . . . better, in fact, to have been some dumb animal. "Lots of little warm, wet places!" It must have been a big night, that night. Some sacred sort of higher beings they turned out to be. That's not love . . . nor luff, nor loove. Whatever they mean by those words, this can't be it.

But look what all those hungry cats are doing. Eating up my minnows. I try to gather the little things up, but they're too slippery. I can't even get one. I try to push the cats away, but there are too many of them and they all seem very hungry. And then, suddenly, Klimp is there helping me, kicking out at the cats in a fury and gathering up minnows at the same time. For him it's easy. They stick to him wherever he touches them. He's up to his elbows in them. They cluster on his ankles like barnacles, but I'm afraid lots are eaten up already. And now he's kicking out at me. Hits me hard on the cheek and shoulder. Stamps on my hand.

"I'm confused," I say, getting up, thinking he can explain all this in a fatherly way, but now he stamps on my foot and knocks me down with his elbow. Then I see him give a kind of hop step, the standard dance way of getting from one foot to the other. He's going to lift. I don't know how I know, but I do. He has that look on his face, too, eyes half closed . . . ecstasy. I see it now — flying, or almost flying, is their ultimate orgasm . . . their true love (or loofe) . . . if this *is* flying. Yes, he's up, but only inches, and struggling . . . pulling at my fingers. This is *not* flying.

"You call this flying!" I yell. "And you call this whole thing being a pure aerial being! I say, cloaca . . . cloaca, I say, is your only orifice." I have, by now, one leg hooked around his neck and both hands grabbing his elbow, and he's not really more than one foot off the ground at the very highest, if that, and struggling for every inch. "Cloaca! You and your 'luff'!" The slime and minnows are all over him. He seems dressed in them . . . sparkling like sequins. He's too slippery with them. I can't hang on. I slip off and drop lightly into the brambles. Klimp slides away at a diagonal, right shoulder leading, and glides, luminous with slime, just off the ground. Disappears in a few seconds behind the trees. "Cloaca!" I shout after him. It's the worst I've ever said to anyone. "Filthy fish thing! Call that flying!"

/ / /

Everything is going wrong. It always does, I should know that by now. I'm thinking that my former husband slipped away in almost exactly the same way. He was slippery too, sneaked out first with younger women and then left me for one of them later on. I tried to grab at him the same way I grabbed at Klimp. Tried to hold him back. I even tried to change my ways to suit him. I know I've got faults. I talk too much. I worry about things that never happen (though they did finally happen, almost all of them, and *now* look).

I hobble back (with cats), too angry to feel the pain of my bruises. No sign of the ewes or the dog, but the backyard looks all silvery. No minnows left there, though, just slime. I have to admit it's lovely. Makes me feel romantic feelings for Klimp in spite of myself. I wonder if he saw it. They're so sensitive to beautiful things and they love glitter. I can see why.

The house is dark. I open the door cautiously. I let in all eight . . . no, nine . . . maybe ten cats. I call. No answer. I lock all the windows and the doors. I check under the beds and in the closets. Nobody. I go into the bathroom and lock that door too. Fill tub. Take off my clothes. Find two minnows stuck inside my sweatshirt. One is dead. The other very weak. I put him in the tub and he seems to revive a little. He has big eyes, four fins where legs and arms would be, a minnow's tail . . . actually big blue eyes . . . pale blue, like Klimp's. He looks at me with such pleading. He comes to the surface to breathe and squeaks now and then. I keep making reassuring sounds as if I were talking to the cats. Then I decide to get in the tub with him myself. Carefully, though. With me in the tub, the creature seems happier. Swims around making a kind of humming sound and blowing bubbles. Follows my hand. Lets me pick it up. I'm thinking it's a clear case of bonding, perhaps for both of us.

Now that I'm relaxing in the water, I'm feeling a lot better. And nothing like a helpless little blue-eyed creature of some sort to care for to bring brightness into life. The thing needs me. And so do all those cats.

I lie quietly, cats miaowing outside the door, but I just lie here and Charles (Charles was my father's name) . . . Charles? Howard? Henry? He falls asleep in the shallows between my breasts. I don't dare move. The phone rings and there's the thunk of something knocked over by the cats. I don't move. I don't care.

/ / /

So what about ecology? What about our favorite planet, Klimp's and mine? How best save it? And who for? Make it safe for this thing on my chest? (Charles Bird? Henry Fishman?) Quietly breathing. Blue eyes shut. And what about all those thousands of others? Department of fisheries? Department of lakes and streams? Gelatin factory? Or the damp basements of those housing developments built in former swamps?

/ / /

I blame myself. I really do. Perhaps if I'd been more understanding of their problems . . . accepted them as they are. Not crit-
icized all that sand tracked in. And so what if they did step on the
tails of cats? I've been so irritable these last few days. No wonder
Klimp kicked out at me. If only I had controlled myself and
thought about what they were going through. It was a crucial
time for them too. But all I thought about was myself and my
blowing-up stomach. Me, me, me! No wonder my former
husband walked out. And now the same old pattern. Another
breakup, another identity crisis. It shows I haven't learned a
thing.

/ / /

I almost fall asleep lying here, but when the water begins to get
cold we both wake up, Charles and I. I rig up a system, then, with
the electric frying pan on the lowest setting and two inches of
water on top of a piece of flannel. Put Charles . . . Henry? . . .
inside, sprinkle in crumbs of wafer. Lid on. Vent open. Lock the
whole business in my bedroom on top of the knick-knack
shelves. Then I check out their room, Klimp's and the others'. It's
a mess, wafers scattered around . . . several pink ones, bed not
made. If they were, all three, men, I'd understand it, but that can't
be. I wonder if they used servants where they come from . . . or
slaves? Well, Charles will be brought up differently. Learn to pick
up his underwear and help out around the house, cook something besides telephone books and such. I find a talisman under
the bed. I shut my eyes, squeeze hard, wondering can I lift with
it? Maybe, on the other hand, it's some sort of anchor to stop
with or to be let down by. Something thrown out to keep from
flying. I'll save it for Charles.

I sit down to rest with a cup of tea, two cats on my lap and one
across my shoulders. All the cats seem fat and happy, and I really
feel pretty happy too . . . considering.

The telephone rings again and this time I answer it. It's a love
call. I think I recognize Klimp's voice, but he won't say if it's him

and they do all sound a lot alike, sort of muffled and slurred. Anyway, he says he wants to do all those things with me, things, actually, he already did. I suppose this call is part of a new campaign. I don't think much of it and I tell him so. "How about breaking school windows and stealing library books?" I say. But whose side am I on now? "Listen," I say, "I know of a nice wet place devoid of cats. It's called the Love Canal and you'll love it. Lots of empty houses. And there's another place in New Jersey that I know of. Call me back and I'll have the exact address for you." I think he believes me. (Evidently they haven't read *all* the books about women.)

/ / /

Political appointees. I'll bet that's what they are. Makes a lot of sense. I could do as well myself. And did, actually. Who was it sent them out with spray-paint cans? Who told them how to cause static on TV? Who had thousands of stickers made up reading: NO DANGER, NONTOXIC, and GENERALLY REGARDED AS SAFE?

We can do all this by ourselves. Let's see: number 1, day-care-aquarium centers; number 2, separate cat-breeding facilities; number 3, the takeover proper; number 4, the lying fallow period. And we have time . . . plenty of time. Our numbers keep increasing, too, though slowly . . . the rejected, the divorced, the growing older, the left out . . . Maybe they've already started it. I can't be the only one thinking this way. Maybe they're out there just waiting for my call, kitchens all warmed up. I'll dial my old friend. "Include me in," I'll say.

Everything will be perfect, and I even have Charles. We don't need them. Bunch of bureaucrats. *That* wasn't flying.

LOOKING
DOWN
/ / /

Those with heavy thighs, flat faces, funny little teeth all in a row. We fly down and knock them over with nothing more than the rush of our air. Not even touch them. And they, yearning after us, try to invent ways to get themselves up into our sky while we squawk by, laughing. We could save them when they fall, but we never do. We let them drop down in their imitation wings, gliders, and such, and they always do drop.

We know what birds mean to them: fire and smoke on the one hand, air on the other. Or should I say, sky — limitless sky. A bird — particularly birds such as we — a bird is better than a mountain top. Better than a tower, and they do build towers. Lightning strikes them. Burns them up. Wind blows them down. Their broken towers lie all across the land. Only the newest ones still stand or those few that are built of stone.

Also we are omens, both for good and evil, depending on the circumstances. We have heard them wailing when the sky darkens with us as though we were the storm, yet it is only us at our fall gathering or our spring dancing.

They dance, too, and sing. Paint themselves in imitation of our colors. Line their skinny arms with fallen feathers and flap about. And always they bow down to us when we sit, as we sometimes do to dry, in rows along their roofs or perch on their tower tops. They leave flowers for us. Not that we care anything about flowers. You can't eat a flower. They leave bowls of milk, too.

Birds don't drink milk. They leave it also for the snakes. Cats come for it.

There are others they bow to. The snakes of course, and even the cats sometimes. I have stolen and eaten both the family snake and the family cat, which shows which of us are lesser. I hadn't done this before, but I had to. (I have even drunk the milk.) The fall gathering has come and gone. I had thought to follow soon — to get well and follow. Not stay until the leaves fell.

Snow will come. I've not seen that nor ever wanted to. The milk will freeze. The tower where I rest is rickety, sways in the wind as though it were a tree, yet is not a tree, therefore will fall. But perhaps I'll not last that long anyway.

I coasted here — no, I fell, having been twisted in a wind devil I'd not avoided in time — fell, torn and broken, hid out until too hungry, climbed down from the tower by hand, one step at a time as *they* would do it. The cat, the snake, my last good meal. Now only milk. I feel dizzy. I wonder, once I climb down for it, if I'll be able to climb back up. Such a thing, for one of us to have come to this low point.

Ah, but this evening I see that the milk bowl is set away from the tower and near to the shack. It's a trap. I know that. They want, no doubt, to catch the one who's eaten their cat and snake. If they manage to do that they'll have one of us in their power, which has not happened before. They've tried, but never succeeded. The flock saw to it that those of us caught in their tree nets were never taken alive.

They bring the milk at twilight. The creatures, such as I, that drink it come out after dark, but I have a terrible thirst and it's the milk I want more than any stray cat or snake or small bird. I climb down almost as soon as the milk is put out. I crawl to the shack on knees and elbows. I see one of the half-people watching me from the window but I'm past caring. When I lean to drink, *she* comes out and stands in the doorway quietly as if she thought she might startle me and that then I would flap away, which is impossible. I don't care. I'm thinking: let it all happen the way it has to happen, there are no brothers or sisters left here to see to it that it is otherwise.

After I drink, she bows down to me, head to ground, calls me, "Lord of Summer, Flight, and Trinity, having incorporated snake and cat whole," she says, "without chewing, therefore having become a sacred three." I raise myself from the bowl, knowing I've milk dripping from my mouth yet, even so, thinking to loom over her displaying myself in all my splendor, but I have a dizzy spell. Can't fall now, I tell myself, and then I do.

Some of us have fallen from great heights, wounded or sick (as, but for the tower, I also, would have done). Some of us have fallen out of cliff nests, too bold when too young, or have been pushed out by a larger sibling. Some of us have caught a downdraft when near the ground. But who would have thought one of us would fall from a half-standing position and who'd have thought that I would be the one to do it.

/ / /

I wake in a musty, dark place void of wind, void of sky. A rack has been made for me to hold my wing in tension, up and to the side behind me. A throne has already been carved and decorated for me. (Or had they been carving at it ever since I'd glided to their tower? Or perhaps they'd always had it, waiting for one of us to be taken alive.) I have been strapped into it. An offering has been set before me: dried yellow flowers and a good goat broth. There's a fire in the fireplace. Also a sweetish smell from something smoldering in a flat dish.

I have never been in such a place, where there's just barely enough room for me to be arranged, as though on display, along one wall, the longest wall. I hang there against it. The rack on one side holds my wing so extended that I, myself, and my throne are almost in the corner. Around my neck there is a heavy chain or perhaps a necklace of some sort, too short for me to see. On my head there's an uncomfortable circle of metal. I suppose it's some sort of crown, as though I needed anything more than my topknot.

I'm still shaking with fever and still thirsty, but I can't reach the broth. Then *she* comes from behind a curtain and holds the bowl to my mouth. I would have bitten her, but I haven't the energy.

She also gives me water . . . a great deal of water, and I can finally drink as I've been wanting to. Then she calls and three of the half-men come in.

"He groans, he sighs," she tells them. "It is meaning that the times will be harsh, the winter cold and early." At first I wonder why she says this and then I think that there are strange things happening and that, rather than protest that I meant no such things, I will keep silent and beware. "Tonight," she says, "or tomorrow, the first snow will be coming," she says. "The tower will fall, having served a good purpose."

"Lucky for him," one of the half-men says, "that we have rescued him in time."

"The gods are lucky," she says. "This one has come to us with a purpose. Do not doubt it."

That night the winds and the snow come just as she said I said they would. The windows in front of me glow with a strange white light. I can see the flakes blowing sideways. And the tower does fall. I had dozed, and I heard the crashing of it as if in my dream and thought that I still lay out on it and had come down with it as it fell. I strain at the bonds and the rack and it's my own squawking that wakes me. One arm comes loose. I'm very weak, but it does come loose and I think that they don't know my strength at all — what it takes to fly south or even cling to rocks by toes and fingers. They've no idea. I will be able to escape whenever I feel like it.

My crown has fallen. In the glow of the coals and the glow from the windows, I can see it lying upside down in front of me, glints of glassy blue stones and gold (that gold they always like so much though I have better in one single breast feather). Rather nice, I suppose, if one must settle for less than myself, but I know my topknot is nicer. I have seen myself, and many times, not only in pools, but in the little mirrors we often steal from the doors of their hovels. I know how magnificent I am, though perhaps not quite so much so here in their dim room.

She comes, having heard my squawking I suppose, but by then I have settled myself so that she'll not see me in some undignified way nor see that one arm is loose. She has again brought me a drink. This time a tisane. I recognize it. Valerian with camomile. We have used the same. Also something fermented in it. Her little teeth don't look quite so funny to me any more, nor her odd, white, edible hand. Edible. We've not done that. We've let them be (after all, they have a culture of a sort, however crippled they and it may be), most of us, that is, though there have been young ones of us, just fledged, who've carried off smaller ones of theirs. But mostly we have an unspoken rule that we let them be, partly just to see what they do next, and if they ever *would* find a way to get themselves into our sky. We'd like to see *that* day, and sometimes speak of it and laugh.

And their women! What use have we for them? Though we've never minded showing off our colors to them. No need for crowns, yet *she* picks it up and puts it back on my head, carefully so as not to crimp my topknot. I could sleep better without that crown and I have a flash of rage. Beware, I think, of the anger of the gods, but the pale hand, the row of teeth, the broth, the soothing drink, all mix — all begin to seem an equation of needs met with the creature who brings the comfort. Also I can see there are qualities I'd not known about before and that I might better take advantage of, especially in my present state, and sights I'd not seen that please me, as the brightness of snow at night.

In the morning the sun is out and all the half-people come to see the fallen tower and the captured god. *She* pulls the curtains wide, lights many lamps and hooks shiny reflectors behind them, puts up mirrors to mirror the sun. Guards come and stand by my side. They wear imitation topknots rather like my own, held on by a strap around their heads, but they droop and flop, and have no sheen.

I know, on the other hand, that the lights shining on me make me glow but I don't have the energy to puff myself up to my magnificence, nor can I, anyway, achieve full brilliance sitting down like this with my scissortail dangling out of sight behind me, and who knows what state it's in. I've had no chance nor energy to attend to it, nor a brother or sister to help me.

Cushions are set out for the half-people, large ones for knees and small ones for foreheads. Then the half-people are allowed to file in. They are warned neither to touch nor to tempt the god, nor to ask about the future, and to seek only one favor. They stand and look at me for several minutes, obviously, even in my present state, awed by me. Then they bow down. The lights and the sun in the mirrors shine into my eyes from behind them so that they can see me but I can't see them except as silhouettes. They kiss my feet though they've been told not to. Some kiss my every toe. They ask their favors — small favors, even so small as for one more little bag of oats. "All I ask is that I be chosen to sing at Solstice." "All I ask is that they buy my spoons."

I keep silent. Had I spoken, it would have been to ask, on my own behalf, that the lights not shine into my eyes, and that I should not be kissed anymore on knee or toes.

I can make a clacking noise louder than their axes in the hills or their hammers as they build their towers. In here it would vibrate from wall to wall. At the same time that I do that, I can warble out a loony, laughing cry. To laugh again would feel good and it would drive them all away for sure, but I also want to continue to be looked after, sheltered until spring, and fed good goat parts.

So it goes on and on into the afternoon. I keep silent. There are, now and then, more serious requests, though always made smaller than one would think to ask. "All I ask," for instance, "is that my daughter should see for just one season, or just one month, or, if one of these is too much to ask, then for just one short day." I think, half-requests, like the half-people that make them. "All I ask is that I be allowed to live through this next month until the birth of our baby so I can see if it's a boy or girl and give the name. Perhaps even last until I see the first smile." On and on it goes. "All I ask is that I should be pleasing to Lutha."

I'm tired . . . tired of the whole thing. "Granted," I say.

/ / /

It had evidently not been foreseen that the god himself would actually take part in any of this. Everyone except the guards leaves, and I can hear there's much discussion both outside near

the windows and in an anteroom I'd not realized was there. I
can't hear much of it for they speak as though to keep their words
from me, but I do find out a startling thing: that Lutha is the half-
woman who has been looking after me, that she is considered the
most beautiful woman of all the half-women and has had many
suitors, but that she has dedicated herself to me alone, that she
has, in fact—the thought is so shocking to me that I almost can't
take it in, and I think that I must not have heard properly—
married me, that she is called the "bride of the gods," that the
ceremony had been performed before I'd come to and that a
proxy stood in for me to say my parts, that she had wanted only
and always to have one of us as husband. I learned all this because
now she is chastised for it. They raise their voices. They tell her I
am a false and a sick god who will continue to interrupt important ceremonies, perhaps even those that are to take place later on
to ensure a happy winter.

We mate for life so it is not a decision we make lightly. That
this half-woman should have been given to me as a bride is
ludicrous. And it's odd, for she has never even seen me at my
finest. Only seen me sick and fainting, with feathers in such a
deplorable state that even if I were healed enough to fly I might
not be able to.

I have to laugh then—to clack and cackle at the same time—
weak as I am. The ridiculousness of everything. I make such a
racket that the guards run away. In here the sound rings out in a
different way than it does at the cliffs, but I see the people outside
run from the windows. I've no idea how far they go, but to see
them scatter makes me laugh all the more. Good to laugh, but
not so good to laugh alone. I wish for the sound of one of us to
alternate my hollering with, so that, at the same time that I'm
laughing, loneliness comes upon me and tears flow. I can feel
them dropping onto the down of my chest. Oh, but none of us
would have nursed me like this. We don't do that. Who would
stay with one of us through the winter? It can't be done. You
would be helped only if you could go south, otherwise you were
to die and best if you were to fall into the sea to be taken by a sea
creature. But if such a thing as that can't be, then at least you were

to stay on the cliffs where even the best climbers of the half-people can't come. This is wrong, though I hadn't planned to do it.

But, for all the noise, *she* hasn't run away along with the others. No doubt the words "for better or for worse" or some such have been said and promises made, so she endures it. Perhaps she has plugged her ears with wool. I stop, though not for her sake, and she takes a soft cloth to wipe my tears. "Sweet, sweet, sweet," she says. (One would think it is she who is of bird and sky.) "How sweet a god this be." Odd that she would say such a thing when I would, and gladly, even at this moment, take a piece out of her hand, except who then would look after me? But I am forgetting she is my mate. Though we haven't done any mating dance that I know of, there are customs to be kept to even so. She, of all of them, I must not harm.

She says, "Next time I will be seeing to it that you will behave as a god should," and I'm thinking she is clever with her herbs. No doubt she will see to it.

But now she's seeing to a different thing. She gives me a drink unlike anything I've ever tasted. After giving it to me, she covers my face with a hood made especially for me. In a few minutes I find out what the drink is. An aphrodisiac. No doubt of that. Why? How? My wing stretching back upon the rack and me fastened to my throne? But now she has untied my feet and legs. (I'll not let her know that my left arm is free. I'll try, that is, not to let her know, but the drug has caught me up so that already I hardly care.) She sits on my lap. She guides me. I feel myself inside her. With my legs and lower body free, I can arch up and down and sideways. As the drug takes hold of me I lose all sense of reality. I know I feel pain in my wing, but I don't care. It's as if I fly again. I glide, I feel the lift of the thermal, up from below. All I need do is spread myself out and balance on the pillow of air pushing up under me. And I have power, the power of a god. Yes, these are god doings. I think I am a god indeed. Truly a trinity of bird and snake and cat but mostly snake or bird-snake. Flying lover. And she says it as though she knows my mind: "Flying lover," and, "My lover from the upper air and of the cliffs." All the things I feel, she says.

And when it's over, it begins again.

Afterward she nestles into my breast; her arms around me. I am feather bed and downy pillow for her for the rest of the night. If she knew, at any time, that my arm is loose, she must have forgotten it, but how could she not know by now! Perhaps she did and would tempt the god. And I will be tempted, of that I'm sure.

/ / /

The next night a ceremony, and the next also, and the night after that. I am both too tired and too drugged to understand or care what it's all about. Solstice. Not now but later. I know that much. And I'm hooded again. I see nothing of any of it. I doze but always wake when I hear *her* telling them what I say, and said, and have predicted. " 'Glory, glory, to us all through the winter,' he says," she says, and often, and, "because he is here among us as Bask, the cat, as Crackle, the bird, and as old Squam, the snake, 'and lo, also, a god child will be born of these three,' he says," she says, "so that we will live with gods among us for ever after this."

They sing in chorus (and it is the one thing that I find really worthy of myself in all that they do), sing, "Who gives the lilies clothing?" and, "Rise, crowned with light," and, "There is an arm that never tires beneath the wings of night," which makes me wonder, do they all know about my free arm and all wish to tempt gods? They sing, "If on joyful wing," and, "Sometimes a light surprises." I like that one best of many good ones and I think, yes, yes, sometimes a light *does* surprise as the midnight light of snow. When they stop I want for them to sing again.

/ / /

Then there is a period of resting. We are deep in winter. I begin to really recover, and no more drugs either, except for the aphrodisiac, especially on stormy nights when *she* is bored with dozing inside all through the day. But even so, I feel like myself. I wake early full of energy. I do what preening I can. (I have a plan.) I exercise against my bonds. They have, anyway, stretched; and often, when she ties my legs again after our matings, she leaves the thongs looser. As though all the care she's giving and the sex have made her love. She hasn't the kind of tenderness to dance and bob, nor for mutual preening, but I see that the half-people have their own ways.

We do not talk. She talks *at* me, that is, but, clearly, doesn't want a reply. I think she feels that if we speak to each other as one fellow creature to another, I might lose my godlike qualities. She wants me silent and remote . . . inscrutable. Clackings, roaring, yes, but nothing of the ordinary.

What she talks most about is our child (it has begun to show).

That it will be a boy and king of the people. (She calls herself and the others, people, not half-people.) I don't trust any of her predictions though some have come true. Chances are it won't come to term.

As I get better I get angrier and I think more about my plan. Am I to live by her whims? Masked when she wants me masked? Drugged when it suits her? (Fornicating. That's all it is.) Hand-fed as though to make me tame? I will show her what the anger of a god is like and that that anger, and my strength also, are beyond the understanding of any half-person. And I will take her on my own terms. I will set god-rules and god-schedules. My anger, also, will be precise and cool as a god's should be.

I wait for a sunny day. Then, carefully, feeling my muscles bulge against the thongs, I stretch them, I break them, one by one. As for the rack, I must loose myself from that even more slowly. My wing, though healed, is stiff and sore. She should have freed me from this rack long ago so I could keep the joints moving. Now I can't fully fold my wing over my back. It's a problem in this small place. Without wanting to, I knock down the herbs that are hanging from the ceiling. I knock the painted pots from the shelves. I knock the little statues of myself from their stands and the little cat gods and little snake gods from theirs also.

By now *she's* standing in the archway that leads to the ante-room, still dressing herself in her long wife-robe. I push her back into the room she came from. There I see that she has a soft bed while I've had a hard throne. She has a fat coverlet of duck down (we have just such in our aeries) while I've not had anything (though I must admit she's seen to it I was never cold). I split her wife-robe with one claw and push her on to the bed. I'm careful. The anger of the gods is careful.

At first her utter nakedness stops me . . . surprises me. Though I already know about the half-people's lack of any fur or feather, I've not seen any of them completely naked. It's revolting. No wonder she blindfolds me. Only when I think to myself, newborn chick not yet dry am I able to approach her, though she looks more like food than anything else; tender, like a suckling pig. She lies quietly looking at me. Her eyes are . . . yes, they *are* beautiful, expressive in a way ours never are. I can see she accepts what is to happen. Welcomes it, even. I would not be able to see any such thing in the eyes of a mate of my own kind, and it is this that turns me back on to her. I sit on the edge of the bed. I touch. Their breasts are larger and rounder than our women's but as soft as though covered with down. I lie upon her then and my wings enclose the whole bed. What an odd way to mate, I think, and such a strange season for it, and I take her . . . at my own time and timing . . . at a god's time. Afterward I rest upon her within the tent of my wings. I'd not seen any such thing before, but I didn't find it bad or wrong. And, since it was *my* lovemaking, I was conscious that she was my mate, as, indeed, she was, even though without any proper dance. I had found it, until now, hard to realize this.

But I must be carrying out my plan, so I get up, see the shelves of jars and bottles and sweep them to the floor. See her loom and crush it into its corner, strings dangling and tangled. See she has been weaving something for the god because it's blue and there are gold and silver threads worked into it. I know why blue. For the lord of sky. I tear my claws across it. What care I, who come from *in* the blue, for gold or silver?

There's no more damage to be done so I open the outside door and laugh out at the village, that this should be the morning of the loss of their god as they know him and become the morning of the god as he knows himself.

It's white outside. Dazzling. Blinding, so that I'm wondering who is the lord of all this snow? I have been too long in the dark. I step out and keep laughing, but I know I don't sound the same and I stop and wait until I can see.

Paths are cleared from here to there, her door to other doors, but the snow is knee high on each side of all those curving walk ways, a god's knee high. In fact even more than that.

I take steps in the stuff thinking to get up speed in order to fly. I sink. I flap. We have always felt awkward getting into the air from a flat place and have laughed at one another and ourselves, but I care how I look to them and they're out now, half-dressed and dressing, pulling their hoods over their heads, and they see me flap and sprawl. The snow rises around me in a powdery cloud. I stand up. This time I follow a path and do get some speed, grab at the air. It's cold, dense air, easier to hold onto than I'm used to. I manage to raise myself, legs dangling in the snow, pump harder, but this is the wrong direction for what light breeze there is. I turn and try again the other way, back toward the shack, and I do get up this time, but there's more pain than I thought there would be. I stagger in the air, turn again, flop and fall, and flop and fall; up, then down, and down onto her roof. Perch there. Feel, for the first time, what cold really is. *This* is cold. I'd not known about it until now. I'd not even suspected. I'd thought to fly to my cliff. Live there, come back and feed on their goats, but that's impossible. You can't build a fire in even the best of nests. I think, for a moment, of living in one of our kilns, but that would be worse than in these shacks. Besides, I know I'd never make it to the rookery.

Sorry sight. The half-people have come out and gathered round to see the sorry sight of one of us (*she* also, now dressed and hooded), to see a lord of the sky (and cat and snake) sit and shiver.

"Now will you believe," I hear a half-man say to her (he is the one to whom I said "granted" before I knew that *she* was mine), "will you believe," he says, "that he is a false god, as I've told you?"

"No," she says, "nor will his son believe it. And where is it written that any human can understand the ways of gods?" (Human, she calls herself!)

Ladders are brought, and chains that I could never break, but I already know that all I care about is to go back where the fire still smolders. I let them take me.

As they do, they sing. "Look upward when the morning shineth . . ." and it does shine. "Heavenly hosts o'er yon horizon, cleaving to the sky . . ." That's us, though I can hardly consider myself as one of "us" any more.

/ / /

The loom is repaired. The blue robe rewoven and tucked around me. I sit chained (often blindfolded, often drugged), crowned; jewels hang about me, hymns are sung, offerings brought. I sit and sit. My strength fails. My wings ache from disuse. Sometimes I howl at night and clank my chains. I wake the whole town. "Deeds!" I cry it out even in my dreams. "The gods must do deeds! Not sit silent, else the gods will surely fail." They don't care to listen. They don't answer.

And *she.* When not blindfolded, I see how she grows bigger and bigger. I keep wondering what sort of funny chick it will be.

Spring is late, but I can smell it. We . . . they, the flocks will be coming back. I look forward to it with both eagerness and dread.

And then the birthing time comes. I hear the bustle of it in the anteroom. I hear *her* groans. I hear its first cries. Impossible to tell if it sounds more like one of theirs or one of ours. Then I hear *her* making a great wailing sound and I wonder, is it dead already? for I have just heard its peeps and squeaks. But no, I hear that her grief and horror is that the chick is female. She needed a god, not a goddess . . . not a rival to herself.

"Kill it," she says. "Do it or let me do it," but instead they bring it in to me. The three men come, one holds it carefully. They ask that I should name my child. I think: Mother, sister, I'll be privileged to use your names. But then I see the creature, face of the real people, yes, but the weak and naked body of those others and tiny, useless wings better cut off altogether. Streaks of yellow down here and there not yet dry. Up on the cliffs we'd have killed such a one on sight and no regrets. I refuse to name the thing. But then I look again more closely and I see the tiny beginning of the topknot shining in the firelight—a golden one such as my own. She will be one of the bold, as we say about ourselves. And is she really any more crippled than I?

All of a sudden I know I want to live, to await the season of my freedom and see summer again. I have let this go on all this time out of foolish pride and because I thought of myself as a person while they were only half-people. "I *will* name her," I say, "but first I must tell you that I'm not a god. None of us is, wings or not. We are half-creatures like yourselves and no better. We perceive the patterns of directions in the sky but we do not perceive the patterns of destiny, and though I am like a cat and like a snake and often feel myself as such, I am not these three except inasmuch as snake and cat are birdlike. I have nothing to give but of myself and of my brothers and sisters if I can persuade them. Let me go free so I can give what I can give. My child is not a goddess either. Sing your songs. Do sing, 'How sweet the truth,' and sing that 'Every flower is full of gladness,' but not in praise of us. These are the first true things I've ever said," I say.

The three men fall on their knees. "You are a god indeed," they say and I'm thinking it will all go on as before or maybe even more so, but it doesn't. They *do* believe me. They get hammers to snap me free. (Who would have thought that freedom could be won so simply?) They give me my chick into my arms. They help me stand up. I'm so stiff I can hardly walk. "My mate is weeping," I say. "Help me go to comfort her." She will be surprised to find me not a god after all, and not a trinity, but I think I know ways to make her happy even so.

ECLIPSE

/ / /

Finding myself improperly dressed and among strangers who all spoke better French than I do, and having forgotten to bring a gift or, rather, not having realized that a gift was called for until I saw them piled up on a table by the door, I was wondering was it the wrong day or the wrong address? Was it even the wrong little town? (I suppose there's a street named Harvard Place in every suburb.) And I was starving. I had skipped lunch in order to be ready to overeat later on and then I had wanted to arrive fashionably late. It was by then after half past nine.

I thought I would just slip in and grab some avocado dip and pretzels and go home, but this turned out not to be that sort of party. Waitresses in black and white passed trays with hot things to be dunked in Japanese sauces kept warm over candles. I moved toward these trays, first one and then another, but either the tray would recede faster than I could make my way through the crowd, or, whenever I reached one, the food was already just gone. All I wanted was a few bites of almost anything to tide me over for the walk back to the train station where I thought I could pick up a stale peanut bar from some dispensing machine. I actually felt weak from hunger and discouragement, and from the idea of the walk back to the station, and then the train ride back to the city. At this hour I knew the trains didn't come often. I would have to wait for a long time on the empty platform nibbling my peanut bar. I sat down in an ornate antique chair wondering, not so much what to do next, but when to do it. All the while, trays of food hurried by over my head on their way to people who were standing up.

I'm not good at parties, anyway. I confuse Hess with Hiss, eschatology with scatology, Simone de Beauvoir with Simón Bolívar. If I drink I fall asleep.

Suddenly I heard loud laughter, louder than any of the others, and looked up to see a tall old woman in a sort of Turkish outfit: turban, several scarves, loose pants. All gray. When our eyes met, she hurried toward me. I guessed she would have an accent and that her teeth would remind me of her skeleton. Have compassion, I told myself. Have compassion for the old. They can't help it if they smell bad. Yes, it was to me she was coming. I could have turned around right then and left, I was still so near the door.

"You have arrived, my darling." She kissed me. She blew on me when she talked. "Why not telling me you're here? Why not speaking up?'

"I should have," I said. "I suppose I should have."

"Come." She held my elbow, pressing on a nerve. It could have been by mistake, but it could have been that she was practiced at holding people by their funny bone. She steered me, with little twinges of pain, through the crowd to the piano. "Here," she said, "what will you be playing first?"

I've never played the piano in my life and I said so frankly, knowing that she would be very angry.

"You *are* Doreen?" she asked.

For a moment I wanted to deny it. I tried to think quickly of other names that I might rather be called, names I've always liked, such as Julia or Eva, but at that moment I could only think of Mary, and Betty, and Joanne, names as unpleasant to me as my own or even more so, and so I found myself answering that, yes, that was my name.

"You were to play the piano," she said, but I insisted that I couldn't. I was watching her teeth. Obviously they were her real ones.

"The flute, then, of course, my darling. I'm so sorry." And she handed me the flute that lay ready on top of the piano. I wondered whose it really was, but I took it without thinking.

"No," I said.

"Your name is Noreen," she said, "and we all know who you are."

"Did you say Noreen or Doreen?" I asked. "I thought you said Doreen. My name is Doreen."

"What a strange coincidence," she said, "that you should play together and that one of you should be named Doreen and the other Noreen. I believe you must have made that up to sound nice, my darling." She put her arm around me. "On the other hand," she said, "I suppose that's one of those things so true to life that it has to be real. No one would ever think something like that up —Noreen and Doreen!"

"I don't play the flute," I said.

"Well then, what are you here for?" She removed her arm from around my shoulders.

Why was I here indeed. Why *was* I here? I certainly had no answer to that and could only stare down at my worn-out blue and white sneakers. She told me to hurry into the kitchen at once, then, and to help out there where I was needed or she would have the police after me and that I shouldn't eat anything until the party was over.

I moved quickly away from her, trying to took as though I knew where the kitchen was. I wandered aimlessly among the guests for a while, hearing bits and pieces of conversations in many languages, some in English.

I didn't suppose that the police really arrested people who got into the wrong parties by mistake; still, perhaps they did in the rich parts of town. At first I didn't notice that I still held the flute. I certainly could be arrested for stealing a flute.

A flute is, actually, quite large, shiny and noticeable. People did notice it, and me. They would look at the flute and then study my face as though they were thinking: So that's what a flute player looks like. At first I thought I would stand it up in with the dieffenbachia, or perhaps lay it down in a corner next to the wall, but I didn't want any harm to come to it and I didn't know what sort of thing would harm it. I was sure whoever's flute it was didn't want it to be carelessly handled by strangers. I held it carefully, back over my arm, one end against my cheek, rather as one might hold a baby, and I wondered how a real flute player would hold it.

Soon there was the sound of the piano (Chopin) and I left, to escape it, through the big glass doors at the back of a hall and found myself standing at the edge of a drained swimming pool (a few fall leaves clustered in one corner of it). I was wishing the lights were turned out so I could see the moon better. I had managed by then to grab a few carrot sticks and some raw broccoli, but they stuck in my throat. I couldn't swallow.

Suddenly I felt myself pushed from behind. I thought I was going to fall into the empty pool, but the arms pushed and then held back. I was safe in the arms of a short, wide . . . in the arms of a powerful man.

All of a sudden I wanted to be dressed in something low-necked, black. I wanted one of those very, very fine gold chains around my neck. I wanted expensive shoes that make your feet look tiny, and a soft shawl . . .

Sometimes I wake up in the middle of the night and know something has stopped . . . a sound has stopped.

And then they *did* turn out the lights. Everyone came outside and there began an eclipse of the moon that everyone but me knew was about to happen. They didn't watch long, though, but wandered back in and soon the lights were on again and the eclipse hardly half over. The man's hand was on my arm through all of this and I had noticed by then that his beard hid several defects or, rather, tried to, around his mouth and jaw, and that his hair was combed to hide his bald spot, but I didn't mind, especially when I found out that he was, though not a full-fledged psychologist, a student of Jung and a specialist in dreams.

"I dreamt," I said, "that I couldn't get over a wall, but that, if I could have gotten over it, there would only have been another wall beyond that one, and another, and another. I also dreamt I was imprisoned in my jacket, but when I finally managed to remove it, there was another jacket just like it underneath."

"Of the three primary emotions," he said, "fear and hope are the easiest to deal with." Then he told me how much he loved the sound of the flute, and then he asked me my name.

"Doreen," I said, suddenly not sure. "Though perhaps you like Noreen better."

We were, by then, seated in deck chairs and he had managed to get me some little cheese dumplings and some champagne. I began to feel light-headed very quickly and such warmth for him for having gotten me some food I could manage to swallow that I decided to confess.

"If I don't play the flute," I said, "that woman will kill me, but I can't play the flute."

He was leaning very close to me and I saw, under the open neck of his wine-red shirt, that *he* was the one wearing the little gold chain.

"I wish I did play the flute, but for you." (This after the second glass of champagne.) "Only for you."

"What you lack is confidence. Though I'm not actually an analyst, I have office hours every Wednesday evening. Are you free . . ." Now he was whispering close to my ear. "Are you free on Wednesdays?"

"Yes." I merely mouthed the word.

"And now, tonight, you will play the flute better than you ever have before. I guarantee it. Lean back and look at this little light." He had a tiny pocket flashlight on the end of a keychain and he held it in front of me, rocking it back and forth slightly.

But I was wondering just then, what about a Jungian who almost throws someone into an empty swimming pool?

"No," I said, looking at it.

"You'll do it for me."

"Maybe," I said. "Maybe for you I'll do it."

"Then watch the light."

Behind him I could see the moon, which now had a misty halo around it. He, too, seemed luminous in that light. A kind of moon himself.

"Noreen, you feel very comfortable," he said. "Extraordinarily comfortable."

"Yes I do."

"Comfortable and confident. The sounds of the party recede into the background. They don't bother you. The light mist feels good. Almost warm. You expand. You breathe deeply. Your eyes shut now. You are deep inside yourself. Deep inside. And deep inside you know you play the flute beautifully. You have a gift to give. Give joy. And beauty. You are calm and ready. Very calm. Clearheaded. Ready. And very calm. Now you will play better than you ever have before. All the notes will come easily. Very easy. Confident. Lucid. All is clear. Bright. Luminous. The full moon. And you are ready. Come, Noreen. Come." He pulled me up.

"But I wasn't hypnotized," I said.

"Yes you were. Come."

He led me off to the old lady and told her I was ready to play. *"Voilà!"* (Her arm around me.) *"Vous avez décidé enfin.* You're not being any more so coy, Mademoiselle Doreen. Thank you, Emmanuel. You always work miracles."

And so they all sat down and the pianist, Noreen (Doreen?) came and Emmanuel (Emmanuel!) stood at the back looking at me with beady black eyes and smiling in anticipation.

I was huge, luminous, confident, lucid at last. Everything he said was true and I was his, Emmanuel's, flute player. First I blew my nose and then raised the flute awkwardly, my elbow out, and stared at the old lady. I was thinking: I can win. I can best her, and it must have shown in my eyes because she took a few steps back. I held the flute as I thought it should be held and pursed my lips and blew. And blew, and blew, and all you could hear was the breathy, noteless blowing. Noreen/Doreen sat at the piano staring at me while I continued blowing until the old lady ran out of the room, her long scarves flying out behind her. She was making tiny little squeaks more like *I* might have made earlier in the evening when she grabbed me by my funny bone. And I blew and blew and when I looked back to where Emmanuel had been standing, I saw that I had blown him away, too. And still I blew. I had the self-confidence. People crept away one by one. I heard their cars go. Pretty soon I stopped (it really hadn't taken all that long) and then I ate. All that I wanted. And then I walked to the station and waited almost an hour for the train, still self-confident and happy. Still glowing. And I never found that house or man again. (I never tried to. I knew I couldn't.) But I will always remember him, Emmanuel, and the brilliant moonlight that one night when I had self-confidence for a couple of hours or so.

THE CIRCULAR
LIBRARY OF
STONES
/ / /

They said all this wasn't true. That there had been no city on this site since even before the time of the Indians . . . that there had been no bridge across the (now dried up) river and no barriers against the mud. "If you have been searching for a library here," they said, "or for old coins, you've been wasting your time."

For lack of space I had put some of the small, white stones in plant baskets and hung them from the ceiling by the window. I don't argue with people about what nonexistent city could have existed at this site. I just collect the stones. (Two have Xs scratched on them, only one of which I scratched myself.) And I continue digging. The earth, though full of stones of all sizes, is soft and easy to deal with. Often it is damp and fragrant. And I disturb very little in the way of trees or plants of any real size here. Also most of the stones, even the larger ones, are of a size that I can manage fairly well by myself. Besides, mainly it's the stones that I want to reveal. I don't want to move them from place to place except some of the most important small ones, which I take home with me after a day's digging. Often I have found battered aluminum pots and pans around the site. Once I found an old boot and once, a pair of broken glasses; but these, of course, are of no significance whatsoever, being clearly of the present.

Gaining access to their books! If I could find the library and learn to read their writing! If I could find, there, stories beyond my wildest dreams. A love story, for instance, where the love is of a totally different kind . . . a kind of ardor we have never even thought of, more long-lasting than our simple attachments, more world-shaking than our simple sexualities. Or a literature that is two things at once, which we can only do in drawings, where a body might be, at one and the same time, a face in which the breasts also equal eyes, or two naked ladies sitting side by side, arms raised, that also form a skull, their black hair the eye sockets.

/ / /

For quite some time now I have had sore legs, so digging is an exercise I can do better than any other, and though at night my back pains me, the pains usually go away quite soon. By morning I hardly feel them. So the digging, in itself, pleases me. There is the pleasure of work. A day well spent. Go home tired and silent. But mostly, of course, it is the slow revelation of the stones that I care about. Sometimes they cluster in groups so that I think that here must have been where a fireplace was, or perhaps a throne. Sometimes they form a long row that I think might have been a wall or a bench. And I have found a mirror. Two feet underground, and so scratched that one can see oneself only in little fish-shaped flashes — a bit of an eye, a bit of lip — but for even that much of it to have been preserved all this time is a miracle. I feel certain that if they had a library, it's logical they would also have had mirrors. Or if they had mirrors, it certainly follows they could have had a library.

I keep the mirror with me in my breast pocket. (I wear a man's old fishing vest.) When people ask me what I'm doing out here, I show the mirror to them along with a few smooth stones.

At night I write. I shut my eyes and let my left hand move as it wishes. Usually it makes only scratchings, but at other times words come out. Once I wrote several pages of nothing but *no, no, no, no, no,* and after that, *on, on, on,* and *on,* but more and more often there are longer words now, and more and more often they are making some kind of sense. Yesterday, for instance, I found myself writing: *Let us do let us do and do and let us not be but do and you do too.* And then, and for the first time, a whole phrase came out clear and simple: *Cool all that summer and at night returned to the library.*

Certainly I would suppose the library, being built of stone, to be always cool in summer, always warm in winter. The phrase is surely, then, true and of the time. It is interesting that the library itself is referred to in this, the first real phrase I've written so far. That is significant. What I have been hoping to do is to reproduce some of the writings from the library, or reasonable facsimiles. Perhaps this is the beginning of one of their books.

/ / /

The circle is sacred to all peoples except for us. We are the only ones that don't care if a thing is square or a circle or oblong or triangular. The shape has no meaning to us. A circle could be oval for all we care. I'm thinking about this because I think I have come across a giant circle. About a foot down I found what looked like a path of stones, and I dug along it all day thinking I was going in a straight line: but when I turned around to look back on what I had accomplished, I saw that, although I had dug only a few yards, clearly I was curving. Though I had thought to finish for the day, I turned and vigorously revealed another yard of the stones, yet knowing full well it would be perhaps a month before I could uncover a really significant portion of the circle. I was thinking that probably here, at last, was where the very walls of the library had been and that, if true, this would be a great revelation of stones (even though done by an old woman . . . a useless old woman, so everyone thinks). I felt happy . . . happy and tired after that and, though I came home very late and my back hurt even more than usual, I sat down, dirty as I was, at my little table. I shut my eyes and let my left hand write: *Let us oh let us do and do and dance and do the dance of the library in the cool in the sanctuary of the library.*

It rained that night and all the next day, and I knew it had filled up all my pits and paths with mud. I would have to do much of my digging over again, and yet I wasn't unhappy about it. Such things come in every life. It's to be expected. (And doing is digging. Digging is doing. Do, not be. That's my philosophy and it seems to be theirs, too.) And my latest discovery was momentous, to say the least. Who would have thought it: a great, white, stone, circular library to be danced in!

Mostly on rainy days like these I do as the other old women do. I knit or make pot holders. I make soup and muffins. While I was there doing old-woman things and looking out the window, I thought, How nice if I found even only another stone with, perhaps, an O on it. People who search as I do must be happy with small and seemingly insignificant discoveries. People who search as I do must understand, also, that the lack of something is never insignificant, so even if there were nothing to be found, I was never disappointed, because that, too, was significant — as, for instance, a library and only one stone with an X on it. Besides, the less discovered, the more open the possibilities. I always console myself with that thought.

That night I let my left hand write. It took a long time to get from scratches to Xs; to *no, no, no;* but finally it wrote: *Let us then stone on stone on stone a library that befits a library each door face the sun one at dawn and one at dusk. Many queens saw it.* (Perhaps they were all queens in those days. Or perhaps when they reached my age they became queens. I would like to think so.)

This was on my mind when I went to sleep and I dreamed a row of dancing women, all of them my age and all wearing crowns of smooth white pebbles. They were calling to me to wake up . . . to wake up, that is, into my dream, and I did, and I was still in my boots, and fishing vest, and my old gray pants. I didn't, in other words, dream myself to be one of them, as some sort of queen or other. I was my dirt-stained self, holding out my grimy hands. And it seemed that they gave me my mirror — the one I had already found — and even in my dream it wasn't shiny and new but just as scratched as when I found it. They showed me that I must place the mirror exactly where I found it in the first place so that I could find it as I did find it — near the former riverbed and on a slight rise. This I did in my dream as the old women beat stones together with a loud *clack, clack.* And of course it's true; that's where I *did* find the mirror. It all fits together perfectly!

(All those old women lacked grace, but perhaps it's not required.)

My daughters . . . I suppose they tell me the truth about myself, though no need to. Why do they do it? Why feel free to say such things? Do I talk too much? Do I go on and on about it or about anything? Why, I've almost stopped talking altogether, wanting, now, other kinds of meanings. My argument in one Xed stone or a particularly smooth one or several in a row. I let them speak their ambiguities for themselves.

I showed my daughters my moonstone. I wanted to convince them. I said it came from the library.

"What library?"

"You know. Out by the dried-up stream."

"You've always had that moonstone. Grandma gave it to you."

"Well," I said, "I found it lying in the mud there." (I knew I was just making everything worse.)

"You must have dropped it yourself. What were you doing wearing that out there, anyway? You ought to be more careful."

I suppose I should have been. I know it will be theirs someday.

Later they told me about a place (I've seen it) where there's a doctor's office in the basement and art rooms, pot-holder rooms, television rooms, railings along all the halls. Everybody has a cane. I've seen that. I told my daughters, "no."

/ / /

Just as crossroads, fire, seashells, oak trees, and circles have special meanings, stones have meanings, too. Some, upright and lumpy on the hillsides, are named after women. All the best houses are of stone, therefore the library also. Molloy sucked them (I have too, sometimes), found them refreshing. Stone doors into the mountain balance on a single point and open at the slightest caress. The sound stone makes as door is not unlike the rustling pebbles on beaches. It is fitting that stones should be open to question, as my stones are. I liked letting them speak their ambiguities. When I was not out at my dig, I remembered stones. I dreamed them, I imagined I heard their *clack, clack*.

/ / /

I told my daughters that if I should be found awkwardly banging stones together on some moonlit night, it would be neither out of senility nor sentimentality, but a scientific test.

/ / /

But then I found a stone of a different kind and color: reddish and lumpy. Essentially nine lumps: two in front, two in back, plus one head, two arms, and two leg posts. I recognized it instantly. Fecund *and* wise. Big breasted *and* a scholar. Fat *and* elegant. I wanted to bring this librarian to her true place in the scheme of things. Restore her to her glory. Clearly, she not only had babies and nursed them, but she read all the books.

After this find, I dug in a frenzy. I knew I should be more careful of myself at my age: follow some rules of rest and recreation, but *I* believe in *do,* not *be.* Do! Though why should I so desperately want more . . . more, that is, than the mother of the library? (My daughters will call her a lumpy, pink stone.) Am I never satisfied?

Never! (My left hand has written: *Stone on stone on stone on stone on stone,* almost as though I were building the library out of the words.)

And then as I dug frantically, my eyes were blinded by the setting sun. Everything sparkled, and I thought I actually saw the library: all white with a great, clear river before it and a landing where the books (stone books) were brought in on little ships with big sails. The glistening of the waves hurt my eyes, but I could see, even so, the librarians dancing on the beach in front of the sacred circle of the library. And they were all old. Old as I am or even older — wrinkled, hobbling women — I could see that their backs were hurting them too, but they kept on with the dancing, just as I kept on with my digging. And I heard the soft, sweet, fluty music of the library and felt the cool of it, for I, too, stood close to the western doorway. And we could see one another. I'm sure of it. I saw eyes meet mine, and not just once or twice.

I stepped forward, then, to dance with them, but I fell — it seemed a long, slow fall — and as I fell, the sun was no longer in my eyes and I saw then my rocky ground and my dried-up stream bed.

After I got up, I felt extraordinarily lucid. As though I had drunk from the ice-cold river. Clearheaded and happy — happier than I'd been in a long time (though I've not been unhappy digging here; on the contrary). I didn't want to go home and rest — I felt so powerful — but I forced myself. I had hardly eaten all day, and most important, if I tried to dig in the dark I might miss something. I might toss away a stone like my important librarian and not see what it really was.

/ / /

When I got home that night I found that someone had been at my stones. They were all, all gone. I was so happy about my little librarian that I didn't notice it at first. It wasn't until I went to put her on my night table (I wanted her to be close to me as I slept) that I noticed there were no other stones there, not a single one. I knew right away what had happened. My daughters decided that I'm being crowded out by stones. They think — because *they* would feel that way — that it must be uncomfortable to live like this. But I was brought up on stones, don't they remember that? I had geodes. I had chunks of amber. I had a cairngorm set in silver. Still have it somewhere, unless they took that off for safekeeping thinking I will lose it out there. Well, perhaps I already have, but if I did, it's been worth it many times over. And now even my hanging baskets of stones, gone, and stones from every surface, every shelf, all gone. Thank goodness I carry my most important ones with me in my vest pockets.

All these old stones. Mother wouldn't have appreciated them either. The work, yes, the care I've taken, the effort — she did appreciate effort and would have praised me for that — but she had no understanding of science and its slow, laborious unfolding. The care, the cataloging, she would have praised, but perhaps not when all this work involves merely stones. Back in those days she didn't even like my geodes (especially those that had not been opened yet). It can't be hoped that she would have liked my little naked librarian. Mother disapproved of nakedness of any sort. I, on the other hand, want to stress the importance of childbearing librarians and so the importance of the bodies of the librarians, and so all the glory of their old-lady sexuality. (And I have seen it at the local library . . . the woman in charge sitting with her breasts resting on the table.)

/ / /

Coming in like that, then, and no stones, my little librarian in hand, I couldn't possibly sleep. I was both too happy and too upset. I sat down instead to draw my new find. If I am, someday in the future, to be judged for this work by someone who really knows what it's all about, I don't want to make any mistakes that will spoil the scientific accuracy of the study. I labeled all the parts: these slits, eyes; that slit, the opening to the womb. (The look on her face is intelligent and self-sufficient.)

I hid the drawings under my socks. (Who knows what my daughters will think worth nothing?) I put the librarian in the top breast pocket of the vest, where tomorrow she will rest over my heart. Then I checked all the other pockets with my most important stones (all there, thank goodness) and went to bed. It was nearly morning.

Even so, the next day I woke still extraordinarily clearheaded. I fairly jogged out to my site. Worked hard all day but found nothing, saw nothing. Once or twice I did think I heard the sound of flutes and perhaps some drumming, but I knew that was just my imagination plus the beat of my own heart in my ears. I always hear that on hot days when I lean over too much or get up too fast.

When I got home I sensed, again, a change. (Why do they always come in the daytime when I'm not here? Why are they afraid to face me?) I couldn't see the changes this time, but I knew they'd been there and I knew things were gone. I checked my closet first, and yes, those few dresses I have that I hardly ever wear weren't there. Also the suitcase that I keep at the back on the closet floor.

A pair of walking shoes were gone, and my best dressy shoes. Also a white sweater my daughters gave me but that I never wear, except to please them once in a while to make them think I like it. Then, in the drawers, I found half my underwear gone and my jewelry, such as I have. (Probably my cairngorm. I didn't see it there.)

They have already packed me up and taken my things off somewhere, and I knew where. From the looks of what they thought I'd need there — dresses, jewelry, stockings — I knew what it would be like: dress for dinner; sit on porches; play cards; watch TV; sing; entertainment every Saturday night. Did they think I was so senile I wouldn't notice what was going on? I knew it wouldn't be long before they'd come for me, and I wondered exactly when that would be. Perhaps very early in the morning, before I was up and out at my dig. Well, I would just have to go back out there right away. The thing was, I wasn't ready yet. Now I would have to make something happen before I really understood anything. Before I went out, though, I thought I would sit down, have a cup of tea, and let my left hand write a bit. I thought it might have something to tell me.

Why not why not lie down and in the sanctuary of the library why not come cool all night and see the shores of the sky?

(My daughters have never been interested in libraries or in anything they can't put their finger on or anything they can't understand the first time they see it.)

Take a white string long and measure and dig in the center of the library a place to lie down with quilts and pillows.

Nothing much else to do that I could think of right then. I didn't wait. I did as they said, got white cord, and quilt, and pillow. I didn't bring a flashlight. The night was clear, stars out but no moon. I could see well enough to find the center of the library. I dug a shallow grave just my size and lay down there, facing up, looking at the constellation Swan. I kept my eyes on that. It took effort, but everything worth doing takes effort. Effort is what makes it all worthwhile, so I held my eyes open and on the Swan, her wings stretched out, flying out there so high I knew I couldn't even conceive of the distance. I forced myself not to sleep. Pretty soon the Swan seemed to move and wobble and then began to swoop about the sky. My God, I'd never seen anything so strange and wonderful as that swooping Swan of stars. And then I heard faintly at first—that *clack, clack, clack* of stones that meant all the librarians were there around me. I didn't see them, but I knew they were there. I was afraid to turn my eyes away from the Swan. Nor did I want to by then. I liked watching it loop and tumble and glide. And then it whizzed by directly over my head so close I felt the rush of air. And after that, there was the fat red Venus, life-size, sitting right beside me. "Sanctuary," she said, but she didn't need to say it. I knew that. "Stay," she said, and all of a sudden I knew it was death, death now, and had been death all along. But I thought, I could be working in the sanctuary of the vegetable garden at the old ladies' home. Or I might even be sitting on the porch, but I'd be alive if only for a little longer . . . not much, but a little bit. "No," I said. But she kept nodding, and now I couldn't have turned away even if I wanted to, and the *clack, clack* of stones was loud, and painful, and right over my head.

"Why not later?"

"It's now or never."

I knew this *was* what I wanted, but suddenly it seemed too easy. I could hear, by now, not only *clacks,* but also the rush and rustle of the great river nearby. I even heard the sound of a boat, the bump of wood on wood as a skiff came up to the dock. I heard the thump of stone tablets being placed upon the shore, and I knew they were full of women's thoughts . . . women's writings . . . women's good ideas. Even *old* women's good ideas. Then the old women danced toward me with flowers, and suddenly I was standing up on my white quilt and I was wearing my old white nightgown, which I know I had not put on to come out here in. (I know better than to walk around at night in nothing but that.) And I worried because I wondered what had happened to my vest with all my best finds in it. But the Venus read my mind. "If you give us up," she said, "you have to give up those, too. You have to give up the proof that there were some little germs of sanity to what you were doing." All the old women came one by one and looked me right in the eye then and smiled; and all their eyes were blue, every one of them, the exact same blue. I could see that they wanted me as much or more than I wanted them and that we would talk and it would be my kind of talk. I knew that my left hand would write, then, many books on stones.

"And they will be found here," the Venus said, "and will be deciphered and all in less than five years from now."

"Otherwise?" I said.

"Otherwise, nothing. No library, no books, no mirror, no Venus."

"I'll take nothing." I said, and the Swan swooped down and knocked me over. I fell, clutching feathers, and I thought, They lied to me. I'm dying right now. They lied to me and took me anyhow.

But it wasn't dying. I woke up to voices and to the sound of a van and my daughters and two men. They don't have to say anything. I know where they're taking me, and I know that I chose it myself. I will go silently and with dignity. I will walk like a queen. I'm thinking that I'll find something there to make an effort for. I'll find something so I can do. I'll not just be.

Odd thing, though. I pick up my vest lying there all torn. It's as though it had been attacked in anger. There's hardly an inch of it without a tear. I check what's left of the pockets. Everything is gone, just as they said it would be — every single smooth, white stone and all the other things — and I'm standing here like a crazy woman, bare feet, nightgown (I feel sure I didn't come out here like this). And I am surrounded by feathers . . . white feathers. When I move they float out all around me. When I shake my head they flutter down.

FLEDGED

/ / /

Two A.M. You could feel the spray. You could taste salt. Sand. Grit in your teeth. Wind blowing miniature squalls across my toddy. I had the sliding glass door open on purpose. And talk about the "brightness of midnight" — everything wonderfully luminous: waves luminous black, foam luminous white, when (and you'd have thought the door wasn't open that far), when, somersaulting at least twice, landing on the far side of the room, water spraying, feathers flying . . . something big, that's all I knew at first, suddenly something big and birdish.

Then it untangled itself from itself . . . from its gray, and white, and black, and I saw it was a winged woman, huge wings, naked woman, but not at all the sort you'd expect would be flying around in seabird colors. Short and plump. I guessed about sixty. I brought her a beach towel to cover herself with and then pushed her into the bathroom, where I thought she'd do the least damage, and started trying to dry her wings with the blow-dryer. A hopeless task. Afterward I noticed there were wet streaks down the hall along the walls and even all across the ceiling. I was put out by the whole thing. I've been told I'm a fussy man, but I was having a party the very next night and I was put out. I don't like to make trouble myself or messes for others to clean up. I'd never be found having been blown, all wet and soggy, into someone else's living room. I'd have taken precautions. It was just like a woman, I thought, not to have listened to the weather report, to be caught out, no clothes on, though I didn't give a damn about that. I certainly wasn't interested any longer in a woman my own age, winged, naked, or not. Certainly not interested in chubby little gray ones with unkempt hair and ragged fingernails. And I found I resented the fact that she wasn't young and beautiful. I could see that in myself. I resented that she wasn't at all what you'd expect in a flying woman, especially not one with such large, white, black-tipped wings. I was thinking she ought at least to be built like a dancer. Maybe small but well-shaped breasts, maybe short-cropped black hair or, better yet, black feathers, little ones curling round her face in a kind of cap, and a nice ring of black around her eyes. I've seen that on some birds. I'd have liked that. But no matter her age and that she looked as she looked, and even though she'd dripped all over my floors and rugs, not to mention what she'd done to the ceilings, I didn't have the heart to shoo her back out onto the deck, though that was my first thought.

Her lips were blue with cold and she was, even still, out of breath. Her feathers stuck out in all directions. I couldn't bring myself to push her back into the storm, but I was worried about what else she would mess up when I let her out of the bathroom and she started swinging those wings of hers around. I had a lot of valuable art books and some pretty good prints on the walls, and then there was my party. I had to have everything nice for that, but she couldn't stay in there all night. I couldn't do that to her.

Strange, though she was part bird, she reminded me of my cat, Pasht. I don't even know why I keep that old cat. Came to me the same way, out of a storm not so unlike this one, and been with me ever since and I don't like cats . . . and birds even less. I did like calling, "Pasht, Pasht" out of the window, knowing the neighbors had no idea why I'd named her that. Perhaps if I looked up some other ancient goddess name for this gull, I'd like her better. (Is there a gull goddess? I doubt it.) But then I thought I'd not do that. I certainly didn't want an old lady hanging around. Not one like this. She looked as though, if one could ever clean her up to that extent, she'd be the sort who'd be wearing medium heels and a flowery dress and maybe do her best to keep anybody from discovering her wings. But it was only her body that looked like that. Her face . . . the look in her eyes . . . that was entirely different.

She wasn't but half dry when I let her out of the bathroom and took her into the kitchen for hot milk and toast. (I'd thought of eggs first, but that seemed insensitive. As it turned out, I needn't have worried.)

All the time I was getting her the snack, I kept having this funny feeling that I'd known her from somewhere: the way she sat on the edge of her chair, leaning forward—she had to, of course, because of the wings, but still it seemed a familiar pose, as though I'd known someone who sat like that all the time, poised for some leap up that never came. Now her legs were crossed, rather primly, I thought, under the circumstances, and it wasn't the best pose for her. They looked terrible, all black and blue. Her circulation must be awful. I knew that wasn't so unusual in a woman her age, but hers were the worst I'd ever seen. And her toenails! Black! And obviously hadn't been cut in ages. She'd been letting herself go. I wondered if she was depressed, and then I thought, Well, with those things on her back, who wouldn't be?

I watched her closely, though I pretended not to, and I couldn't get over how all her gestures seemed so familiar. I'd known that way of holding a cup, handle facing away from her as though other people's germs—left-handed people *and* right-handed people—as though the only safe place to drink from was opposite the handle. Except that sort of thing didn't fit with the look of her eyes. I thought, *of* her eyes, not *in* her eyes, because you couldn't see *in*. I'd never seen eyes like that on a person. Close-set. Wild. Fish-wild actually. All surface. And then there was the way she swallowed her toast. I'd never seen a person do that before.

"Coo," she said, finishing her hot milk. "Oh, coo."

Color had come back to her cheeks, but her eyes were still . . . well, in spite of the cooing, she looked like somebody who'd tear the wings off wrens for fun. I wondered if she had.

Lots of birds fly up from South America this season, but I don't know much Spanish, and I get it mixed up with Italian. And there certainly wasn't a Spanish or Italian look about her. I tried though. *"Parlate espagñol? italiano? . . . oder Deutsch?"* I tried all the languages I had smatterings of. I was thinking she might look familiar because I'd met someone who looked like her on one of the business trips I used to take. She responded . . . or, rather, sort of responded only to my bad French. *"D'où venez-vous?"* I asked, in polite form. *"Où allez-vous?"*

"Ici, ici, ici," she said, like a bird would say it. I wasn't even sure it was French. Perhaps it was only "Ti, ti, ti," or maybe she meant "tea."

My empathy for wild things is practically nil, though I don't consider myself a cruel person. My Pasht, for instance, has her special cushions and the best cat food I can get. I often cook up a batch of liver as much for her as for myself. I think that's the reason she's lived so long in such good shape. And the same goes for me. I take the same good care of myself. You'd never guess my age any more than you'd guess Pasht's. I don't take care of her like this because I love her so much. It's just a matter of pride to have a sleek and handsome animal. She matches me. We go our independent ways, but there's mutual respect. But what was happening now was . . . I don't know, all wrong. It's odd to say, but I didn't feel philosophically ready to tackle this sort of thing, especially not right before a party. I couldn't cope. And how could I have once known a bird-person when I had never heard of such a thing?

It wasn't until the next morning (I was in that half-awake state they always say is the most creative) that I knew who she reminded me of—who she, maybe, was, though I wondered how in the world that could be.

I had put her to bed in the guest room. First taken out everything breakable including the pictures off the walls, floor lamp, night table, mirror, and so forth. Took the quilt off the bed and left her a good warm blanket. Shut the door and braced it with a chair so she'd not get out without my knowing, and left her to find her own way of sleeping as best she could with those cumbersome things on her back.

Then I went to bed myself, and it was only toward morning, half awake, that I knew, or thought I knew (though I wondered, was I making it all up out of some kind of guilt, or fear, or remorse — but I'd simply done what I had to do and under the guidance, actually, of a psychologist), I thought that she resembled, to a remarkable degree, my first wife. I hadn't seen her for twenty years. (I was alone again now, after a short second marriage.) She would have aged more or less this much . . . if I wasn't imagining the whole thing. But if this were true, then I'd have to speak to her in no uncertain terms. After all, we'd gone our separate ways long ago, and she was not, by any means, a stray cat. Her size alone precluded that I take her in. This time, though, I'd have the sense to talk to her in English. (Why had I not thought to do that before?) This would not do, feathers all over the place, the smell of the sea permeating everything. I would not tolerate her imposing herself uninvited, and so forth, throwing herself in by the back door in the middle of the night . . . And those ridiculous encumbrances! How could anyone live like that? I'd help. I've always been willing to help when help was really needed. I'd pay to have them removed, should it come to that — and I really felt it *should* come to that — I'd help out in that way, but she couldn't stay. I had just, not so long ago, found myself — if that's the way to put it. I needed my own space. The house is small. Living-dining area smaller even than the deck.

It was early, but I found it impossible to sleep anymore. The storm was past. I swept the feathers out into the sunshine, where they blew away. There were an awful lot of them. I wondered if she was sick, or maybe moulting, though perhaps it was just due to the storm.

After I cleaned up, I took care to put away the breakables in the rest of the house. Party or not, this had to be done. Sculpture off its pedestal and into a corner, my best pictures into the closet, room divider up against the wall. I worried about the bookcase and the books. Also about the shelf of dishes (Mother's old china) hanging on the far wall in the kitchen. I'm a six-foot man,

and I'd have trouble knocking them over even if I tried, but she
. . . who could tell?

As soon as I heard sounds from the guest room, I opened the
door. She sat, naked again, in the middle of the bed, her wings
stretched partly up and partly out behind her at the angles that
cormorants hold theirs to dry. Even half-folded like that, they
touched the ceiling. Her feathers still looked ragged, her hair was
still a mess, but she looked a lot better than she had the night
before. "Hawk," she said. Rather disagreeably, I thought.

It was Julia all right, you couldn't mistake her, but really sort of
magnificent. Wings even larger than I'd remembered. Nose
quite grand. No wonder I'd not recognized her at first. And,
actually, she did look older than she should have, though perhaps
only worn down. Perhaps the stresses of twice-yearly migrations.
The cold of the upper air. The outdoor life. They say being in the
sun ages one, and her face did look chapped and weathered. And
of course those awful legs and feet (she'd had varicose veins years
ago before I'd left her, but nothing like this). Her hands, too, had
suffered. The rough perches, no doubt, and cold water. No hope
of keeping even one or two decent fingernails, I suppose. She had
suffered. I knew I wasn't entirely blameless in that myself. No
wonder her eyes were blank and black.

But then, suddenly, I was wondering where was Pasht? I
hadn't seen her all morning. That wasn't unusual, but I worried
just the same. The question of eggs (and bacon!) for breakfast
took on significance, so I had them and it turned out they were
fine with her, but then I remembered she'd always liked them.
And chickens. Fish. Raw clams. I decided, however, that I
wouldn't be cowed by any of this and that it was time for a
serious talk. "What about my cat?" I asked, though that wasn't
what I'd meant to take up first. What I needed to know was how
long she thought she was going to stay, especially since I was
having my party that night. My God, I thought, what will I do
with her?

Looking straight at me, she picked up three slices of bacon and
swallowed them all at the same time in one gulp. I didn't know
whether to take it as a warning to myself or a statement about

what had, maybe, happened to Pasht. And then she did just what I'd been worried she'd do: got up, turned around, and — it didn't seem on purpose, just the turning around — knocked every single dish off the shelves across the room. "Hawk," she said — I could tell she wasn't sorry — "hawk," with the self-confidence of a gull and a look of either all understanding or of no understanding whatsoever. I couldn't tell which. "Hawk, haw, haw."

"Laugh away," I said, "but you'll have to get rid of those things by this evening."

I didn't have the slightest idea how this could happen. It looked as if it would be quite an amputation. And of course it takes time to find the right doctor. I wouldn't want just anybody, any more than I would take Pasht to just any veterinarian. But then I had the idea that I'd make it a costume party. It was hard to think that anyone wouldn't notice even so, but I'd keep the lights low. I'd hurry and call everyone right away and tell them that I'd just thought of it and they didn't have to come in costume but it would be nice if they could manage something because there was someone coming to the party who had a great one.

The only way to dress her would be in scarves and veils or towels. Nothing else would fit around her wings. Of course, there were sheets. If I could find some white ones she could be an angel. Except there wasn't anything about her that was angelic. It turned out I didn't have white sheets, anyway. Then I thought of a sort of Renaissance avenging angel, my dark gray sheets, Harlequin mask, yellow bathrobe cord. I did have a white silk scarf — two, in fact. I could use both. I worked so hard on her costume I never did get a chance to fix one for myself.

Strange how they accepted her — how she seemed to fit right in in spite of her occasional squawks. Her laugh wasn't that much louder than some others, and she had that glazed-eyed, not-understanding, not-really-listening look almost everybody had as the evening went on. And people liked her. I don't know why. (But then, people had always liked Julia.) Perhaps because she said so little. (She'd always said little.) Actually she said nothing. Absolutely nothing. Laughed in the wrong places as well as the right ones. And I couldn't believe how little they seemed to notice or care about the wings. My sheets and wrappings hadn't done much to disguise that they were real, huge, factual wings that fluffed out when she laughed. But they *did* notice — on some level, anyway—because the conversation went from aviaries to omelets; from guano to condors, the demise of, or rather, the last few (it's strange how that always happens—how one manages to mention what seems unmentionable), through Lindbergh, budgies, passenger pigeons . . . Gulls, strangely—or perhaps not so strangely—weren't mentioned at all.

And she! Laughed a lot, said "clock" and "rack" and "gack," "cheek," "eat," "ork," "currr . . ." but they were enough. Ate more than her share. Drank. No, it was I who drank, and as I watched her, I became more and more fascinated. I admired her in spite of myself. How grand she had become. She had achieved a strange sort of dignity.

Centered, that's what she was. What *I'd* always wanted to be, though this was the first time I really knew what it meant. And, though chubby, she had a kind of grace. Swooped herself about. Guests, like Mother's dishes, seemed swept before her, spun in and out, scattered as the feathers scattered. People picked them up and put them in their buttonholes, in their hair, or behind their ears. They were having fun. Wherever Julia was they were having fun. And there was that touch of danger. They liked that, too. Some of the guests hung so close to her, leaning forward as they spoke, looking into her half-open mouth, I had to keep watching, wondering was I close enough to get there in time just in case. I *had* to be near . . . but for lots of reasons. It was as if I had been living someone else's life and now I was back to *the* question. The same old question as then—Did I or didn't I love her?—had to be rethought, and who would leave whom, and when, and *would* one of us leave? I thought I had become whole over the last few years, but now I felt halved. Humpty-Dumpty ever since she'd come.

As I drank, warmth spread through me, and, suddenly, I wanted her to stay. I needed her to stay. Of course the wings would have to go, no question about that, but then, I'd be making sacrifices, too. I already had: my walls and ceilings permanently ruined, my books, Mother's dishes . . . and, after all, I'd lived alone for quite some time now and liked it, or thought I did until this moment.

As they left, everybody said they wanted to see her again. Everybody made me promise to bring her along to the next parties. Some went so far as to hug her good-bye. I worried what she'd do, and when some gave her a peck on the cheek, she looked at them as if she'd peck them back, but she didn't.

When the last guests had gone, I told her she could stay, though she'd have to get rid of those things, and I said how we'd both have to make compromises, which was only right, though I did understand that hers would be the greatest, physically at least, and that maybe hers had been the greatest, mentally, too, even before, from the beginning.

"Aw," she said, and "How?" and shook herself, fluffing out her feathers and looking large. "How!" But this time it didn't sound like a question, and it didn't look as if a compromise (on her part) was going to come about.

"All right," I said, "stay any way you like, but stay. I don't care. I don't even care if you ate Pasht, but I want you to know that I think you did." (Actually I *did* care. It was only just then that I realized I probably *had* loved Pasht all this time.) "But I'm willing to forgive."

"Grackle," she said. Obviously she didn't care much about forgiveness.

She went to the sliding doors, pushed them open, and stepped out into the dawn. I could understand her wanting to get into the fresh air to think about it. I stepped out, too. Off on the horizon it looked stormy again, but it looked as if there would be a spectacular sunrise. I was thinking how nice it was, being with somebody, sharing the rising sun. I came up behind her and put my arm around her waist.

"How," she said, but again with finality. She seemed not to mind my arm around her, to hardly notice it in fact, but she turned and looked at me with that fish-bird/bird-fish stare, and I took my arm away. I couldn't help it. And then she stretched, reached both wings and arms up as far as they'd go, and, my God,

I'd not realized. I'd not understood at all. I just kept saying, "Oh, my God," over and over. I mean she could never live here. Those wings . . . they'd *have* to go. There was no way a person could get around like that. There was no house (that I could afford, anyway) that could contain them. Probably no house anywhere that could. I didn't even know how she managed to sleep. And think of her getting into a car. I mean trying to. Think of getting into an airplane, for heaven's sake.

But now I could see, storm or not, she was going to leave. She was going to take off in this wind. "Stop," I said, "you'll be blown away. You'll be struck by lightning." But perhaps she had been waiting for a wind like this all along in order to take off. She kept on stretching and making practice motions with her wings. They kept looking larger and larger and sounded like sails when the ship luffs, out of control. Suddenly I didn't care how wet, and cold, and hungry I might be. I wanted to come along to whatever rocky cliff she must live on. Nest on. "Take me with you," I said. "Let me hang on. I can."

"Quack!"

Then there was a great flapping and I reached for her. I had her, for a moment, by one awful, blue-streaked leg, but there was all that wind and sound . . . a great sound, and I dropped to my knees to keep from being blown off the deck. She headed out over the ocean toward the storm. I heard her "Hawk, hawk" blow back to me as she lifted into the wind.

And here I was, down . . . down here with the mess of the party, more drunk than I'd meant to be, and no Pasht to talk to. I couldn't face my own house. I sat on the deck and watched the storm come, and as soon as the rain started — really started — Pasht came back, not eaten up after all, except she'd lost her tail. Of course I don't know whether Julia did that or not, but I suspect. It takes away a lot of the snaky gracefulness Pasht had, but I keep her . . . I love her anyway.

VILCABAMBA

/ / /

Some kind of rain — some soft kind of rain first. Then the prickle of imagination or remembering; I'm never sure which. Another mist almost like this one, though, and tunes of old songs I wonder if I'll ever hear again or if I really heard before. A different language. *Guaya gocomadi. Guaya go comaditu.* What does it mean? And there is a sign: the hand palm up, then turning over and back again, and repeated. A graceful gesture. I remember, too, a funny little backward step-dance. And whistles! Each child had both a name and a whistle to be called by, and the whistles echoed sharp and clear about the mountains. I've forgotten my special whistle but I think I remember my name. I was Akuhu. And I think I remember they told me I was Ipa. "You are Ipa," they said. "Ipa! You will marry Ipa and no other. There will be no children, and there never have been children, unless Ipa marries Ipa." (I think not all of us, even there, were Ipa.)

It turned out to be true: there are no children. I married one of these women. She left me for one of her own kind and now she does have a child. If I do not find Ipa, I fear I will be childless. But are there any Ipa — and what is Ipa?

I do remember they said Ipa had dogs that came from the wombs of pumas, Ipa had cats from eagles' aeries. I remember this, but I forgot the language I learned it in.

Here they call me Mac, though some call me Joe. Also Big Nose, Nosey, Nose it All, Slanty Head . . . Sometimes it seems they took me only to laugh at me. (They had, by then, and as a favor, cut off my two sixth fingers.) I imagine all of us looked more or less like me back in that place, and I think that the burden of proof of my ugliness is on them. I think I remember Mother, or perhaps big sister . . . Yes, a sister: Woialala. I rode on her back sometimes in a little yellow sling with tassels. I remember her . . . I *do* remember her because it's her face I began to see in the mirror, more and more, as I grew older. My nose, her nose. My black eyes, her black eyes. My long, strong fingers, hers. When I think of her, I think this is a good way to be looking.

They took me from the food I knew and loved and fed me pickled fish, onions, sour cheeses. I remember the first crab I ate. There was nothing else to eat, so I ate it. (We are mountain people. Such food is alien to us.) They never let me do any work that I wanted or felt suited for. First I was set to polishing their shoes. Later to polishing their vehicles. I polished silver, brass, and bronze, glass, glasses, doorknobs . . .

Always they tell me my people are gone. Even the kindly ones tell me I have no more people, our land a broken wilderness: bridges, roads, and terraces fallen into the valleys. All now impenetrable. Also I know it's not a trip to take alone, but I have nothing to lose, and I would be happy if I found even one person like me, or one a little like me, or one like Woialala. I want to die in that place, somewhere near the terraces and tarns of home even if in ruins. But it's been so long I wonder if it will seem like home anymore.

I have a box of things I came with—what I had on when they took me: a sort of vest of stained white cotton with a border of red and gold threads. Much too small for me now, of course. I've often wondered if the stains are blood. They're the right brown color. I don't think it's my blood, but I don't remember whose it could be. I don't know who was hurt or maybe even killed when I was taken. Perhaps I don't want to remember. There's a rattle-snake-skin belt with no buckle. I think they took the buckle. There's a red wool hat. That still fits. I remember clinging to these even after they'd dressed me in their clothes. It was as though something of mother, aunt, or sister might be in them.

They saw how the things comforted me and they gave me a box and let me keep them.

> *Kopi, kopi,*
> *Bra ta apu.*
> *Kopi, kopi,*
> *Bra ta pu.*
> *Kopi, kopi,*
> *Rintu kopi,*
> *Bruha tapu,*
> *Tapapu.*

Children said that. Over and over.

"Ama sua, ama llulla, ama quella." I do not steal (*sua*), but I have stolen, I do not lie (*llulla*) but I have lied — already five lies. Or, rather, the same lie to five different people. What I have stolen is only the exact fare and not one penny more, but it is stealing none the less, even though I, myself, could be said to be stolen goods. Can't I steal, then, in order to restore myself to myself and to the place where I was stolen from? But I know something about that place. I know I left my golden bracelet on the edge of a cliff and would come back and find it still there. Though perhaps I only dreamed this and that once I had a golden bracelet.

My heart is a stone. (An idea I think I learned in that place: golden heart, silver heart, a heart to reach the top of the mountain, a heart to go on a long journey.) I cried after they first took me. I have not cried since. I looked for love after they first took me, I have not looked since, nor believed in it, not even in my marriage. "Go," I said to Lillian. "You haven't broken your word for there was only a stone to make promises to." My trip, then, not only to find my people and Ipa, but to make my heart the navel, the *cuzco* of my being, where all directions merge.

/ / /

Now the happy dawn of the first steps into the desert of the coast. Leave behind the ocean foods. In my pack, dried corn and potatoes, nuts and fruits. Also my little red- and gold-trimmed vest and my snake belt. Only now, three hours' hike into this damp desert, have I dared to take out my red hat and put it on. It's a funny little hat with a fringe along the edges. It must have been loose and rather like a beret when I wore it as a child, but now it fits more like a low fez. In the center of the front I think I once had a golden ornament — must have been real gold because that was torn from it when I was first taken. Now there's a ragged hole there. I've not tried to repair it. I've left it as it was. A hat with a hole. I would like my heart, one day, to be as open as my hat.

For the first time in my life — that I can remember — I'm full of hope and eagerness. I don't care if I find my own mountain. I have come here to be in that brisk air. I have come here to taste the little round seeds of home. I have come here to see, if not big noses, then at least the groups — the *majorities* in fact! — of small, brown people.

But of course I've seen them already, when I first landed. People, not exactly like me, but rather like me. Some almost as small and some hawk noses. But a strange thing happened. I tried to come close to them to see if I remembered anything of their language, but they turned their backs and whispered. They covered their mouths with their hands or their hats and stopped talking. They looked in some other direction or kept their eyes on the ground. I thought I heard one of them whisper *"Nawpa runa"* and I remembered — or thought I did — that *nawpa* meant old and *runa* meant person, but I am not old. That they turned away worried me, but not much because I have little to do with these people of the hot lowland cities here on the coast. Also I'm used to being looked at as the stranger. I'm used to the hand that covers the mouth, though of course I'd hoped that here, at least, that would stop.

At this early part of my journey I feel I should avoid the roads, stick to paths. I cross the edges of banana plantations. The people I see all do as the ones in town did, whisper, turn away . . . I keep to a more or less straight course. Not hard since I can see my goal: the heights in the East, snow on the tops of some of the peaks. The ground is flat here, so I walk as fast as I can. I don't stop to rest. Even at noon, I don't look for a shady spot. I nibble parched corn and sip *chicha* as I walk. By late afternoon I come, already, to the cliffs. I look for seldom-used trails. I want to sleep at least part way up, out of this heavy air and away from these people who seem less like my people, even, than those others, my captors, though they look more like me. I wonder if, the closer I get to my own, the less comfortable I'll feel?

At the head of one trail a serpent is sunning itself. Large and beautiful. A series of diamonds, yellow, tan, white, black . . . It comes into my mind that this is Serpent-Ipa. Ipa-Serpent. Fully fledged birds fly out of its eggs. If a snake should lead the way, then so be it, I will be led, especially by this prince of snakes. Yes, I think . . . No, I think, no. I tell myself I am no longer superstitious. All very well, but how else shall I pick the trail? I move forward. The snake coils off his rock. *"Ama sua, ama llulla, ama quella"* I say to it, and, *"Guaya comaditu."*

The snake looks at me with its little eyes, making me realize I have not been looked at since I came except by this prince. We stare at each other and then he moves aside to let me pass.

I manage to climb out of the damp heat before dark, so I sleep where I can breathe and where I can see the stars, clear and close.

Before I left the town, I had bought not only food with the last of my money, but a poncho such as these people wear and a heavy sweater. I had thought perhaps then I wouldn't be looked at as the stranger . . . the peculiar stranger anymore. I'm wearing these as I reach the top of the cliffs the next day and see before me the grassy plain with the mountains . . . my snow-touched mountains . . . beyond it. I see three clusters of little thatched houses and not far off—perhaps a mile or so from me—I see a group of farmers planting in the old-fashioned way, six or seven pairs of them, each man with his digging stick and each woman leaning toward the man and laying in the seeds.

I'm thinking that these people of the high plain will be more like my people, and now that I'm dressed more like they are, they'll see I'm one of them even if I can't speak as they do.

But first I rest a bit after my climb, my lungs . . . even my heart . . . opening. I will greet them, palms up. I angle toward their hill. They're singing a planting song and they're working so hard they don't see me. I hold out my hands. *"Ama sua, ama llulla . . ."*

I begin the greeting, but they're running off before I finish it. It seems they hardly have a chance to look at me and they're running away. In the distance dogs bark.

"Per qué? Pourquoi?" I shout and, *"Imatataq?"* but they're already into the valley beyond the hill. I'm upset and yet elated. I have remembered, *Imatataq*. It popped out—in the right place. And I know I will remember more. But why did they run?

And now almost the same thing has happened again; I've crossed the high plain and here behind rolling hills, I see another village. I think to ask for shelter for the nights up here are cold. Also for something to eat if they'll share with me. At the nearest house I see an old man in a yard behind a low, stone fence. He is threading red wool tassels into the ears of a llama. When he sees me he's so startled he pulls on the tassels and frightens the beast. It jumps the low wall and runs off in front of me while the old man hides in his hut, squawking out, *"Nawpa runa. Nawpa auqui."*

"Per qué? Por qué?" (Which is right?) But then I shout, *"Imatataq,"* as though it were a curse. And then yet another "why" comes to me: *Kotpo*. What language is that? Is there yet another language I used to know? *Guaya go cocomaditu? Kotpo?*

Away, then, from the people of the high plains. These are not my people. I will walk all night or at least as long as the moon shines. I will get into the heights as fast as I can.

Have good heart, I tell myself. Even my captors said, "Take heart," and "Don't lose heart." Walking keeps my courage up. (Now there's another word of hearts. *Coeur*. I will keep up my *coeurage*.) *Auqui?* the old man said. Didn't that mean prince? Or was it magic mountain spirit?

They told me my people were gone. Is that why these people treat me as though I am a ghost? Or am I so very different? But, yes, perhaps I am, for what I haven't let myself think about, nor do I ever let myself think about, is that I had been put to the board as a baby. I have a head like no other head that I have ever seen except—and even these are rare—in drawings and on statues.

Sometime after midnight I lie down, flat out on the plain, sheltered by nothing. The moon has set. I look up at the stars. I look from under my flat, slanting brow; (I must admit it). I watch them until I fall asleep, dreaming fires on the hillside. These are my fires. I have set every single one but I don't know if they are the fires of rage or fires of celebration. Then I dream falling and landing here on this plain as if from a great height, and wake as the sun is coming up over Vilcabamba and begins to warm me.

How can I stay angry, how can I be discouraged on such a bright morning, my lungs expanding? My chest, I can feel it, becoming a chest like the chests of my people? And it's always been a chest like this, but never, till now, had a chance to breathe to its full capacity. Sky bright. Air thin. Morning. Sun. And my singing heart has remembered another old tune. I will go, singing it.

And now I come upon the royal road. Here it's forty feet wide and still well used. I'm passed by mountain people coming down to get corn because they can't grow it where they live. Again, these people don't look at me or speak when they pass. They hurry by even though I lean over as though weighted down by my pack though it's not that heavy. But I lean over more than I need to. I remember that is the polite way. It says, "I am burdened. I am like a beast of burden." I keep my eyes on the mountains or on my feet. I never look at anyone passing.

The road is well kept up. I cross a wonderful, swaying bridge. Armies crossed on bridges just like this, six or eight men abreast. But they told me this would end, as I near my jungle home, the roads would not be left, and that's true. As I turn away toward my own land, the road dies. One needs a machete to chop one's way along it. I don't follow it. I strike straight out — no reason not to — into the "eye-teeth," the "tusks" of the world. Now I cling to the slopes with fingernails and toes and sleep half standing up or wedged into some cleft. No way to go but up or down or crabbing along crosswise, but soon I find trails, hidden trails. I follow them, but each trail rises up out of the jungle and then ends suddenly with a drop-off as though these were all dummy trails to fool the enemy. I try again and again, always with the

same results. Three days of it. Now four. I have walked all day
sometimes and then retraced my steps to try some other branch
and to sleep huddled on the trail. I see no one. I go nowhere, but
I'm being watched. Bird calls come too clear in places where no
bird seems to be. Pebbles come down on me. At first I didn't
think they had been thrown on purpose, but now I think they are.
Sometimes they come from a great height, many small stones
that sting. Three times a boulder has come down just behind me.
Purposely missing, that's clear. A warning, perhaps, but I keep on
trying. Now, at the end of the fourth day, I come to yet another
drop-off. No sign of a path along the far cliff. Nothing to dare to
leap for. Why? Why so many false trails and not one single one of
them a real trail? This one has a stepping stone at the end as
though to stand on and leap off into nothing. Others have had
that, too. I eat the last of my food and settle in to spend the night
behind the stepping stone to nowhere. It seems if I die here it
may well be of starvation unless I find a trail soon that goes
somewhere.

That night I have a dream that all the boulders and pebbles
coming down on me are friends and are sending me messages, the
small ones whispering, the large roaring. I wake with a headache. I
stare out over the mountains, puzzling over the dream for a while.
There's nothing to eat. I try to concentrate on the dream so as not to
think about that. Then I get up to start back, but I take one more
look over the drop-off and there's a rope of thick pilu grass hanging
over beyond it . . . a great leap beyond it. It wasn't there last night. Is
it to lure me to my death in one jump, or is it to help me on my
way? And if to help, why do they hang it so far from the last step?
But I had said that I would die here, and what better place than with
this view of snow-capped needles.

I call upon the sun and wait for it to warm me. I remove my
gloves. I will also leave my backpack here so as to be as light as
possible. I will even leave my little vest and snake belt. Then I have
the idea to take off my boots and leave them, too. It's as if, if I do
that, it will be in answer to what the pebbles and boulders of my
dream were saying. And of course the boots are heavy. Then I call
upon the sun again, as well as the mountain peaks. I worship the

view one last time, my Vilcabamba: up, down, out. I let my heart fill. I think I remember . . . yes, I do remember, Grandmother told me I had a heart of gold . . . that my heart was like the sun. *Guaya,* gold! Shall I leap to my death just when I'm remembering words in another . . . in the secret language of my birth?

I leap. I touch. I *just* touch the rough fibers of the rope but it is jerked away from me at the last minute. But I'm so light! I'm such a small, thin man! The joints of my fingers and, yes, even my toes . . . they're not like the joints of other people's. Have I always known that! My slanted head against the rock as if pressed to a breast, and I cling (*easily!*) like a spider, to the tiny rough places of the cliff. I cling and then I climb. And I know for sure that there is another language. There is Spanish, then Quechua, and then this secret language and these gestures and whistles, these secret other people, they, watching me.

At the top they've left me a pair of sandals that leave the toes free. I put them on and climb down this side as I climbed up that other, over and down and down again, until I drop beneath a false forest planted on platforms. I enter my hidden land. Men, women and children come to me. They're small with thin, strong hands. Six fingers. Noses like the condor's beak. Their heads are slanted, but I understand now that they were never put to boards. These are their natural heads. These are the people from which the idea came that others tried to imitate, tying up heads, wanting to make themselves and their children more like us. No doubt these people had once roamed all this land before the conquest.

They're singing in that language. *Guaya go. Guaya gocomaditu. Go comaditu.* Here the Ipa, all in white. They make way for me. They bring me to the once-gold chair, to the once-gold dais, to the once-gold house. *Guaya yaputu.* Gold is gone. *Guaya go comaditu.* Long live your golden heart. They bring the woman, Woialala. "This is your sister. This is your wife." I understand it. I answer, "*Gatu. Gatu.*" They put a yellow glass bead in the torn hole in my hat. No gold here, yet all is gold. It shines in their eyes and hearts and in the sun. "Go *as* gold," they tell me. "Go *in* gold," they tell me, "to the end of your days."

THERE IS
NO EVIL ANGEL
BUT LOVE

/ / /

She is eighty-two and in love. Impossible to be in love now, but she is in it. Dried up just there where love takes place, so no more of that for her. Yet she loves. And cries about it. Not cries for any real reason because so far nothing lost. Nothing gained, that is, in order to have lost anything yet. Still she cries, but only a few tears. Hardly enough to bother taking a Kleenex to, though perhaps her tears have also dried up like that other part of her.

She hasn't ever really loved until now — at least not that she can remember. But why not? And why never married? Why never had a real life like everybody else has, with husband and children? Or even just one child? Was that too much to ask? Just one man and one child?

The man — that man she loves now but hasn't met yet — isn't as old as she is, yet he's white-haired. (If she had ever had a son, he would be white-haired by now, too.) He has a sad expression. That's what made her fall in love. But she doesn't want to change it — doesn't want to make him happy. She likes him as he is. Something mysteriously wrong inside him. Secret sorrows. She likes that.

She knows he drinks too much — or at least too much in her opinion. She sees that every evening, looking out her window and into his window one story below hers and across the street. He comes home tired. She can tell by his walk. And then, inside his apartment, the way he flops onto his ragged old couch and stares into space before he gets up, finally, to turn on his music and make himself a drink. She knows what the music is even though it's winter and all the windows are shut. She's heard it in the summer — Beethoven symphonies for the most part. None of it, except maybe the slow movements, the kind of music you'd think somebody would listen to when tired.

So she doesn't want him not sad and she also doesn't want him not tired. She just wants to be there when he comes in. Share the tiredness and sadness. Make the drink and turn on the music so everything will be ready for him.

She's seen him naked. Sometimes at night he stands at the window, but the light is always behind him so she only sees a dark silhouette. He looks strong. Wide, heavy bones. Only a little bit paunchy. Not balding though. Lots of curly white hair. He stands at the window a long time sometimes, though usually not naked, looking out, but never up toward her.

She has stood there naked also. Three times. Twice (they were hot nights) when he was naked, too. Why doesn't he ever look up? But then, at her age, even though she's not fat, things sag. Not just breasts, but under arms, over knees . . . What if he *had* glanced up when she hadn't noticed and didn't like what he saw?

After five-thirty she always hovers by her window. Sits knitting (a man's tan vest now — she has already made a man's long scarf), knitting and watching at the same time. She never turns on her TV in the evenings anymore.

Lately it's been getting harder and harder for her to sit still and just look out at him. She keeps having the feeling she should hurry up. Do something before it's too late, though she doesn't know quite what. It's hard to look out the window and see him so calm and tired and lying back on his couch, cushions under his head and under his feet, drink on coffee table (she can only see the corner of the table), and that look of listening, his toes bobbing to a beat she can't hear. How many years now, looking down at him? Three or four? If she had acted back then she'd only have been in her seventies, but then she had thought that too old. Now seventy-eight or seventy-nine seems so much younger. And had been. Fewer aches and pains, better memory for where she'd put things and for what she planned to do next.

What *should* she do next? She didn't want to have to begin. She wanted it to have already happened. She, there in his apartment, his supper prepared. She wasn't asking for much. Never had asked for much and now, still, only for a little bit. Not even to be loved. Just to be with somebody, anybody, but especially him.

And it isn't conversations that she wants. It's a melancholy quiet. Or that she might walk with him, a few steps behind, which she could do right now, actually, but hadn't thought of before. And to be just a little bit younger. Is being sixty-nine too much to ask? In a flash it could be so. One magic word, or not even that. One sideways shift — a tiny jump and into a new world. "There's a whole other universe next door." She remembers reading that or something like it. Perhaps, just as she was thinking about it, it had already happened. She *had* felt the lurch, and then the moment of dizziness just afterward. She had staggered. She'd had to sit down. It had been a subtle shift, but it might not take much for a big change. And the plant on the window sill — *there* was sure proof — all of two inches shorter. Maybe now she can say she is only seventy-eight. She will say it. Or avoid saying anything at all about it.

And him? What time is it? Only two-thirty and coming home. Is he sick or has he lost his job? There he goes, into his building. A minute later she sees him through his window and then at his window. He looks up. It *is* a whole new world, and the half-moon never seemed so bright in the daylight sky. He's looking right into her eyes. Is she dressed right? Old baggy sweater she only wears when in the apartment. Why didn't she get ready for that glance? Especially right after that dizzy spell? But in this new place it might not matter because they must have already met. The hard part is done. She waves, but he's looking down again. And now he pulls the shade. He's never done that before. It definitely i whole new world.

Should she go down, ring his bell and ask him if he's sick and can she help? But what if, in this new place, this is his usual time for coming home? She mustn't act as if she doesn't know. But what if he *is* sick? Maybe she should wait and see. Except the shade is down.

Anyway, no time for long-range plans. At her age only time for action. If she goes down and rings his bell, when he asks who's there, she'll say, Charlotte, or perhaps Isabel. In this world her name could be anything. Maybe Julia. She would have been a jewel, not a left-out person.

She'll wear her best dress and go on over. Third floor, right side of building. Maybe someone will be coming out just as she's going in. She'll not even have to ring the bell. Surprise him.

/ / /

And the surprise turns out to be even more than that. His apartment door is unlocked. He *must* be sick. Or in some sort of agitated state. People don't leave their doors unlocked around here.

But she won't just walk in. What if he's in his underwear, or even less? It's different when she watches from across the street and can only see little slivers of him, except when he's on the couch or at the window. She shuts the door and knocks. "Who's there?" comes out in a kind of croak. She's never heard his voice before, but she recognizes sickness in it. "Julia . . . Juliette," she says. (It sounds younger being Juliette.) "You know. Your neighbor from across." He opens the door a crack, then wider when he sees it's just her. His face is oddly puffy and pale. There are circles under his eyes. His hair is damp and some sticks to his forehead. Reminds her of a feverish dog she once saw. Close up, he looks even sadder than she'd thought he looked when she watched him out her window. It's not just an ordinary sadness. Bigger than that. All-encompassing. Inborn. She loves him for that look. She wants to take him in her arms right away.

She's exactly the same height as he is, neither one of them very tall. He's just the right size for her to reach out and hug. She steps forward, he steps back, and she's already inside. It's easy.

"What do you want?" There's irritation in his voice, but she knows that's just the sickness talking and she forgives him.

"You're sick," she says. "I could tell from my window." She's thinking how lucky that he *is* sick. That makes everything so much easier, whether a whole other world or not. "I want to help," she says and shuts the door behind her, locking it properly this time.

He backs up and sits down on his couch. She can see he hasn't the energy to argue with her or throw her out, thank goodness. "Dear," she says, and then, "Poor, dear man," because she doesn't want to have called him "dear" just yet—not until she finds out how far things have progressed between them. But it's the word "man" that catches her up—that sticks in her throat and almost makes her cry. How long since she's had occasion to say it or to be standing so close to one—a flesh-and-blood, not a shopkeeper, not the plumber, not in the movies, not on TV, man?

She dares to go even closer. Plumps up the cushion where he usually lays his head. Then to the other side of him and plumps up his foot cushion. (She can tell it's been a long time since anybody plumped them up.) She can hardly breathe with the wonder of being there, so close she can smell the sick sweat of him. "Lie down," she says. "Please do lie down. I'll get you tea." She hopes there is tea. She can't go get her own because she might not be able to get back in so easily. She's never seen him drink anything except something from the bottles on the end table, but she doesn't think that would be good for him. Especially now.

He does lie down. She's surprised to see him do it—to see how things are turning out so well. "Music?" she asks, but he turns on his side and doesn't answer. There's a record of Beethoven's Fourth on the turntable. She turns it on and then goes to find tea. There is some. Funny how people always have plenty of the things they never use because they never use them.

After she makes the tea, she finds he's already asleep, so she opens the blinds, sits down to drink it herself, looking up at her own windows across the way, thinking how this is *his* view. She's feeling contented for the first time in a long while. She can almost see her poor old self up there, yearning at her window.

When she finishes the tea, she looks around his apartment, first pocketing his keys, which are on the end table along with the bottle of Scotch. Now she can go home and get him anything he needs from her place and come back in. (He needs plants. She noticed that right away.)

She checks the bedroom. It's tinier than she'd thought it would be. And, after all that Beethoven, she hadn't expected so many dirty socks on the floor. The bed is unmade. She can't tell if the sheets are gray or haven't been washed in a long time. She'll bring over a laundry bag, and her cheerful, yellow sheets with daisies on them. Good for a sick person. She'll bring the throw she crocheted last year. She realizes she'd made it for his couch. She'd had that, though hardly known it, in the back of her mind all along.

There are no pictures on the walls, but there are two photos stuck into the frame around the mirror. One is of a white-haired little boy and the other is of *him* in a battered hat and hunter's vest. Behind him there are woods and, in the distance, mountains. She pulls that picture out and puts it in her pocket. His bedside lamp is broken. The base is propped up with a little book of Shakespeare's sonnets. Shakespeare and Beethoven. A little obvious. Surely not particularly intellectual. Or is it? Anyway, it's clear he really likes them. There's a big book of Shakespeare's plays on the floor by the foot of the bed, a sock on top of it. She has a brass Shakespearish lamp at home—a mannish sort of lamp. She's sure he'll like it.

She comes back to the living room and carefully puts the photo of him in her purse. Then she starts to hide the bottle that's on the side table. Decides to put it under the sink, but there are more bottles in there already. She should empty them all out. It's hard for her to bring herself to do it, but she does, all of them, including the six-pack of beer she finds in the refrigerator. It's a good deed. Sick people shouldn't have alcohol. Nor well ones either.

Then she moves the chair from the window to just across the coffee table so she can look at him. He's in a sick sleep, jerking his head every now and then as if trying to avoid something and making noises of discomfort.

She has him right where she wants him. She can study his bushy, still brown, eyebrows; the lines crossing his forehead. His mouth looks grim, but then, of course, he's sick. How wide and muscular and hairy his forearm that lies across his chest!

She sits, leaning forward, looking, studying. She wants to have him memorized for any future references that might be needed in some sadder days to come – if there would be any more of those, though she thinks not. (His main flaw is a short upper lip. Perhaps, later on, she can persuade him to grow a mustache.) She watches for a long time until he seems to be sleeping more deeply, then she runs – actually runs – across the street. (Could she run like this before that dizzying shift? Surely not.) Once there, she takes out two big shopping bags, gets the crocheted throw, juices (he should have plenty of juices), yogurt, the lamp. She'll make other trips for the plants.

Hurrying back to his apartment is wonderful – as if they're already lovers and about to have their second rendezvous, which is true. (Could she have already undressed in front of him? Maybe could have in the dark, but even that would have taken courage. In this world, though, it seems she does have courage.)

He's still asleep, snoring lightly, when she comes back. She changes the bed, throws away his broken lamp, arranges her crocheted throw across him, though not covering up his wonderful arm. She makes a second and then a third trip across the street for all her plants. She uses a shopping cart to bring over the biggest one. She can look after them better over here now. Finally everything is ready. She sits down and wishes he would wake up. If he doesn't soon, she'll make some loud noises. She wants to see what's going to happen next. But for the time being she waits in the chair across from him, contented with how nice she's made things look.

The record player clicks down the next record. A slow movement. She dozes without meaning to. Dreams she's pregnant with his child and wants to name it after him but can't because she doesn't know his name – doesn't yet know what name it is she cherishes. She saw his last name on his mailbox as she was going in and out, but she still doesn't know the precious, private first name that she would have named her son if he hadn't been just a dream. (Would he have looked like that white-haired child in the picture in the mirror's frame?)

She wakes with a start when the music moves on to the scherzo. She'll check his mail for his first name. There's a little desk across the room, and here's A. E. Housman right on top. *"When I was one and twenty . . . ."* (She'd never wish herself that far back.) And, *"Oh, when I was in love with you, then I was clean and brave . . . ."* Does this mean he's old-fashioned and sentimental? That would be nice. Perhaps he writes poems himself and that's why he looks so sad. Except she hopes they're not the sorts of poems you'd find in newspapers.

Under the book she finds the bills. John. As simple as that. Who would have thought she'd ever like the name John? But suddenly it's full of magic. Just like this whole new world.

First she says it softly and then louder and then quite loud. In a minute she will wake him, but first she moves his desk over by the window where the chair used to be so he can look out as he does his bills or writes his poems. Then she gets a glass of juice, banging things about in the kitchen. Comes back and kicks the arm of the couch just enough to shake it. Calls out, "John," again. The music has come to a bombastic finale, but she has to kick the couch twice more before he finally opens his eyes. She holds out the drink.

He's having a hard time waking up. Then he looks angry and even shocked. "What are you doing here? Who the hell are you?"

"Genevieve. Don't you remember me?"

"I'll call the cops."

"Drink this. You need to keep drinking."

He pulls himself up on his elbow and looks at the end table where there's no Scotch anymore. "Where's my Scotch?"

"This is better for you," she says and dares to go right to him, hold the juice glass to his lips. He flinches away and sits up, but then leans back, hands to head.

"Oh, God," he says. Takes the juice, drinks it all at once as if it were only a little glassful instead of a large one. She's thinking: *That's* the way men do it. Women never do that.

As soon as he puts the glass down he says, "Where *is* my Scotch?"

"Gone," she says, "but I brought you some aspirin to take down the fever."

"There's some under the sink," he says.

"Not anymore."

"Damn it, who *are* you? What right do you have to . . . ?" He's getting up, staggering over to the sink to see for himself, breathing hard. Looks as if he's going to cry. Looks as if, after he squats down to see, he can't get up again. His shirttail is coming out in back and there's a large, sweaty spot in the middle of it. Now women wouldn't have that. She can hardly keep her hands off him he's so *man*. But she should help him get up. She had the same trouble getting up from there herself and she's not even sick. He pushes her away. She knows that's just because he's sick. She was that way the time she had pneumonia — irritable when there wasn't even anybody to be irritable at. She'd had to go through it all by herself, but now *he* doesn't have to.

He gets up by holding onto the sink. "Shit," he says, and, "Shit, shit, shit. Do you know how much that stuff costs?"

He's so dizzy he can hardly get back to the couch. She grabs him just before he falls, her arms around — like a hug. How warm he is! How damp! How alive! Especially that. What a strange thing it is to touch another person. Like a stove. And men must be more like stoves than women.

"My cold's gone into my ear," he says. "Inner ear. I've had it before. Oh God, it makes me feel sick to get up."

She's thinking, good. All the better if he's helpless, but she says, "That's too bad," hoping it sounds sincere. "But I'm here now. You don't have to worry." She still has her hand on him even as he lies down. It's as though he were the central core from which all life's energy emanates. Now that she's found it, she knows exactly what she hasn't had all these many years. Never had. Not even for a little while. When had she hugged, and who?

Why, not even that dour woman, her mother. But now there's been this shift and things are better. Over here she probably had hugged her mother and been hugged, too. And here she is, happy to have her two fingers touching his arm, the same arm she'd looked at for so long before that she knows it by heart. She keeps her fingers there even though she has to stoop awkwardly because she doesn't dare sit on his coffee table. It's not very steady.

But then he tries to see around her — pushes her away. "What are those plants? Why is the desk over there? What's happening?"

"That's a golden pothos and a jade, and that big one is a ficus. They're for you."

"I don't want plants."

"But you *do. 'The loveliest of trees,'* for instance, ' . . . *is hung with bloom along the bough.'* You do. You know you do."

"Oh God, I can't think about it now. Just go away."

"Don't think, then. And you really ought to get in bed." She can hardly wait till he sees her daisy sheets and Shakespeare lamp. Also she had brought over a large photo of herself when younger to put in his mirror frame next to the white-haired little boy, to take the place of the picture she had stolen.

"In a minute." He says it as though he thinks he'll never have the energy to walk that far.

It occurs to her that he hasn't had anything to eat yet. "Are you hungry?"

"There's some beer in the refrigerator."

"That's gone, too."

"Goddamn!"

"You don't mean that."

She makes him toast and tea. He's so nauseous when he sits up that he nibbles at it lying down with the plate on his chest, but he does seem a little better afterward. He lets her help him to the bedroom, flops down, puts his head on the pillow, but won't take his feet off the floor. "I can't sleep on these," he says.

"Yes you can." She likes the way he sounds like a little boy, though being his mother isn't what she wants. She wishes there'd be one more lurch, one more little thunk like before, and one more dizzy spell and she'd be . . . well, whatever age, of all the ages that women can be, that he likes the best.

"I will not sleep on these things."

"Don't be childish," thinking, be childish.

"Is that *another* plant?"

"Just a little one. African violet."

At first she thought he'd said, "another planet" — that he knew, as she did, that it is a whole other world.

He looks half-asleep already. She tries to lift his legs onto the bed, but he resists. "Who are you?"

"Don't you even remember? You must be really sick. I'm Harriet." (He finally does let her lift his legs.) "You haven't forgotten . . . all those things. Beethoven in the park. We held hands." (Of course they had.) "We even . . ." But she can't speak of that. Had they really gone that far? But he looks to be already asleep, and thank goodness.

She takes off his shoes. Doesn't dare take off any more (in spite of what they may have done together some other day when he wasn't sick). She does unbutton his shirt and peek inside. Lots of white hair across the middle of his chest. He's snoring lightly again, so she dares to rest her hand on his fuzzy chest, the stove . . . the furnace of life. What a nice world this is turning out to be!

She'll go sleep on the couch where he lies so often, her head on his cushion. She'll try to lie there gracefully in case he comes in during the night, though, at her age, what good will that do? At least she won't let herself sprawl.

Before she settles down, she takes out the photograph of him she had put in her purse. He's actually smiling in it—a little Mona Lisa sort of smile, though his eyes, she's glad to see, look just as sad as ever. It's such a sweet smile, it *has* to be rare.

She props up the picture on the coffee table so she can study it while she eats her yogurt. She wonders about that other picture of the little boy. Perhaps she should have taken it also. It would be nice to have a picture of such a beautiful child. If she had ever had a child, would he have been as beautiful as this boy? Why not? She hadn't been bad looking and John must not have been either.

After eating, now what to do? She doesn't feel like sleeping yet and there's no TV, only all this fancy old-fashioned music equipment. How settle down when she has so much energy over here in this world? She'll sit at his desk. She'll read his poems, his letters, or whatever there is, and if there isn't anything like those . . . well, you can learn a lot of things about a person from his bills, too.

And here's the electric bill, second notice. Second notice on the telephone also. She'll get out her checkbook and pay them right now. She'll pay all his bills. Mail them tomorrow. And she'll get him some decent food: whole wheat bread, brown rice, broccoli . . . She'll go home and change her clothes. Wear something she can clean up in. What sort of clothes does he like women to wear? What *do* men like? There's probably a book on it. These days there's a book on everything. She'll get all there are. She can hardly wait till morning. (Should she buy herself a padded bra?) How courageous she is over here! Why hadn't she ever taken action before, even there, in that old, drab world next door?

/ / /

She wakes up early even though she went to bed late — wakes to find herself in exactly the position she wanted to be in, on her side, legs together, curled up, but she doesn't think he's been in to see her like that. She lies there, watching the glistening dust motes, watching the oblong of sunlight move across and down the wall. She'd not done either since she'd been a child. She's thinking how sweet to be so like a child again. Then she thinks back to all the things she had memorized about him the night before. She hopes she hasn't forgotten one single precious thing.

First thing after breakfast it will be down to the laundromat and over to the store. Then to the library to get books on what men want, though if she starts thinking about it, she already knows a lot about them — like, even though they always say men put women on pedestals, she knows it's the reverse. Men want to be the ones on pedestals and they don't like women who don't put them up there and keep them there. But she won't have any trouble doing that for him. She'll let her feelings shine out from her eyes and she'll say it, too, though it's probably too soon to tell him that she loves him so.

She's getting bored and thinking of waking him, when she hears him (she'd left the door partway open) sniffing and coughing and saying, "What the hell? What the hell?"

"I'm here," she calls. "I'll be right there."

She's by his bedside right away and he's still saying, "What the hell?" and looking at the brass lamp as if he'd never seen it before. "Where did that come from?" and then, "Who are you?"

Doesn't he remember anything! "I'm your friend from across the street. I'm Gloria." (Gloria! That's exactly how she feels, absolutely glorious!) "We've known each other for a long, long time. Don't you remember anything?"

"You said your name was Juliette."

"I ought to know. You can't remember anything." She's glad to see he's looking puzzled.

"Where did that lamp come from?"

"My gift to you. A long time ago."

"I can't say I don't need it."

"You like it. You said you liked it. Before."

He *does* like it. She's sure of it. Probably likes everything but won't admit it. She knows that about men, too.

He struggles to sit up. Clearly he's still dizzy, though not as bad as last night. (If she's lucky, he'll get worse again in the afternoon.) Looks like he'll hardly make it to the bathroom, though. She grabs his arm and he lets her help him. She's thinking, again, how warm, how damp.

He won't let her come in with him, though she tries to at first, but then thinks the better of it. Lets him shut the door. When he staggers out she's right there, ready to put her arms around him and help him back to bed. "You've sweated up the sheets," she says, thinking: like a man. "I'll bring over some fresh."

"Yes, you go on and do that."

She can tell he doesn't know she's here to stay. She won't say it, not quite yet, but she tells him that she paid the bills. She wants him to know that. "I paid them all," she says. "I have to mail them now and then I have to get you some decent food. All there is for breakfast is my yogurt so that's what you'll have to have. If you like, I'll get some steak." Men always like steak.

"I remember you now. You threw away the Scotch. Don't bother coming back unless you bring some."

"Orange juice," she says, "and milk."

He says he won't eat her yogurt, but she leaves it by the bedside anyway. "I know I've told you this lots of times before," she says as she leaves, "but you're wonderful."

He groans, but she's sure he likes that she said it. Who wouldn't?

/ / /

At the library they only let her take out three books at a time. She gets: *Intimate Sexual Play, Women Who Don't Love Enough* (she rejected the opposite title), *How to Kindle Passion.* Glancing through them as she was picking them out, she learns that being playful and childlike is good during sex, that one shouldn't give advice (she'll just clean up and not say a single word), that most men fear intimacy and commitment (she saw that in him right off), that men like a woman with joie de vivre. Joie de vivre! Perhaps her name over here is Joy.

None of the books has any advice on how or who to be. She'd wanted a book to tell her whether to wear skirts or slacks, and what to do about her hair — a long time since she's done anything about it at all. She decides before she goes back she'll have it dyed and curled even though she isn't sure which, of all the possible styles or colors, he'd like best.

While she's under the drier, she reads more about men and about love: one should not use sex to manipulate the loved one. (She won't.) Most men don't want to marry if they can get what they want by other means, though women are always thinking they'll change their minds.

/ / /

Back at his front door, there's the music — too loud. She can hear it from downstairs. He must have gotten up. She had hoped he wouldn't be well enough. Upstairs, her arms full of groceries, laundry, and books, she unlocks the door and pushes with her knee. The chain is on. She calls out, but the music is so loud he can't hear, or pretends he can't. Nothing to do but wait for the slow movement. She puts her packages down and sits on the floor. (She had thought that maybe *now* it would be easy to get that far down, but it isn't. She wonders how it will be trying to get up again.) She puts her foot in the opening so he can't close the door, thinks maybe all that memorizing of him will come in handy after all — even right now. Delicious to remember all those things. She's so deep in thought that, when the tender, slow movement comes, it fits so well into her daydream she almost forgets to call out.

But he doesn't answer.

"I'm not going away. I'm not leaving this door."

Finally he comes and looks at her through the gap. He's had a shower and combed his hair and he doesn't look quite as sick, but, happily, his eyes look even sadder than before, and he looks confused. Stares at her.

"You've changed. Have you changed your hair?"

She had almost forgotten she'd had it done — that she looks (she hopes) maybe years and years younger with these jet black curls. "No," she says, "it's always been this way."

"I don't believe it."

"Believe what you like."

"One thing's sure, you won't get back in here again unless you bring some Scotch."

She supposes she'll have to. She'll *have* to. And Housman wrote it. No wonder he likes him. Two of a kind.

> Look into the pewter pot
> To see the world as the world's not.

She, on the other hand, would rather see reality, especially when this is such a nice reality.

/ / /

She buys the best. Chivas Regal, and two imported beers. Catches sight of herself in the liquor store window with her new hairdo and color. She'd been letting herself go — even after she'd fallen in love and watched him walking home everyday. She must have thought there wasn't any hope.

/ / /

He seems relieved just to have a bottle in his hand. He even smiles — one of those rare, treasured smiles, and all for her. "Thank you, Gloria," he says.

"Gay. I keep telling you."

He's sighing. He's drinking and looking more mellow all the time. He's going to let her cook the steak. (They'll not have steak often once she's settled in. Fish is better for him.) He's lying back and shutting his eyes. He's sighing again, but it's a different kind of sigh this time. Now is probably one of those times the books would say to keep quiet. It's hard to do when she's so happy. But now he's getting up and putting on a record and there's a man's bass voice singing out with the gravel and rumble of masculinity. She isn't tempted to do anything but listen.

The air is fragrant with steak and onions. The late sun slants in again, but from the other side. Dust motes look like tiny diamonds. The man on the record sings while her man lies humming along. Her man's voice is not quite so deep, but it's raspy. (If liquor makes him feel so good and makes him let her in, she'll be sure there's plenty of it — or, rather, just enough.) Things couldn't be more perfect than they are right now.

Oh, but they could. The doorbell rings from downstairs and she buzzes the front door open, puts the chain on so she can see who's there before she opens the door all the way. It's the white-haired boy! Older now, maybe ten, but just as beautiful as ever.

More so, here in the reality of him. Except he needs a haircut. She can take care of that.

The boy draws back, looks frightened, but she opens the door all the way and reaches out for him. No need to wonder who he is anymore. *This* is who.

"Come on in," she says. "I'm Aunt Joy."

IF THE WORD
WAS TO
THE WISE

/ / /

It is written that what is written shall be done as it is written, and that the sacred books and secret words shall remain sacred and secret. It is written that what is written shall be the law of the land and that those who rule the words shall be the leaders of the land. It is written that the leaders shall live in the towers and turrets of the library, and that they shall heed the words of the books therein, and shall take an oath to do so. Because the library opens on Monday, Monday is the first day of a possible five-day communion with books, so Monday will be a sacred and a joyful day, and on that day the flags of the library will fly.

The word for *word* will be *word,* and the word for *library* will be *library,* and the word for *law* will be *law* and it will be obeyed.

/ / /

The library is the tallest building in the city. No other building is ever to be as tall or as magnificent. It has nine white towers where eighty pale blue flags fly. Inside, silks hang along the walls. Alabaster lamps in niches give the interior a soft, mysterious glow in keeping with the mysteries of the words. In summer, the bronze doors that face east are opened at dawn in order that the first light should penetrate deep into the malachite lobby. Anyone can enter, but over the door there is a warning: BEWARE ALL YE WHO ENTER FOR HERE IS UNDERSTANDING BEYOND ALL UNDERSTANDING.

In the several subbasements of the library there are two safes. One contains the secret, sacred writings of the laws of the written word, which are the laws of the library and the laws of the land. This safe is opened frequently in order for the members of the central book committee to refer to the written word. The other safe is larger and more secure. This one contains the banned books. Someone did, they said, enter this safe many years ago and read, they said, several pages of lewd and antilibrary writings. They said he even wrote down what he had read, but that was found and burned, and the person was not killed, not confined, but deprived of communication. His tongue was split and his upper teeth pulled out, the tendons of the thumb and fingers of both hands were cut so that writing was out of the question also. This was so long ago that no one today, they said, remembers exactly what that safe contains, and we thank God for that. We had, they said, wiped out, once and for all, all the evil books by appropriating them and locking them up. We lived, therefore, in harmony and with only good words.

The princes of the library are housed in the subbasements also, for they are the ones who guard the safes. I was one of them. (It's an honor and a privilege and I took pride in walking about the library and being called prince.) We were the ones who saw to it that those who visited the safe that contained the words of the laws were qualified to do so and had permission from the chairman of the central book committee. Of course there was no permission, ever, for visiting the banned books, even for the members of the book committee. They said the only possible reason for entering that room would be in order to bring more books in, and this hadn't happened in all the time since I had become a prince of the library.

None of us princes has ever entered either of these rooms, though we know the combination, but we guard each other as much as we guard anyone, and we've made vows. I had never been tempted to enter the safes, nor had I allowed myself to wonder what could be in those rooms in all my eighteen years of service. (I came here as a boy of fifteen, having sworn the oaths, and being, already, six foot tall, and having, already, learned to take words seriously.)

/ / /

But then there was Josephine. She was older than she looked, but I liked it that she was my age. I wouldn't have known what to do with her if she had been a teenager, which is the age she looked. I had lived so much of my life among the princes that I'd lost the "family" touch. I'd forgotten what it was like to have people of your own. Josephine took the lead. She went after what she wanted. She offered me a captaincy and a space of my own on the eighteenth floor and she had the power to get it for me. At least she said she did, and I believed her because she was the daughter of the head librarian. It was not as powerful a position as if she were the daughter of the chairman of the central book committee, but still her mother was a person to be reckoned with and I thought might actually have the power to do as Josephine said she could. Josephine said the room would have to be small, pieced out of someone else's apartment, and it might not look toward the river, but inward toward the towers (which I would find—I would *still* find—as beautiful as any outside view could be, for the white, glazed tiles of the towers reflect the colors of the sky and so are endlessly changing and, on sunny Mondays when the flags fly, I can't think of anything I'd rather look out at. Eighty! Imagine that. Eighty blue flags.).

The view from Josephine's balcony was exciting in a different way. Daytimes the river was full of sailing vessels (some quite large), and skiffs and barges—often library barges full of books, sometimes small boats rowed by several princes such as myself, but in the service of some lesser library. At night the lanterns on the far banks looked as though they were lit up for a festival. It was a view not many princes of the library had been privileged to see. I was grateful for it. In fact I wasn't sure I wanted an apartment on the eighteenth floor. I just wanted Josephine and that things should stay as they were.

I wasn't sure what Josephine wanted. Perhaps she didn't know herself. I often thought she chose me not because of me at all, but because I was a prince and had access to forbidden rooms. Any prince would have done as well. She even told me so to my face, laughing at me, but then she would take it back—say that that was her idea at first, but that it wasn't anymore—that she loved me for me. I didn't know what to believe, but actually I didn't care, as long as I had the privileges of her balcony and bedroom.

You might think that I would regret the promises I made to her in our moments of passion, but what else had I to give? She already had everything and she gave so much to me, including the river view, and boats, and lights along the shore. What could I give her but my one and only gift, access to words that we had probably forgotten the meanings of, let alone the pronunciation, access to excesses neither of us could imagine in our wildest conjectures.

Yet for all this, she was an innocent—in many ways as innocent as she looked. Perhaps her desire to see forbidden documents was out of that same innocence. How could she foresee, being who she was, words that might be dangerous—that might harm?

It was this innocence that lured me. I especially liked it in her voice. She sang, but not professionally. Her voice wasn't powerful enough. It was fluty, breathy, young . . . She never suspected that her voice was too small ever to amount to anything. She was even innocent of the fact that she couldn't carry a tune and that her rhythms were often off in odd ways. Yet her voice was to my taste. It was all of a piece with her pale beauty. Like her voice, which no one but me thought worth listening to, no one but me thought she was beautiful. Perhaps she could read this in my eyes. Perhaps this was why she picked me.

Though it was she who tempted me, I knew full well that if the thing were done, I couldn't blame *her* for it. And it was I who had sworn the oaths, not she.

I didn't rush into it. I asked her, over and over, why anyone would want to see subversive books, least of all she. Didn't we already have more than enough words? More than enough concepts? More, in fact, than we could handle as it was? More than any one person could learn about in a lifetime? We already had ideas that ought to be voiced only in the privacy of one's own home, and we had words for no other purpose than to be said in anger; there were even books that came in plain brown wrappers. Why would anyone want or need even more outrageous ideas than we had?

"Because they're there," she always said. "Because they exist."

I told her she shouldn't be overawed by what she didn't know. I said she ought to learn to live with a little bit of ignorance. I tickled her toes as I said it so she would think I was just teasing, but I wasn't. "Might just as well," I said, "write down wrong words and things not true, so that what is written is lies." Even as I said it, I felt I had blasphemed.

Josephine turned away and looked out the window to the far side of the river, squinting. I stopped stroking and tickling her feet and we were silent for a long time.

We were lying sideways across her hammock, I facing upriver, she, facing down. My boots were on the floor, my cap of honour carefully on top of them. The cap was the pale blue of the library— the honorable blue of honorable words.

Suddenly we turned to hold each other for comfort, and the holding turned into caresses, and she said (and it wasn't the first time), "What lewd things do you suppose they have in that safe about how to make love? What evil ways that we can't even think of?" And we began to think of the ways and to laugh, and then we tried to find the ways: backward, forward, upside down, until we fell out of the hammock (and it wasn't the first time).

Afterward Josephine wondered if everything in the safe might be hilarious, but I said that was unlikely.

At that time I wasn't sure if I would open the secret safe for her or not. In fact I really thought I wouldn't. I didn't want anything to change. I stalled her. I kept questioning her. But then things changed.

/ / /

Normally Josephine's mother never bothered to come down to her daughter's apartment. Normally Josephine's mother never bothered with her daughter at all. I wondered about this sometimes, but then I knew that the head librarian had a busy schedule. And then Josephine was a grown-up—in her thirties as I was. Yet I did think that she and her mother might have been friends and talked now and then, but they never did that I knew of. But then her mother did come and it was clear that she had come in anger, for she bounded in, slammed the door and shouted for Josephine, whom she called Joe. (Josephine was so unlike a 'Joe' that I was almost as shocked by that as I was by what happened afterward.)

We never did find out what that first anger was about because she was even angrier when she found me there, naked, and her daughter dressed in what was, essentially, nothing but mosquito netting. (We had been, again that day, playing the same game of "What is written in the forbidden safe?")

"Not worthy of the word," she said. "Either of you." And to Josephine, "Must you pick lovers from the gutter?"

I thought she hadn't noticed my uniform and my cap on my boots beside the couch. "I'm a prince of the library," I said.

"Rats," she said, "from the cellars. That's what everybody calls you."

It wasn't the first time I'd heard this. We even called ourselves cellar rats sometimes, but I never expected to hear it from the very people who were the bosses of our bosses, people we considered our kings and queens, and for whom we were the princes. Here was one of the very ones who had told us we were princes and should conduct ourselves as such, saying, "Rat, rat, rat . . ." I was not only shocked by that, but also by the fact that one of the leaders of the library could be so out of control.

When she could catch her breath, she told Josephine that she might at least have had a smidgen of dignity for the sake of her mother and her mother's job, and then she turned to me and told me that, if she found me on any floor higher than the first basement, she would have me de-capped and forbidden to wear library blues ever again.

That I couldn't be on or above the ground floor meant I had no access to the library books that occupied the first seven floors of the library. We princes had access to all seven floors if we were so inclined, which was more than most citizens had. I had (I realized it right then) not taken advantage of my privileges, and now access to "understanding beyond all understanding" was out of the question to me forever.

And then there was the fragrance of the library on those days when incense burned in the lower halls! And the soft light from the alabaster lamps! Often I sat among the books, not to read, but to be in the silence and the glow. And I knew I was welcome—that the patrons of the words liked to see the princes come and sit with them. They would smile and call me prince. The library was, in a way, father and mother to me after I had left that distant village in order to come here to be a prince.

What Josephine's mother said also meant that I had no access to the elevators that took me up to Josephine's rooms.

And how could Josephine's mother say we were rats to every-body? When I walked the streets I could see that the whole world of words knew we were word-proper men in responsible positions. I was thinking it would serve Josephine's mother right if her daughter did enter that safe and if she did read whatever there was in there that was the most lewd and the most subversive. I no longer had any desire to save either myself or Josephine from her crazy wishes. In fact I hoped she would be caught and her mother shamed by it. And yet I did . . . I really did love Josephine. But I wanted her to share my fate—to be dragged down with me so we would still be together one way or another. I was partly banned and partly cursed, why not both of us completely cursed? Or blessed as the case may be. "Then shall your eyes be opened and ye shall be as Gods." Our eyes will be opened and we will know what is to be known.

Josephine's mother said she would talk to Josephine later—that she had to leave right then because she couldn't stand the sight of me.

As I dressed, I told Josephine to meet me in a lower hall the next night . . . that we would go into the safe. That we might as well do it, and it would have to be now or never.

She looked frightened, but I thought she was more frightened of her mother than of breaking any forbidden laws. She said she would be there, but I could see the desire for it had left her. It wasn't a game anymore. I wasn't sure if she'd be there or not, but I thought that if she was, it would be a sign that she cared about me—that she could be with me without the tickling, and the giggling, and the pretending, and that she could defy her mother for my sake.

/ / /

And she was there. She was even early, waiting for me. I couldn't help but smile—though I was worried about my future, which didn't look good no matter what happened now. She came into my arms as if she really loved me and we held each other a long time. It wasn't dangerous for us in those lower corridors. It wasn't that unusual for princes to bring girlfriends here. There were few places a prince could take someone where they could be alone for a while. We wouldn't be noticed when other princes came by.

After we had held each other long enough to soak up comfort and courage, I told her my plan. It wouldn't be hard if I could be quick with the combination. Things were quite lax, actually. We princes were serious about our guarding, but it had been decades since anyone had tried to get into those safes without authorization. We put in our time, dutifully, but we didn't expect confrontations. Changing of the guards took place in a front hallway some distance from the safes and the ceremony had, in recent years, evolved into an elaborate rite that we princes felt was worthy of the word and of the library. We liked the pomp of it and so did our bosses. Josephine and I could simply wait in an adjoining hall listening to the clump, clump of the guards until they clumped away for the ceremony.

But, just as the footsteps faded and Josephine and I were about to make a run for the safe, there was a squeak and grind, and, not three feet from where we were standing, a section of a malachite panel seemed to split and out came the head of the central book committee and hurried to the safe. If he'd looked about anxiously he'd have caught us, but he seemed sure of himself as though he'd done this so often he no longer thought much about it. It took him only a second to open the door. He bypassed all the complicated turnings of the dials and simply pulled a single small lever and the safe opened. He is a bulky man, but graceful for all that, and he slid in sideways and the door shut behind him silently.

Josephine and I looked at each other as though the world had turned upside down, which, for us, it had. We hesitated only a few moments and then we followed, using the same little lever. The door swung open and we were in. Only when the door closed behind us did we wonder how we would be able to get out of there. As it happened that was taken care of.

It was a large nondescript room and nobody was in it. There were only a few book racks along the walls and these were more than half empty, the books that remained lying helter-skelter on the shelves without dignity. There were several mismatched long tables and a few cast-off chairs, none of them worthy of the library. (We princes had better than these in our barracks.) On the tables there were several books lying as though recently put down. Some were open and turned over, their backs broken. There were even some on the floor, corners bent from having been dropped and pages dog-eared. Neither of us had ever seen books that had been treated this way. Though there was dust everywhere, there were signs of recent use, clean spots and smudged spots. Obviously people read here. We turned to some of the books to see what they were about. What we glanced at didn't seem to have anything new to us: bondage, rape, sex with animals . . . We'd heard of these before. But we didn't want to spend much time with the books. We were too worried about where the head of the book committee might have gone and when he would be coming back. There were no good hiding places in that room.

We found the secret door by the smeared place along the wall where many dusty hands had worked another lever. You could see, along the floor, that one of the bookcases used to be pulled over to cover it but, obviously, nobody bothered with that anymore. Above this door someone had pencilled rather carelessly the same words that were over the library doors: BEWARE ALL YE WHO ENTER FOR HERE IS UNDERSTANDING BEYOND ALL UNDERSTAND-ING. Behind the door I thought I could hear the sound of running water and strange cries. Also I thought I heard a horse whinny, and birds, and laughter, and I remembered what Josephine had said about it, maybe, being hilarious, and I felt the prickle of gooseflesh along my arms.

All through this Josephine and I had kept looking at each other, frightened and awed, not knowing what to think. And now we looked at each other again. She nodded. "We've gone so far," she said, "one more thing won't make any difference." I pulled the lever then and as the the door opened the sounds came clear. Yes, water, shouting, squeals, but not a single word.

Inside was a garden . . . a jungle . . . fountains, hanging plants, bushes, huge ferns. Great purplish lights overhead, and people all naked, all pawing at each other, making animal sounds and laughing hysterically. Here were the elite of the library—even Josephine's mother—scorning the word and living out the forbidden secrets of the forbidden safe. There was a horse and a goat. There was a peacock making dreadful squawks, but no more dreadful than the squawks of the people. There were yaps, yowls, howls, caws, caterwaulings, and great ha-has. They, at least, found it hilarious.

Josephine and I quickly took off our clothes in order that we might hide among the naked bodies. Josephine pulled her hair down to cover her face as much as she could and we stood there, holding hands, knowing that all the words we had learned were lies—that the word was not the word as we understood it—that things were not done according to what was written, or, at least not according to any writing we knew of.

Of course being naked didn't hide us for long. Josephine's mother recognized her at once. We were seized and, in a drunken, laughing frenzy, knives were brought out, and hammers, and pliers. All the people looked as though they finally had, in us, what they'd been waiting for and hoping for for a long time. I saw Josephine's mother give the first blow that knocked out her front teeth, screaming at her the only words I heard in that place at all. "Stupid," she yelled. "Crazy, crazy. You could have been down here any time you wanted if you'd picked a proper lover from the right class of person. You could have been down here with the best of us any night you wanted to, wordless."

You might think this was the end of words for Josephine and me, but I have someone who knows my signals, even after all these years, she still knows. My mother reads my eyes and lips, counts taps, knows my gestures. She writes it out and I nod yes or no. Then she will tell.

And Josephine and I still have each other. Our eyes say all that needs to be said.

LIVING AT
THE CENTER
/ / /

Oh the beached women of Omphalo . . . lolling, lazing, leaning
back into the sand, raising their heads to the sun, eyes shut, eyes
that, when they open them, are as round as fish eyes and the color
of the water, whether gray, or green, or blue. Sometimes they
darken even to the deep coppery shades of indigo, or so 'tis said,
and, oh, the sing-song of their language and the sing-song of their
songs . . . the clink of their wine glasses, the whiteness of the sails
of their boats, and the blackness of the heads of their black-headed
terns!

The mountains behind them look as placid and stolid as the
women of Omphalo might be themselves, there on their beach,
but every afternoon clouds gather around the peaks and there's
thunder, fireballs rolling down. Those women would hardly
understand how, now and then, a boulder, struck by lightning,
might turn bright red, though that's been seen and not just once.
Hair sometimes stands straight up. Air is thin. As are the men and
women who live there. Shoes hardly lasting even through one
season. Marmots' shrill clicks clang out warnings all day long. It's
from them that the mountain men and women learned to whistle
and to beep out their own echoing calls from cliff to cliff.

But, ah, those women of Omphalo! The mountain men have
never seen them or been down there, but they've heard tell, and
they've only glimpsed the ocean from their eastern passes, but
they've seen how it sparkles. They've seen how blue it gets, or

green, or gray, or, now and then, indigo, and they've seen the thin, white edge of the shore line, and they've seen what they think are white sails, and once an old man said he saw—he's sure he saw—a stately sea serpent swimming across the bay. Every evening those who live on the eastern slopes watch the lights flickering down there, and on still nights . . . on those rare, very very still nights, the mountain men even think they can hear those women singing, though how could that be?

Send a boy down first. Look things over. Always send a boy down first just as they always send a boy *up* first, but how about a half-grown girl? Dressed as a boy? A thin one, not to be found out. Or an old lady? What about an old lady? She'd not be missed. One that can still jump around like a goat.

The men keep talking about it, but they don't *do* anything. They make a lot of plans. Sometimes they think to go on down there themselves, either alone or maybe two or three together, or maybe all of them, but they don't do it. It's as if they don't really want to know too much about the women of Omphalo. It's as if they just want to think about them a lot. They want to laugh and whisper about what those women might be doing and *right now!* Or might do if one of these mountain men came on down to show them a thing or two. And it's as if they want some kind of women they can always be telling their wives they should be more like, so they're always saying that the women of Omphalo are, if nothing else, sexy. They even pick out one woman that they name Opal who's the sexiest of all. It's her they talk about the most, but nobody goes there to find out if there is an Opal. You'd think they'd want to, always talking, as they do, about those fandangoes and violas da gamba, while up there they only have flutes à bec, and little tambours, and dances that are more like stamping, knees high and coming down hard on their heels, though sometimes those men get together and do a long, slow dance such as they think the women of Omphalo might do.

Now there *is* an old woman who can jump around like a goat. She'd not be missed and she knows it, because she's taking up good space in a small house. Sometimes she wishes she would be missed . . . had somebody who'd follow her off on those never-used trails of the eastern slopes and say, "Come on home now, Ma," and, "I've made you some broth. Come sit down," and, "You don't need to be doing this silly thing." And she could answer, "It's not silly," and keep going on down. But she knows that, on the contrary, if they saw her they'd say, "Good, she's going on down." They wouldn't be thinking ordinary "down," but "down" like the old people do when they get useless—"down," right off the cliffs, but that's not what she'll be doing, and if they want to look over toward Gem Lake for Grandma in her red hat, there won't be anybody there.

Even when she was young and her husband was alive, he'd not have been following her off somewhere—not that she needed or wanted anybody to do that then, since she was doing it herself for all the others, keeping the babies and the goats herded together as best she could. He, also, that husband, talked about Opal and the women of Omphalo and died—as they all do—not even knowing anyone by that name, or any Sapphire, Ruby, Rose Quartz, Amethyst, or Lapis Lazuli.

She is thinking that, should Omphalo, by any chance, really be the center of the universe, as it's said it is, how would anyone know? Though if it really is, then certainly the trip would be worth it just to see such a place. But then she's wondering how and why the center of the universe has already been agreed upon and so long ago that no one remembers when or who decided? And why have the mountain men so easily taken "down there" to be the center and not, more logically, one of their own mountains? (The highest of all, for instance, Old Man Magic Mountain, would seem to her to be the logical center of the universe from which everything else fell down, the earth and branches—sometimes even trees—rushing down in the streams, the rocks rolling along beside them, the boulders tipping over, bouncing down, and knocking everything in their way to the bottom which is Omphalo and which is perhaps why it's called "Omphalo, low, low, low" in the songs.) But perhaps they take "down there" for the center simply because it really is the center. And once they, on the other hand, a long time ago, with the seeds of the trees, and the bushes and the wild flowers in their backpacks, had climbed up from there with everything. That's possible, though not so logical.

She worries about going down, not so much afraid that the journey is to be over old unused trails, but that she might learn more than she ought to know, or is good for her to know. Just how much should one know, that is, about the things the men were always whispering? And might she stay there forever? It's said 'tis warm . . . that people lie around naked (except maybe for a scarf or two or a hat) even at night. So what if she never came back when all her life she's called the mountains, "Comrade, friend"? What would she call comrade, then, down there? The seaweed? The oysters? (She knows about those . . . or at least she knows the words for them, from the old songs, the "Down, down, bounce, bound, down, down," and, "Doodle, doodle, going on down," and, "Gooseberry, down, oh down oh," songs from some other time when the mountain people and the people of Omphalo must have lived more comfortably together, exchanging treasures and verses so that the mountain people have songs about seaweed and oysters that they haven't yet forgotten. (No doubt that's how silk scarves came to be among the mountain men, handed down, father to son, and how polished amber came to be among the mountain women, handed down, mother to daughter.) But, anyway, why shouldn't she be, for once in her life, at the center of things? Perhaps Opal would be her friend.

"Old Man Magic Mountain," she had said, seeing him through rising skirts of fog, "let me go, Old Man, that I should make it to the center of the universe before nightfall if I start before dawn." She had said this several times, nodding at him, over her left shoulder, and then she'd not slept, but waited for the moon to rise and started down. And Old Man Magic Mountain had granted her wish just as though it had been made upon the first star, and she was down, or almost, and it wasn't quite dark yet. She could lie under a fir tree, hidden in its lower branches—a fir tree much bigger than those she'd been used to up there— untie her skirts from around her waist and wrap them about her and sleep the sleep of somebody who's climbed all day long and half the night before, too. In her sleep she sings a song she had forgotten . . . a song

from her great-uncles and her grandfather. She sings it all night
long.

> Oh the queenly women of Omphalo
> Sing low, sing low,
> Sing down by the sea,
> Sing breasts, sing bellies,
> Sing up to the sky,
> Sing high, sing high, sing high.
> Sing lie down and die.

Even as a child she hadn't liked that song, wondering why she, a
girl of the mountains, or her sister, or certainly her queenly
mother, thin and straight as a sheltered pine, wasn't worth singing
about. She'd forgotten the song, most likely on purpose, and when
she wakes up, she has forgotten it again.

/ / /

The sounds down here are all different. Bird calls such as she's
never heard before. Something's squawking just around the slope
from her tree, another thing chirps nearby, and far out in the bay
there's some sort of groaning going on. If that's the women of
Omphalo, they don't sound happy.

She creeps out from under the fir tree branches. It's very early,
but that's her usual time for getting up. The sun is hitting her
mountain tops, though down here, it's barely light. But it's not
cold. She begins taking things off, one by one, and still not cold.
As she does this, she walks toward the beach, hunkering down,
trying to hide behind rocks and trees, not knowing what might
happen if she were seen by one of those women. She crosses a
wide plain full of unfamiliar flowers or large . . . huge versions of
ones she already knows, lupin that makes her lupins look like
dwarfs, though the columbines are here, exactly as they are on the
peaks. She can see almost the whole bay now, sparkling between
the trees. She comes to the edge where there's a drop-off, and
beyond it lies the beach, all flat and smooth. It isn't what she
thought it'd be. For one thing, it's mainly pink, not white, and it's
not soft sand. It wouldn't be comfortable basking there. She can

see, even from here, that it's made up mostly of broken shells and a group not broken lying, pink or striped with red, in a little line of their own at the edge of the water, and there's another reddish green line of seaweed and another thicker line of foam, and then the water, sucking in and out. There's nobody there. Not even a goat.

She's stripped down by now to her gray knitted petticoat and undersocks. It's not a bad petticoat. Her best, in fact. There are seven little Indian paintbrush flowers across the top, alternating with six little sulfur paintbrush flowers. She'd not only embroidered them herself, but dyed the yarn. There'll be no shame in going down on the beach wearing nothing but that.

She piles her bundle and her outer clothes beside a bush that has rose hips on it. There are rose bushes—well, they hardly deserve the name bushes—almost like these in the mountains, though so much smaller, both the bush and the hips . . . not even a quarter . . . not even a tenth the size of this one, though the hips are just as sweet. Perhaps a tiny bit sweeter.

That makes her think of the fir tree where she slept, how lush it was and how it came down all around like a tent, and not a small one, either. She had a little shiver thinking of this. What, she wonders, what about the large, round women of Omphalo? But where is it? And where the women that are supposed to loll along the shore all day?

Now that she sees the place, she does believe this might well be the center of the universe. What else could be so blue and sparkly? What else could be so large and round and edged with pink, almost all the way around, a luminous pink, like a baby's lips?

She climbs down the short, steep way, over rounded rocks to the beach. (Where she comes from, she'd hardly call it a cliff.) Even before she crosses the line of weeds and then the line of shells, and puts her toes—socks and all—into the line of foam, she already knows the water won't be anything like the cold of the mountain streams, yet, when she does put her toes in, it's warmer than she expected—warm like having been kept in a kettle at the back of the damped stove so there'd be something warm to wash with in the morning. She wouldn't have thought that such a thing could be—as though the center of the universe was one warm, big pot, though why not?

But now that she's out in the clear, standing up to her knees in the water, she turns around to get a good view of the curve of the bay. She looks in a great circle, trying to see if she can get a glimpse of any of the white palaces of the city, or any white towers, for it's known, or at least it's always said 'twas known, for its towers, and balconies, and pillars, and for its great halls where they dance all night and then lie down on beds of snowgoose down, and there, do all the strange things that they do with each other. But all she sees are the red and white rocks of the cliff, red on top and white on the bottom, curving away for more than half the arc of the world, and finished off with the line of the sea behind her, and not even one small tower . . . not even the tiny edge of anything white or pink peeking out from among the trees that line the drop-off to the beach. She studies the whole of the borders of the bay over again, slowly, and she begins to see that there's more here than, at first, there seemed to be. There are fissures and caves and, yes, even balconies right in the cliffs, and windows, and pillars, and pilasters, and balusters, and balustrades, if you look at it all in just the right way, squinting your eyes. And even tables and chairs here and there in front of the portals, mushroomlike tables, big and little, with red tops and white bottoms. And there are towers, red ones, though not very many and not very tall. These and the caves and balconies line the bay as far as she can see, all in the round, carved curves of Omphalo, the rocks looking soft, just as you'd expect them to, and pink, red, and white, just as you'd expect.

Is this great curve of cliffs full of holes, then, Omphalo itself? Are the eyes of Omphalo all facing, then, out toward her? Out of their niches, windows, vents, crannies, portals, watching her secretly and laughing at her tiny breasts?

She's so startled at the thought, she can only stand and stare out, both arms crossed over her chest. A black-headed tern flies by, not two feet from her, and looks at her sideways with one beady eye that has no feeling in it at all. Just so, she thinks, just so, no doubt, the eyes of the women of Omphalo when looking at a woman of the mountains.

But all of a sudden it's as though there's nothing more to lose than standing here so small and in her socks and petticoat. She puts her arms down and heads for the nearest portal. Changes her mind halfway across the beach and turns to a much smaller cave.

When she gets up to it, there's nothing to knock on. She tries knocking on the stone, but that makes such a dull thunk she can hardly hear it herself. Well then, she'll go right on in and apologize for it straight away. The opening she's chosen is so small she has to stoop to enter. It's like their houses up there, small doors to keep out the cold. Before she gets quite through it she calls out, "Kutch koo, kutch koo," but softly, almost a whisper, rather like a dove, and yet it echoes off into other, connecting caverns, to the left and right of her, and on and on, seeming to get louder and making itself into a kind of round, so that she thinks the women of Omphalo have answered her in a great chorus and that their voices are shriller than she thought they'd be and that they're laughing at her again. But when the last "kutch koo" sounds out, almost by itself, she hears that it's her voice, as though she mocked herself for thinking there were others who were mocking her.

Nothing more to lose, indeed, after that racket, so she calls out, louder and bolder, "Hoo haa," but, again, no answer but herself, echoing back at her. She steps completely in then, and through what seems a vestibule, and on into what seems a great hall, and then to another, and another beyond it following the curve of the beach. Yes, yes, here are, certainly, the quarters of the women of Omphalo, and worthy of them, too, one cavern connecting to another through huge halls and doorways, smooth and round, sometimes the walls curving in like great bellies. Sometimes the floors balloning up . . . and there are balconies leading on to other balconies, porches leading on to other porches, and every single one of them with views of the sea and the beach.

She finds only one object. A curious thing, too. A round silver bell, smaller than what one might put on one's best pet goat. An odd thing, she thinks, for the women of Omphalo to have, and just a tiny sound to it, too, which would hardly be heard across a room, though here where, in lots of places, it echoes so, the sound would be adequate. After she finds it, she rings it as she goes along.

She hopes, apologetically. She does not want to intrude, but if she'd known that everyone had gone away, she'd have brought more food. Rose hips and raspberries will hardly do.

She goes a long way through the caves down one side of the bay. The place is so big, though, she doesn't try to do even half. When she finds a balcony she likes a lot—it's just her size and she can sit on a red knob and look out at the view . . . all along the floors there are these strange lumps, and knobs, and tables. Certainly the women of Omphalo don't dance the way the men say they do. Or if they do, they do it on the beach. Maybe in the moonlight? . . . When she finds that place, she decides she'll spend the night there, honored to be spending it even in this corner of Omphalo—small corner, but a small corner at the very center of everything and from which everything else rose up. She's glad she didn't put on a red hat (and wouldn't ever now) and jump over—"down" beside Gem Lake.

The doorway to her chosen place is small, exactly the size of the doors she's used to, and there's an alcove on the far wall that's high enough so that, even when she lies down in there, she can still get a good view of the sea over the balustrade. She brings up seaweed to make herself a soft bed and then sits a while looking out at the view and wondering if she'll have to hold her nose and swallow some of the little soft things along the beach. The snails . . . periwinkles . . . She might be able to manage those little ones.

As she sits, she catches a glimpse of something white far out beyond the mouth of the bay. At first she thinks it's just more sparkle, but then she sees that it's a sail. As it comes closer, crossing the mouth of the bay, she sees it's a cluster of sails, two square ones and two triangular, front and back. So much sail that the ship looks tiny underneath it. The way the sails belly out makes her think it must surely be a ship of Omphalo, but it just goes straight on as though Omphalo wasn't the center of anything important. For a while, the sails glow pink in the setting sun, and then it's too dark to see anymore. She lies down in her niche, but she doesn't sleep well. She keeps wondering what there'll be to eat the next morning.

/ / /

Though she's hungry when she wakes up, that doesn't seem to be a problem, at least not for the moment, because the sky is so full of the sunrise and the water's lap-lapping in a way that makes all the little shells sing their own songs as they rustle up and down the beach, and the breeze, as she comes out from her balcony, is touching her cheeks as she's not been touched since she was a child, and not often then, either. So that, before she even thinks about it, she's taken off her petticoat and socks and gone right on into the water, lain down in it, her face up to the sun, arms out, and lolled and basked away half the morning just as the women of Omphalo would do.

But then something starts happening behind her out in the bay. She feels it in the water before she hears or sees anything. This is something big and possibly dangerous. She hurries out and back up the beach to stand just under the umbrella of a mushroom-shaped stone and turns to watch whatever it is that's happening out there. There's a spot, far out, where the water is roiling, but also something is nearer and coming in fast. Whatever it is leaps a great, last leap and lands up on the shore, half in, half out of the water, a huge thing, whitish, and, here and there, spotted with ugly calluses. And she knows, right away, that, as mountain rose to beach rose, as mountain fir to beach fir, just so, is she to this being. She had begun to suspect that such would be the case even before she'd gone into the caves.

The creature sighs, or perhaps groans. It sees her, too. She can tell that, and she's looking back at it, right into its tiny, unblinking eye (tiny, that is, only compared to the size of the rest of it). It sees and seems to her to understand everything so far. With one hand and arm she covers her small dry breasts and with the other she covers her skinny ribs, for this calm, sad, understanding eye is more than she can bear.

The creature makes that sound again. Is it speaking to her in some language she knows nothing about? She moves closer, "Opal?" she asks, and waits. "Opal?"

But suddenly here comes another one, and then three more, and four, leaping out and lolling there, leaning back into the pink shell beach, until so many she's stopped bothering to count. The first one is already changing color, turning blue and purple, shivering a great shiver. Its skin has begun to have a dry look. She squats in the sand beside it, not afraid any longer. "Opal?" she says, "Opal? Opal?" for this is, clearly, the largest and the leader.

She knows by the look in its eye that it's dying. She's seen that look before. "Poor friend," she says and strokes what might be the forehead. The creature shivers just there, where she touches, as though the rough skin were exquisitely sensitive. Then she walks among them, patting and stroking as the breeze had done to her, and calling them, "My poor friends," and she calls one Amethyst, and one Ruby, and one Sapphire, and one Rose Quartz, and one Lapis Lazuli, and, at the same time, tries to chase away the gulls that are gathering, and the vicious little things that walk sideways.

She knows by their eyes when they die, and they all die. The gulls and the others peck at them even before that happens. When they're all dead, she lies down among them to keep company with them till they get used to being dead.

/ / /

A long time after, in the middle of the night, with all the little things still tearing at the bodies, eating and eating . . . the sounds of eating all around her, she realizes how hungry she is. Like them. No different from them.

Opal will be, soon enough, gone, that's clear. Opal and all the others, nothing but bones. She'll be sorry to see it. Perhaps Opal would be glad if a little of her flesh didn't go to gulls and crawly things. Perhaps Opal would like to contribute . . . to go on . . . in her . . . as her. (That had happened once up there one terrible winter when some of the grandparents gave themselves for the sake of the others and it had been a grand and useful gift.) Something of Opal would certainly live on in her, then, just as she, herself, had become more and more goatlike. And she would thank Opal, just as they always thanked the goats who were also friends. And some of Opal could be smoked and dried and put away in the right sort of cave and kept a long time there.

She goes up to get her knife. When she comes back she sings to them, "Dead and gone, dead and gone," before she touches any of Opal.

/ / /

So that's how there came to be a fat woman on the beach at Omphalo, who, every day, watched the sailing ships go past the mouth of her bay, and every day lay on a torn piece of sail upon the shells among the bones, and ate periwinkles and floated on her back in the warm water, and sang "Going on down" and "Gooseberry down" songs, and, on clear nights, lit fires along the beach so that the men of the mountains could see that Omphalo was there and would know that Opal waited for them at the center of everything.

MOON
SONGS

/ / /

A tiny thing that sang. Nothing like it mentioned in any of my
nature books, and I had many. At first no name we gave it stuck.
Sometimes we called it Harriet, or Alice, or Jim. Names of kids at
school. All ironies. More often we just called it Bug. This mere
mite—well, not really that small, more the size of a bee—pulled
itself up by its front legs, the back ones having been somehow
bent. Or so it seemed to us. Perhaps it happened when we caught
it.

How can such a tiny thing have such a voice? Clear. Ringing
out. Echoing as though in the mountains or in some great resonat-
ing hall. Such a wonderful other-worldly sound. We felt it tingling
along our backbones and on down into the soles of our feet.

My sister kept it in a cricket cage. Fed it lettuce, grains of rice,
grapes, but never anything of milk or butter, "in order to keep
down the phlegm," she said, even though we didn't know how it
made its sounds. We asked ourselves that first day, "Is it by the
wings? Is it the back legs? Is it, after all, the mouth?" We looked at it
through a magnifying glass, but still we couldn't tell. Actually we
didn't look at it long that time, for (then) we didn't like the look of
it at all. There were hairs or barbels hanging down from its mouth
and greenish fur at the corners of its eyes. We didn't mind the
yellow fur on its body as that seemed cuddly and beelike to us.
"Does it have a stinger?" my sister asked, but I couldn't say yes or

no for sure, except that it hadn't stung us yet . . . me yet, for that first day I was the one that held it.

"I would suppose not," I told my sister. "Maybe it has its voice to keep it safe, and besides, if it had a stinger it would have used it by now." I did look carefully, though, but could see no sign of one.

To make it sing you had to prick it with a pin. It would sing for ten or fifteen minutes and then would need another prick. We knew enough to be gentle. We wanted it to last a long time.

How we discovered the singing was by the pricking, actually. The thing lay as though dead after we first caught it and we wanted to know for sure was it or wasn't it, so we pricked it. One prick got a little motion. Two, and it sat up, struggling to pull its poor back legs under itself. Three, and it began to sing and we knew we had something startling and worthwhile—a little jewel—better than a jewel, a jewel that sang.

My sister insisted she had seen it first and that, therefore, it was hers alone. She always did like tiny things, so I supposed it was right that she should have it, but I saw it first, and I caught it, and it was my hand first held it for she was frightened of it . . . thought it ugly before she heard it sing. But she had always been able to convince me that what I knew was true, wasn't.

She was very beautiful and it was not just I who thought so. Heads turned. She had pale skin and dark eyes and looked at everything with great concentration. Her hair was black and hung out from her head in a sort of fan shape. She wore a beaded head band she'd made herself with threads and tiny beads.

We were in the same school, she, a full-blown woman about to graduate, and I in the ninth grade, still a boy . . . still in my chubby phase before I started to grow tall. I felt awkward and ugly. I *was* awkward and, if not exactly ugly, certainly not attractive. Her skin was utter purity, while I was beginning to get pimples. For that reason alone, I believed that everything she said was right and everything I said was wrong. It had to be so because of the pimples.

Beautiful as she was, my sister wasn't popular, yet popularity or something akin to it . . . something that looked like it, was what she wanted more than anything, and if that were impossible, then fame. She wanted to make a big splash in school. She wanted to sing, and dance, and act, but she had a small, reedy voice and, although graceful as she went about her life, she was awkward when on stage. Something came over her that made her like a puppet—a self-conscious stiffness. She was aware of this and she had gone from the desire to be on stage to the desire not to expose herself there because she knew how, as she said, ridiculous she looked—how, as she said, everyone would laugh at her, though I knew they wouldn't dare laugh at her any more than I dared. People were afraid of her just as I was. They called her "The Queen," and they joked that she had taken vows of chastity. They called me "Twinkie." Sometimes that was expanded to "Twinkle Toes," for no reason I could tell except that the words went together. I certainly wasn't light on my feet, though perhaps I did twinkle a bit. I was so anxious to please. I smiled and agreed with everyone as though they were all my sister and I always agreed with her. It was safer to do so. I don't remember when I first figured that out. It was as though I'd always known it as soon as I began to realize anything at all.

"I wish it would have beginnings and ends to its singing instead of being all middles, middles, middles," my sister said and she tried hard to teach it to have them. Once she left it all day with the radio tuned to a rock and roll station while she was at school. It was so exhausted—even we could tell—by the end of the day that she didn't do anything like that again. Besides, it had learned nothing. It still began in the middle and ended in the middle, almost as though it sang to itself continuously and only switched to a louder mode when it was pricked and then, when let alone again, lapsed back into its silent music.

I wouldn't have known the first time my sister took the mite to school, had I not sat near her in the cafeteria. She never wanted me to get close to her at school and I never particularly wanted to. Her twelfth graders were nothing like my ninth graders. She and I never nodded to each other in the halls though she always flashed me a look. I wasn't sure if it was a greeting or warning.

But this time I sat fairly close to her at lunch and I noticed she was wearing the antique pearl hat pin we'd found in the attic. She had it pinned to her collar, which was also antique yellowed lace, as though we'd found that in the attic, too. She could laugh a tense, self-conscious wide-mouthed laugh. (She was never relaxed, not even with me. Probably not even with herself, though, now that I think about it. Sometimes when we lay back, she on her bed and I in her chair, and listened to the mite sing . . . sometimes then she was, I'm sure, relaxed.) She was laughing that laugh then, which was why I looked at her more closely than I usually allowed myself to do when in school. I was wondering what had brought on that great, white-toothed derision, when I saw the hat pin and knew what it was for, and then I saw the tiny thread attached to her earring. No, actually attached to her earlobe along with the earring, right through the hole of her pierced ear, and I saw a little flash of yellow in the shadow under her hair, and I thought, no, our mite (for I still thought of it as "ours" though it seemed hers now), our mite should stay safely at home and it should be a secret. Anything might happen to it (or her) here. There were boys who would rip it right out of her ear if they knew what it could do, or perhaps even if they didn't know. And the hat pin made it clear that she was thinking of making it sing. I wondered what would happen if she did.

Also I worried that it wouldn't be easy for her to control her pricking there by her ear. She'd have to hold the mite in one hand and try to feel where it was and prick it with the other, and she couldn't be sure where she would be pricking it—in the eye for all she knew.

I wanted to object, but instead, when we were home again and alone, to let her know I knew, I asked her if she was hearing it sing to her all through school? If, tethered that close to her ear, she could hear its continuous song, but she said, no, that sometimes she heard a slight buzzing, and she wasn't even sure it came from it. It was more like a ringing in her ear. Still, she said, she did like the bug being there, close by. It made her feel more comfortable in school than she'd ever felt before. "It's my real friend," she said.

"What about if it stings? What if it *does* have a stinger? We don't know for sure it doesn't."

"It would have stung already, wouldn't it? Why would it wait? *I'd* have stung if *I* had a stinger."

And I thought, she's right. It hadn't been so well treated that it wouldn't have thought to sting if it could have.

So we lay back then and listened to it. We could feel the throbbing of its song down along our bodies. We shut our eyes and we saw pictures . . . landscapes where we floated or flew as though we were nothing but a pair of eyes. Sometimes everything was sunny and yellow and sometimes everything was foggy and a shiny kind of gray.

It was strange, she and the mite. More and more she'd had only male names for it: George, Teddy, Jerry—names of boys at school—but now Matt. Matt all the time though there was no Matt that I knew of. I began to feel that she was falling in love with it. We would sit together in her room and she'd let it out of the cage . . . let it hobble around on her desk, flutter its torn wings, scatter its fairy dust. She was no longer squeamish about studying it in the magnifying glass. She watched it often, though not when it sang. Then she and I would always lie back and shut our eyes to see the visions.

And then she actually said it. "Oh, I love you, love you. I love you so much."

It had just sung and we were as though waking up from the music.

"Don't," I said. And I felt a different kind of shiver down my spine, not the vibrations of the song, but the beat of fear.

"What do you mean, don't. Don't tell *me* don't. You know nothing. Nothing of love and nothing of anything. You're too young. And what's so bad about having barbels? You don't even shave yet."

I was beneath contempt though I was her only companion—not counting the mite, of course. She had no friend but me and yet I was always beneath contempt. I did feel, though, that should I be in danger, she'd come to my aid . . . come to help me against whatever odds. She'd not hesitate.

She wore the mite to school every day after that first day. As far as I could tell she told no one, for if she'd told even one person it surely would have gotten back to me. Such things always did in our school. I began to relax. Why not take it to school if it gave her such pleasure to do so? It wasn't until I saw the list of finalists in the talent show that I understood what she was up to. She'd already used it in the tryouts. She (not she and her mite), *she* was listed as one of the seven finalists.

She was a sensation. She left her mouth open all the time as though in a sort of open-mouthed humming. She moved just as awkwardly as always, as though deciding to hold out one arm and then the other, alternating them, and deciding to smile now and then as she pretended to sing, but she looked beautiful anyway. The music made it so . . . made it flowing. Also she was dressed in gray (with yellow earrings and beads) as though to make herself a part of that landscape we often saw as we listened. I knew nobody would make fun of her, whisper about her afterward, or imitate her behind her back.

She was accompanied on the piano by the leader of the chorus, who was pretty good at improvising around what the mite was doing. I thought it was a good thing she had the accompaniment, for it made the music a little less strange and that seemed safer. There was less chance of the mite's being discovered.

Everybody sat back, just as the two of us always did, feeling the vibrations of it and no doubt seeing those landscapes. After ten or so minutes of it they clapped and shouted for more and my sister pricked the mite once again and pretended to sing for ten more minutes and then said that was all she could do. Afterward everybody crowded around and asked her how she had learned to do it. Of course she got first prize.

After that she didn't exactly have friends, but she had people who followed her around, asked her all sorts of questions about her singing, interviewed her for the school paper. Some people wanted her to teach them how to do it, but she told them she had a special kind of throat, something that would be considered a defect by most, but that she had learned to make use of it.

Because of her I became known at school, too. I became the singer's brother. I became the one with the knowledge of secrets, for they did sense a secret. There was something mysterious about us both. You could see it in their eyes. Even I, Twinkle Toes, became mysterious. Talented because close to talent.

After that she was asked to sing a lot though she always said she couldn't do it often. "Keep them wanting more," she told me, "and keep them guessing." Sometimes she would come down with a phony cold just when she'd said she would sing and the auditorium was already filled with people who'd come just to hear her.

But something stranger than love . . . more than love began to happen between my sister and the mite. Or, rather, the mite was the same, but my sister's relationship with it changed. That first performance she'd pricked it too hard. A whitish fluid had come out of it, dripped down one side and dried there, making the yellow fur matted . . . less attractive. She felt guilty about that and said so. "I'm such a butcher," she said, and she seemed to be trying to make up for it by finding special foods that it might like. She even brought it caviar, which it wouldn't touch. And she *wanted* punishment. Sometimes she would ask it to sting her. "Go ahead," she'd say. "I deserve it. And you have a right to do it and I don't care if you do, I'll love you just the same. Matt, Matt, Matt, Matty," she said, and it occurred to me perhaps it was a name she'd made out of mite. She had called it sometimes Mite, Mite, and now had made it clearly male with Matt. "My Matt," she said, "all mine." I was out of it completely except as watcher and listener. Its song had not suffered from the wounding. It just had more difficulty moving itself about. My sister had tried to wash the white stuff off, but that had only smeared it around even more, so that the mite was now an ugly, dull creature with, here and there, one or two yellow hairs that stuck out. "Sting me," my sister said, "bite me. I deserve it."

Now she would lie on her bed with her blouse pulled up and let it crawl on her stomach. It moved with difficulty, but it always moved, except now and then when it seemed to sit contentedly on her belly button. "I don't deserve you," she'd say. "I don't deserve one like you." And sometimes she'd say, "Take me. I'm yours," spread-eagled on her bed and laughing as though it were a joke, but it wasn't a joke. Sometimes she'd say, "You love me. Do you really? Don't you? Do you?" or, "Tell me what love is. Is it always small things that once could fly? Is it small things that sting?"

I sat there watching. She hardly seemed to notice me but I knew it was important that I be there. Even though beneath contempt, I was the observer she needed. I saw how she let it crawl up under her blouse or down her neck and inside her bra, how she giggled at its tickle or lay, serious, looking at the ceiling.

In the cricket cage she'd placed a velvet cushion and she'd hung the cage over her bed by a golden-yellow cord.

"I'm your only friend," she'd say. "I'm your keeper, I'm your jailer, I'm your everything, I'm your nothing," and then she'd carefully place the mite in its cage and I would know it was time for me to leave.

At school she became known as an artist with a great future and she walked around as though it were true, that she *was* an artist, that she could dress differently from anyone else, that she was privileged and perhaps a little mad. "I live for my art," she'd say, "and only for that." She stopped doing her homework and said it was because she practiced her music for hours every day.

I told her she might be found out. "Can you live with this secret forever?"

"Not to sing is to die," she said and it was as though she had forgotten it wasn't she who sang. "I will die," she said, "if I can't sing."

"What if *it* dies or stops singing? It might. It's not that healthy by the looks of it."

"Why are you asking me this? Why do you want to hurt me?"

"I'm scared of what's happening."

"Love always scares people who don't know anything about it, and art does too. I'll always be this . . . in the middle of the song in the middle of my life. In the middle. No end and no beginning. I had a dream of such a shining rain, such silver, such glow, as if I were on the moon, or I were a moon myself. Do you know what it's like to be a moon? I was a moon."

But I knew that she was frightened too . . . of herself and of her love, and I thought that if I weren't there she'd not be this way, that I was the audience she played to, that without me she'd not believe in her drama. Without me there'd be no truth to it. That night . . . the night I thought of this, I stayed away from our evening of music. I went back to my nature books and, it was true, she did need me. She brought me back with a bribe of chocolate. I even think her sexual dreams, as she ignored me and stared at the ceiling, were of no pleasure to her without me there to be ignored. I did come back, but I wasn't sure how long I would keep doing it.

And she was, in her way, nice to me then. To show her gratefulness, she bought me a little book on bees. The next night she threw it at me while I sat, again, in her chair and she lay on her bed. "It's nothing," she said, "but *you* might like it."

"I do," I said, "I really do," because I knew she needed me to say it and I did like it.

"I'm going to give a program all my own," she told me then. "It's at school, but it's for everybody in town and they're charging for it and I'm to get a hundred dollars even though it's a benefit for band uniforms. It's already beginning and I haven't even tried. I just sat here and didn't do my homework and everything's beginning to come true just as I've always wanted it to."

I began to feel even more frightened thinking of her giving a whole program. We'd never had the mite sing more than about forty minutes at a time at the very most. "Well, I won't be there," I said. I had never challenged her directly before, but now I said, "And I won't let you do this, but if I can't stop you, I won't be there."

"Give me back that book," she said.

I was sorry to lose it, but I gave it back. I would be sorrier to lose her. It was odd, but the higher she went with this artist business, and the higher she got in her own estimation, the more she, herself, seemed to me like the mite: torn wings, broken legs, sick, matted fur . . .

"It's just like you," she said. "This is my first really big moment and you want to take my pleasure in it from me." But I knew that she knew it wasn't at all like me. "You're jealous," she said, and I wondered, then, if that were true. I didn't think I was but how can you judge yourself?

The mite inched along her desk as we spoke and I had in mind that I should squash it right then. Couldn't she see the thing was in pain? And then I saw that clearly for the first time. It *was* in pain.

Maybe the singing was all a pain song. I couldn't stand it any longer, but she must have seen something in my face for she jumped up and pushed me out the door before I hardly knew myself what I was about to do . . . pushed me out the door and locked it.

I thought about it but there was no way that I could see how to stop her. I could tell everybody about the mite, but would they believe me? And wouldn't they just go and have the concert anyway even if they knew it was the mite that sang? Maybe that would be an even greater draw. I had lost my chance to put the creature out of its misery. My sister wouldn't let me near it again. Besides, I wasn't sure if what she said wasn't true, that she'd die if she couldn't sing . . . if she couldn't, that is, be the artist she pretended to be.

She was going to call her program MOON SONGS. There would be two songs with a ten-minute intermission between them. I decided I would be there, but that she wouldn't know it. I would stand in a dark corner in the wings after she had already stepped on stage.

The concert began as usual, but this time I was changed and I could hear the pain. It *was* a pain song. Or perhaps the pain in the song had gotten worse so that I could finally understand it. I didn't see how my sister could bear it. I didn't see how anyone in the audience could bear it, and yet there they sat, eyes closed already, mouths open, heads tipped up like blind people. As I listened, standing there, I, too, tipped my head up and shut my eyes. The beauty of pain caught me up. Tears came to my eyes. They never had before, but now they did. I dreamed that once everything was sun, but now everything was moon. And then I forced my eyes to open. I was there to keep watch on things, not to get caught up in the song.

We . . . she never made it to the intermission. After a half hour, the song became more insistent. It was louder and higher pitched and I could see my sister vibrating as though from a vibrato in her own throat that, then, began to shake her whole body. Nobody else saw it. Though a few had their eyes open, they were looking at the ceiling. The song rose and rose and I knew I had to stop it. My sister sank to her knees. I don't think she pricked the mite at all any longer. I think it sang on of its own accord. I came out on the stage then and no one noticed. I wanted to kill the mite before it shook my sister to pieces, before it deafened her with its shrieking, but I saw that the string that held it to her earlobe was turned and led inside her ear. I pulled on it and the string came out with nothing tied to it. The mite was still inside. My sister was gasping and then she, too, began to make the same sound of pain. The song was coming from her own mouth. I saw the ululations of it in her throat. And I saw blood coming from her nose. Not a lot. Just one small trickle from the left nostril, the same side, where the mite had been tied to the left ear.

I slapped her hard, then, on both cheeks. I was yelling, but I don't think anybody heard me, least of all my sister. I shook her. I hit her. I dragged her from the stage into the wings and yet still the song went on and the people sat in their own dream, whatever it was. Certainly not the same dream we'd always seen before. It couldn't be with this awful sound. Then I hit my sister on the nose directly and the song faltered, became hesitant, though it was still coming from her own mouth and nowhere else. Her eyes flickered open. I saw that she saw me. "Let me go," she said. "Let *us* go. Let us both go." And the song became a sigh of a song. Suddenly no pain in it. I laid her down gently. The song sighed on, at peace with itself and then it stopped. Alive, then dead. With no transition to it . . . both of them, my sister and the mite, stopped in the middle.

I never told. I let them diagnose it as some kind of hemorrhage.

In many ways my life changed for the better after that. I lived for myself, or tried to, and, the year after, I became tall, and thin, and pale, and dark like my sister and nobody called me Twinkie ever again.

EMISSARY

/ / /

"Greetings to the men and women of the garden that is Earth and to all the important creatures alive there at this very moment. Greetings, though we, at the time you receive this, will be dead. Others of us will have replaced us, even down to the longest lived of our creatures, but we, ourselves, will be long gone. You, on the other hand, will have been born, and will be there to receive our greetings and our message of good will.

"We have looked at your world and found it to be as beautiful as you, yourselves, must be finding it right now as you look up and down and around in the wide arcs of your eyes, at the gardens of your yards, and the gardens of your pastures, and the gardens of your forests, and the gardens of your deserts—deserts that, even so, do bloom. You must be frolicking with joy all the days of your lives as you step out into your world and go up and down and around saying, 'Good,' and, 'Good.'

"But we are making do with less here and so we are coming to see how to make do with a little bit of what you have so much of, hoping that we should live with you on your planet with no less joy than you do. Those of us from the lesser worlds will call you 'friends-of-the-lesser-worlds' and will thank you with gifts. The time for coming is soon, so collect the bonnets and banners of celebration."

/ / /

Of course nobody believed the message, and rightly so. We thought it was a hoax originating right here on Earth, and then, when that was (more or less) proved not true, everybody wondered what these beings were up to and why was everything in English instead of some other language? Though perhaps that wasn't so strange, considering it's the language of pilots and the main language in India, and lots of other places you wouldn't think it would be.

We did believe something was coming, but not that it would be of any use to us. And what was all this "Good, good" stuff? Already the rivers were polluted and the air acid, the climate changing. Last winter had been the warmest on record and this summer was beginning to be the hottest. A yellow haze hung over every city.

And then *she* arrived, wafting down at Kennedy Airport. In her palace. She said she had come "home."

She was enormous, ungainly, lopsided. Even so, when she first crawled out (backward) and stood up, it looked for a few minutes as though she was trying to dance for us—crutches, props, and all (clearly our gravity was too much for her)—but she gave that up, thank goodness, when she got a good look at us. Then she began, instead, to try to make herself look smaller, to squeeze herself down into her pantaloons as though she hadn't realized, until right then, how small and thin we were compared with her.

Right away she began telling us how much she loved us. Of course nobody believed her. Love, we all knew, doesn't come that easily. You have to earn it. You have to make sacrifices for it. You have to really know the other person and accept some faults, though not all, and be strong enough to make changes in yourself, too. We knew all about love. We had studied it, read about it, experimented with it (double blind).

Her palace had settled right across the main runways and that was a bother because it was there permanently. "Only built for coming down," she said. "It won't be going on up anymore." She tilted her hand right and left to show the way the palace had landed, drifting back and forth as though of no weight at all. "When down," she said, "is down." Our bulldozers couldn't budge it. From then on, 747s had to land all the way up in Boston or down at Dulles.

We had seen the huge hips first and took them for some sort of big, blank alien face, but then she turned around, stood up with the aid of her props. Her first words after landing were the ones she always used. "Good, good. I like it. I like it a lot."

What was there to like about the vistas of Kennedy Airport? "If she says good, good, to that, she'll say good to anything," we said, and she did say good to anything and everything. She could see the sunset lighting up the haze over the New Jersey gas-cracking plants and liked what she saw and even what she smelled. She could examine a thin-shelled egg that would never hatch and say she loved it even so. She had small, close-set eyes—big compared to ours, but small for her bulk—and she seemed nearsighted, always squinting down at us, or any creature or thing. It seemed as if, to her, the smaller the better: bugs and bees and seeds and tiny sprouts . . . studying, puzzling over. If looking was any indication, she loved the tiniest things the most of all.

It really was a palace that had come down—or looked to be more palace than spaceship with its turrets and towers, and it occurred to us that, even though they knew a lot about us, they didn't know enough. It also occurred to us that she, herself, had been made purely to impress us—that she might be as artificial as her palace/ship seemed, but they had got the head too small, the stomach and hips too big, and the overall size way off.

She had gifts for us. When she first mentioned them, we thought of scientific or medical advancements, new metals, the secrets of her spaceship, but it turned out her gifts were picture frames, all sizes. One of the first things she did was to stand a large one up in front of her and look at us through it, saying, "Good."

Though she was large, there was a mildness about her so that no one was afraid. She was like Gulliver, though smaller, and she let herself be tested and sampled: urine, blood, even large chunks of skin. So many of us wanted these that she ended up quite scarred and pale. (The skin was merely skin. The blood merely blood.)

She let us listen to her great, slow breathing and her great, slow heartbeat. We (all the rest of us) saw the whole process on TV, heard the breathing and the heartbeats amplified. Some of us still couldn't believe she was real. I doubted, too, but I was won over the evening I heard her heartbeat on the news. I listened as though to the waterfall of life—the seashore of life on a calm day; and when they focused the camera, closer and closer, on her close-set eyes, they loomed like sunrises and seemed to look right through me and yet love me anyway. Her breasts, in yellow silk (or what looked like silk), also rose up in the same way as her eyes, as if over the mountains. What can one say about those breasts! They, like her eyes, could see right through me. I knew everybody else was thinking the exact same thoughts—for if I, then certainly all of us.

As for love, I had done a lot of research. I had a postgraduate degree in it. I knew enough about it to doubt that she knew anything about it except the word itself, but, because love seemed to be her main topic of conversation and because of my credential, I was given the assignment of asking her to marry me in order to get to know her more intimately—find out who she was behind all this "Good, good," what she really came here for, and what she meant when she said she "loved"—if she meant anything at all by it.

There was certainly danger in the assignment. I'd learned in my studies not only that it's the quiet ones who are the most passionate, but also that the quiet ones can be the most violent. I knew that, because of her size alone, there could be danger in her passion as well as in her anger. Perhaps, of the two, her passion would be the most dangerous.

"Ask her to marry you right away," they told me. "That way you'll get close to her before she finds out it's not our custom to get married so quickly (if at all these days)."

When I first saw her "in the flesh" (good word to describe her, "flesh") I wondered, all over again, if she were real, if there might not be a dozen puppeteers inside making her move, except they probably wouldn't have been that awkward. They would have practiced until they could work smoothly together. And there were too many mistakes. The warts, for instance, and she wasn't at all as good-looking as she'd seemed on TV. The lights had been so bright they hadn't brought out the real color of her skin. It was grayish, tending to purple around her eyes and under her chin. There were large, whitish warts here and there that they'd covered with makeup. What I noticed most, though, after the first shock of seeing her so large and so gray, were the circles under her eyes and how she kept blinking. If one could judge from how we look when exhausted, then she, too, was exhausted.

I think when she said yes to my asking her to marry me, she hardly knew what she was doing. She was simply saying yes to everything anyone requested of her—another sample of her skin, some strands of ropy blond hair, or if she'd marry me.

I wondered why the others didn't see her exhaustion or didn't pay any attention to it, and I thought I knew how to get on her good side quickly. "We'll have a honeymoon," I said. "Do you know what that is? We'll go away by ourselves and you'll get some sleep."

I explained my strategy to my bosses; they approved and made it possible for us to go off alone even though that wasn't easy.

(Do you, Leonard, take Harriet—that's who she insisted she was—to be your lawful, etc. "Oh, I do, I do, I do. I really do, and forever." She was always saying too much.)

An L1011 had to be gutted so we could travel, and an area cleared for a mile-long airstrip, with another clearing beside a lonely lake so an army tent could be put up and stocked with food and drinking water. And it all had to be done secretly so we really would be able to be alone and she really would be able to get some rest. And I must compliment them. They did find us a beautiful, wild, and lonely place in the mountains.

/ / /

I was so patient and kind I hardly knew myself. I'd never been that way with any of my girlfriends, but of course this time I was being paid for it. Also this was important research, and for the welfare of humanity in general. I could make good use of the skills I'd learned in my studies on the four main kinds of love and their subcategories. I could give all of myself in the service of my science and not feel I was giving more than my share. I *expected* to give more than my share whether or not I got back what was due me from my partner. But engulfed! There was not only the figurative but also the real possibility of that. I was determined, though, to keep the upper hand, and I was determined, as I'd never been before with my girlfriends, *determined* that she should love me, and more, and in a different way from this love, love, love she was always talking about. She didn't even know me and already she'd told me that she loved me "like the ocean and the mountain, and you are my mountain." (I felt more like her mouse.)

I told her to forget love and that she should lie down on the air mattresses they'd lined up for her. I said, "Relax and I'll rub your back. Good old American back rub." I called it American though of course it wasn't, but I wanted to get her on our side. Nobody knew yet what her capabilities were or if there would be other gifts that might be more useful than picture frames. If there were, we wanted them to be for us. "American lake, American honeymoon, American moon in the big American sky," I said.

She lay down and I pulled her big, loose blouse up and thought to myself, I have to do it in spite of the warts and the little hairy patches. I just have to shut my eyes and do it, but she was snoring monstrous snores almost as soon as I began kneading the back of her neck.

She slept a great, three-day sleep, looking like some big beached thing, flattened with gravity, out of her element for sure. I wondered why in the world she said she liked it here—had even called it home—when it was obviously uncomfortable for her. I thought she was probably well trained to do her job, but then so was I, so we were even.

/ / /

I was lying on the dock when she finally woke and came crawling out of the tent—again, hind end first—not bothering with her crutches or trying to stand up. I suppose not wanting, quite so soon after waking, to face gravity. She crawled over to the shore, carefully skirting a patch of iris.

"Don't drink," I yelled, and just in time. "God knows what's in the water, not even counting *Giardia*." But I told her swimming was probably OK so she went on in, rolled onto her back, floating high and waved her arms over her head as though in some ritual of greeting the day. She had with her, hanging from her shoulder, a picture frame like the ones she'd used for gifts.

"I thought all you people lived under bright lights," she said. "I thought you were always asking questions and staying up all night giving little pricks and cuts. Now I see a different side. You do good things for me. I have slept a great, good sleep of love because of you. What's next on a honeymoon?"

The honeymoon part, I hoped, could wait. Now I would begin a different study. "What's all this talk of love about, anyway? What *is* love to you?"

"Oh, you know love," she said. "It has more meanings than can be spoken of, and there's always danger in it." (I knew that well enough.) "It's a big risk, but, best of all, it's full of surprises." Then she held up the picture frame and looked through it at the far shore. "Look how everything is so green and new," she said.

It didn't look that way to me, but I didn't say so. Dead maple trees dotted the forest (I had been sorry to see the maple syrup come to an end even though we have flavors that can imitate it fairly well), the tops of almost all the spruce were brown and many of them, too, were dead, but I had to admit it *was* still beautiful anyway. The water *looked* clear. Some hardy birds still sang. A woodpecker still pecked. Bees were rare, but other things buzzed about.

"I feel as if I fell down from the sky right onto this sweet new place here where everything likes me. Look, even the flies like me."

"Dragonflies," I said, "and thank goodness."

"I think how love is, is how to dance. It's hard, but you do it anyway. You practice and learn the positions for it. Bring me my crutches, lover dear, if you wouldn't mind, so I can dance love for you. Then you'll see all about it. It has to be shown and not talked of."

I went and got them, the two crutches and three props. "Dance of death" was what was in my mind, but I was here to take risks and, as she'd said, love is a risk. Even true love with my own kind is a risk. I knew that from my experiments.

She had a lot of trouble getting up. I went to help her, but she waved me away. "Everybody has to love all by themselves," she said. "That's one of the risks of it. Just like with death, you're all alone with your love. Now watch me through the frame."

Those frames were nothing but normal picture frames. We'd tested them carefully, but I picked it up, anyway, and looked at her through it. It was just as I knew it would be, exactly the same except with a frame around it. She'd given out thousands of those frames, and I'd thought then, as I thought now, we'll kill ourselves off for sure if we sit around looking at everything through frames. That will be how they'll take us over. Though I guess it's no worse than TV. Maybe better for us than TV. Perhaps the frames are to wake us up—take us away from TV. That would be doing us a favor. But I didn't believe they'd really want to do us any favors. I thought maybe, instead, they wanted us to leave well enough—or, rather, *not* so well enough—alone. That would kill us all off. These laissez-faire frames were so we'd see that everything looked about as good as it could and we'd leave it that way. Maybe that was their strategy.

She began her big, dumb dance, stumbling and wobbling. No danger in it to me that I could see, unless she fell on me. Holding up the frame made me awkward—as awkward as she was, so I kept well away. At the end of the dance she tried to twirl around faster and faster and did fall—into the iris patch. "The best of love," she said, lying there panting, shaking all over, "was in that last part." Then she saw she'd ruined the iris and looked as if she might cry, but held herself back. "Death is everywhere," she said, "as usual, and right in the middle of love."

She crawled into the tent and brought out another picture frame and then she sat near the edge of the dock. (I was glad to see she had better sense than to walk out on it.) "Now we sit," she said. "I'll rest up and we can watch this world together." At that moment I couldn't feel any menace in her even though I thought certainly they will win over us. All they have to do is wait.

In the water minnows no longer clustered under the dock, though a few lay, belly up, along the shore. Crayfish no longer shunted from rock to rock. But turtles were still there, sunning themselves on the dead tree trunks that had fallen in near the banks. And we could watch the mating beetles, and the mating frogs, and the luminescent dragonflies, mating as they flew.

"What's next on the honeymoon?" she said again, after several minutes of watching through the frame. Then she said what had been on my mind . . . what I'd been worrying about all this time. "Sex," she said. "When is that?"

"What about real love?" I said. "I mean *really* real love?" Of course I was stalling.

"Oh, I can prove that. Come close."

"Wait," I said. "Wait a minute!" Then I thought back to my training and turned it back to her. (Always ask a question if you don't know what to do next.) "What do *you* think should happen now?" I asked. "And how do they do things where *you* come from? After all," I said, "I don't want to be selfish. We should do things your way sometimes."

She looked pleased, but then she said again to come closer. "I'll show you," she said, and she reached out with that big picture frame—I stepped back, but not fast enough. She hooked me around the neck with it and pulled me to her. I was right up against her big, naked stomach, breasts hovering over my head—resting on it, actually, one big boob actually resting on the top of my head. I couldn't breathe. Nothing was covering my nose or mouth, but I felt as though I were suffocating. Right in front of me was one of her biggest moles and it had five or six thick, black hairs growing from it. A part of me felt sympathy for her for having a mole like that, but another part of me was terrified—especially terrified because I began to have an erection. I told myself it was from fear, except here were these big boobs drooping over me, soft against my forehead, the puckered areola, a huge nipple, erect, hovering, wobbling back and forth in front of my mouth.

"No!" I shouted. I couldn't help myself. I put my hands—lost them actually—in her soft belly and pushed with all the weight and strength I had, and she, her balance never good, went down backward. As she fell, the frame came up over my head and I was free. I ran. Up the mountain. I thought that would be safest. I could hear her struggling to get up behind me and I knew I could get a good head start. I didn't look back until I was out of breath and had to stop.

She was coming faster than I expected. No props or crutches, but then it was a steep climb and she didn't need them as she would have on flat ground. I went on, angling more to the side, but I knew that wouldn't help much. She could always lean into the mountain even going sideways and support herself. In going up, I had just made it easier for her.

I headed for a pile of boulders. I was getting tired and hoped there'd be a place to hide. I found what I was looking for, a crack between two huge stones that I could wriggle into but she couldn't and where I could go farther in than her arm could reach. I waited there, listening to the loosened rocks clattering down, to the scrape and rustle of bushes, to her great breathing and to her breathless calling. "My love," she called. "My only one. My dearest heart. Honey bunch. My heart will break." Where had she learned all these clichés? Certainly *we* don't use them anymore. And how could a people invent a great civilization and communicate—God knows from where or how far—travel through space, arrive in a "palace" that couldn't be moved or even blasted out of the way, and then keep talking like this all the time? And I mean *all* the time.

But already she had come up and was leaning against my rocks. "It's love that helps to find the lover," she said, breathing hard and looking in at me. "Love needs no sense of direction, nor of smell, nor to see the tracks. Love finds its ways." (She had probably heard me. I was, as she was, breathing hard.)

I couldn't stand it anymore. "Cut the crap," I said, but she went on.

"Dear heart," she said, as though out of some Victorian novel. "Dear, dear, dear, dear heart."

"Look," I said. "You can't keep loving everything that comes in sight. And I'm sick and tired," I said, "of hearing about it." Then I said all sorts of things you're not supposed to say if you want any kind of lasting relationship with a person. I said she was sappy. I said no one—not a single person on this planet—could put up with her for a minute, least of all myself. "Love!" I said, "I don't even like you. Nobody here does."

She sat down then, and I could see her better from between my stones. She was looking at the ground, scratching into it with one big, fat finger, and, again, I had a feeling of sympathy for her, but then she said, "There's a sweet little bug here."

"Crush it," I said, and she did.

"What about all these other ones?"

"Same," I said, "and keep doing it." She did and then looked for more little things to crush. I felt a wicked sense of satisfaction.

"OK," I said, "now no more picture frames. Promise."

"All right," she said.

"And stop doing everything I say to do. I can't stand that anymore."

She didn't answer. That was a step forward.

"Everything isn't good, good. Look around at all the dead trees. Dead and half-dead. Well, that's what this planet is, half-dead, and we're a half-dead people. Tell that to your crowd up there on the so-called lesser worlds. Tell them all they have to do is wait and they can have the whole planet for nothing, though by then who would want it?"

"What about sex?" she said. "I thought we were going to have some fun with that. I thought you people did that a lot here."

"It's not for you," I said.

"But that's what makes everybody and everything grow and come to be."

"It's not for you."

She sat quietly, seeming to think, but who knows what went on in her big, lumpy head. Then she began banging on the ground with her left hand. "I want," she said. That big hand could make a thumping noise as though to call a herd of elephants. I could feel the vibrations of it where I lay back under the boulders. She shook the whole mountain. There was no sense asking her to stop, I'd told her not to do what I said anymore, but I *did* ask her anyway, just to see if she would. She wouldn't.

I began to hear little trickling-down sounds and then the thump and clatter of larger stones. She was starting an avalanche or, rather, a lot of little ones. I worried about where I was, under these boulders. I'd have to come out.

She wasn't paying attention to me. She was pounding, now, with both hands, and making a low, singing sound. I came out just in time. My boulders toppled over and started down with the rest of the stones. But she *was* paying attention to me, because just then a head-sized stone rolled right at me from above and she reached out, seeming not to be looking, and stopped it. Others, too, larger ones, came down toward me. She saved me, over and over, even though she was pounding at the same time, making them come down. Finally she stopped. "Now we go back," she said, "you and I." And she started down, mostly falling, and sliding, and setting off more little avalanches.

I followed her. Keeping well behind, though. I didn't know if I should be afraid that she'd hurt me or if I should count on her to keep me safe. I didn't know if it was good or bad that she seemed to be taking charge, that she had such confidence that I would follow. And I wanted to follow. Like seeing something to its ending or seeing that it *does* end. And I was responsible for her and for how it would end—*if* end. I was being paid to be courageous. I wouldn't get paid at all if I didn't stick by her.

When I came into our clearing, she was already back on her crutches and props, stumbling around putting her picture frames up on stands. "We won't be caring what or who is half-dead now," she said.

Then she moved fast. I wasn't ready for it. She turned and caught me again over the head with a long, narrow picture frame that looked made for the purpose of catching people. She threw me down and put one big thigh over me. Then she twisted around so she was lying alongside me and began to take my clothes off. *Very* slowly, brushing my skin lightly with her fingertips every so often. You wouldn't think someone so big and so gross could stroke so exquisitely gently. She leaned over me as she did this, and her big breasts moved as though filled with water—milk, I should say—brushed over me, undulated over me, big nipples rising.

Then she pulled my jeans off. "I see," she said. There was no keeping it from her. After that I lost track of things, only knew I was enmeshed, enveloped, lost, just as I'd feared, except I wasn't afraid. Everything was fat, rippling, jiggling, pulsing. I mean *everything.* I was on top, but mostly in, a breast on both sides of me, her stomach a great sea I floated on. With my ear pressed against her chest, I heard (again) the great waterfall of life, all the more impressive in the reality of it this time—beating for me, it seemed, as much as beating for her sake, keeping me alive as well as her—making me live. Everything's not quite dead yet, I thought, even in the midst of it. Everything is still possible.

When she got up, finally, and left me, it was as though the great sea of life—*la mère,* the mother, the mare—had left me. I had ridden the mother-horse of the sea—of the world—and suddenly I knew what all those sappy words of hers meant and why she said them.

But she . . . it was as if she'd gone crazy. She was smashing all the frames and throwing them in the lake. She was stamping on the last remaining iris. She pulled down the tent with just one sweep of her arm. After that she took two steps out on the dock and broke it. I was already backing away toward the mountain again when I saw her pull up three young spruce trees by the roots and throw them in the lake, too.

"Don't worry," she said. "I go, but not to you. Make things dead now. You said, crush. I do that now, but not you. You're already crushed, only now you know how good we have sex on our lesser world so you know one good thing. We wouldn't like this place. It has great beauty, but it's all squash, squash. There's no really real love in you or in any of you."

Then she left, skirting the lake. I came back and walked out over the sunken, broken part of the dock to the end of it where part was still above the water and sat down.

They would probably get to her before she did much damage, though her damage wouldn't make much difference anyway. I hoped she would know enough to hide, and I thought, with her gray coloring and whitish spots, she could hunch down and look like just one more lichen-covered granite boulder. They would come for me this evening. There was supposed to be a flyby when I was to signal them to pick me up or not. I thought maybe I wouldn't tell them which direction she'd taken, though it would probably be clear. I'd tell them we were safe now—that I had managed it so that the creatures of the lesser worlds didn't want to come here anymore, but it didn't feel to me like much of a victory.

I sat and listened to her go until the crashing sounds faded away and everything was quiet again, and the bird and the bug sounds started up and the things that were mating went back to their mating, and I thought, good, good. I love. I love.

PERI

/ / /

Margaret's right. She always is. I don't argue with her. As she says, I ought to see a psychologist. I ought to have done it a long time ago, and not only because of wasting my talent. I ought to see one because I'm always holding back. I'm always waiting, who knows for what? I'm blending in. I wear nothing brighter than brown. In fact I wear nothing except brown. I shouldn't just stand there. I ought to go and *be* something.

Mother spoiled me. Money spoiled me. I admit all that, but I tell Margaret I never took to drink or drugs or frittered money away on crazy schemes. I think she'd like me better if I had. She even says it. She says it drives her crazy that I don't have any bad habits . . . that I haven't any habits at all, though I don't see how that can be. She says, what's to love or hate about me? And she can't understand why I insist on keeping my ability hidden. She says I'm frightened. She says I'm scared to death to be *anything*.

Well, it isn't as if I could really fly. I never manage, even when in the best of spirits, to get more than about a foot off the ground. Mostly I'm hardly up six inches. As she says, I haven't practiced. I feel silly. I feel dumb being only a few inches off the ground and I know I look funny doing it: my toes point, my legs dangle . . . I have to lead with my left shoulder and hold my right hand out in front, left hand back. And I bump into things along the way— anything that sticks up higher than I can lift: stones, front steps, bushes . . . Even flowers sometimes get in my way. The worst of it is, when I bump into them or get tangled, I lose my balance and fall, always down on my left elbow or shoulder. I lose my hat. I drop my cane. My suit gets mussed and the knees of my pants get scraped. Once I went down into a puddle. And then why do it, anyway, when I can't go along much faster than a brisk walk? Why bother?

Balance is the trick. Margaret doesn't realize how hard it is. But I know she's right: I could work at it. I could practice. I have a feeling, though, that she wants me to be more than I ever could be—that she wants people saying about me, "Look, look. He's walking on the water!" or some such, and I can't even swim.

Instead of practicing, I do it less and less. I don't even walk briskly anymore. I slump along. Oh, I stand up straight enough when I go out with Margaret on weekends now and then, but when I'm by myself, which is most of the time, I let myself go. Sometimes I find I've buttoned up my overcoat or sweater all wrong and I don't even care. I don't wonder that she's disgusted with me.

Even our son . . . He doesn't say anything, but he doesn't have to. I know the look. I ought to, I see it every day on Margaret's face. But Isabel, our grandchild . . . Now she's the only one I never see looking like that. Perhaps she hasn't noticed me that much, or doesn't care, whichever. I don't get to see her as often as I'd like. I suppose I'm considered a bad influence. She's nine. Or is it seven? Naturally I can't keep track. I try, but birthdays come and go. You'd think I could at least remember Isabel's, but I don't, not even hers, and yet I care about her. I really do.

And now it turns out that Isabel is coming to stay with us for a whole month while her parents have a big second honeymoon down in Brazil—Ipanema. They have been fighting so much (they confessed it to Margaret; needless to say no one confesses anything to me) that they thought they needed a long, private time on some beach to clear things up.

Isabel comes on a Sunday morning, all dressed in blue, which makes her green eyes look blue, too. And she comes with a long list of things not to do and things to do and when to do them: not stay up after eight, not watch TV, not too many movies, not be out after dark, and, most especially, NO CHOCOLATE! *Can* go to ballet and concerts. *Must* go to piano lessons and dance lessons and tennis . . .

As it turns out, I get to be the one to take her to all these last things. As it turns out, I get to take her everywhere. Also it turns out she's only six, going on seven.

I don't know where Isabel comes from. She looks like none of us. You'd think she walked right out of the sea on a foggy day: pale skin, circles under her eyes (she always has them, sick or well), hair almost white, though I suppose it will darken with age. You'd think, with those looks, she'd be quiet once in a while, but she talks—and quite precociously, I think—talks and talks. After half an hour of it, Margaret says to me, "For God's sake, do something. Get her out of here. Take her for a walk in the park for a few hours. Go to the movies." But on the list it said not too many movies, so I thought we'd not do that so soon.

For my kind of person, who never knows what to say next, somebody like Isabel, even if only six years old, is a great relief— somebody who always knows just what to say and isn't a bit worried about changing the subject right in the middle of some other topic of conversation.

So Isabel and I go out to the park and she skips along holding my hand. We do the zoo. We pet dogs. We return other people's balls. We look at the babies going by in strollers. We have popsicles with only a little bit of chocolate around the outside. Isabel thinks it's not too much. She thinks we could each have a popsicle a day and it wouldn't be too much chocolate. She thinks popsicles are perfect for weather like this. She says you can get popsicles that don't have chocolate on them but that she likes these better. She says chocolate isn't good for children and it isn't good for old people like I am either because it does something bad, she says, to the calcium, which is why her mother doesn't want her to have it and why I shouldn't have too much either. And I say I won't have *any* at all after she's gone, and she says, good, because she won't either, so then we'll be even. "Mother can smell it on you," she says. "I wonder if Grandma can smell it on you, too?"

We have so much fun that, on the way home, Isabel cuts a kind of caper: kicks both feet up in front of her and falls down on her bottom, quite hard. She almost cries, but she holds it back. Mainly she worries because she tore some lace on her panties. I tell her we'll get some new ones. (Margaret would say I'm spoiling her as much as I spoil myself.) I say we'll go right away and get another pair, but of course it's Sunday, which we both forgot. The children's stores are shut. But then we do find a store, except it only has things for grown-up women. Isabel says she wants to look there anyway.

She chooses a blue bikini-style panty with tan lace around the legs and along the top, more lace, actually, than blue. I know Margaret would disapprove. I even disapprove myself. It's too much. It looks like Forty-Second Street, but I also think the panties extraordinarily beautiful. Baroque. No, rococo. I'm not going to say anything to Isabel that might make her feel bad about her choice. We get the smallest size they have, and I think, well, it doesn't matter because they're much too big and Isabel will never be able to wear them. I tell her to put them in her shiny little blue purse that she's been carrying all this time and didn't even forget when we stopped for hotdogs. I tell Isabel not to bother Grandma with any of this. "It's our secret," I say. I know how much Isabel loves secrets, so I know she'll not tell on purpose, though I also know it may pop out by mistake.

By Monday, it's clear that Margaret can't abide Isabel for more than fifteen minutes at a time, so I'm the one to take her off to tennis that afternoon, and afterward we go to the Plaza for strawberries and ice cream, and Isabel tells me she hates tennis *and* piano. She doesn't mind dance so much, but she wishes the piano were an oboe instead.

"How in the world do you know about the oboe?" I ask.

"I go to concerts all the time, you know. It's good for you. And there's nothing to do there but think or, if you're sitting in the first row of the balcony, which I like the best, you can see who's playing by who's getting the reddest face, so I found out what the oboe is and the sound of it and I like it so much I wouldn't even care if I got red and my cheeks puffed out while I played it." What she likes about the sound is that it's piercing and nose-ish and, she says, kind of like it comes from some other country . . . from the Arabs or some place that has tents and red and orange stripes on things. And she likes it because you don't have to have a piano around all the time. You could even take it outside and practice walking around. You could practice in the woods or on the top of a mountain, which would be the best of all. She has read up about it, too, and she knows all about shaping your own reeds and wetting them.

So then I wonder out loud, how can we work it so that she can take some oboe lessons while she's here. "Well, why not?"

And she says, "Well, why not?" too, so we decide that we won't do the piano anymore—that I'll call up and say she did something to her thumb. And she *can* do something to her thumb so we won't be lying because neither of us, Isabel says, ever wants to lie, and she's right. "And why not, while we're at it," Isabel says, "change tennis to karate?"

All through this I can't believe she's six going on seven. On the list she came with, it said she should behave like a lady and she does behave like a lady. How could anyone doubt it? The waiters at the Plaza don't doubt it. The head waiter doesn't doubt it. The man who brings the water doesn't, the bellhops in the lobby don't, nor does the doorman as we leave. And I don't doubt it as I give Isabel my elbow and we go out and down the steps.

I find a teacher, same time as piano. I find two oboes. We take them out and practice in the park so Margaret won't suspect. Even in the rain, we always find some secluded place to get under, such as the bridges where the traffic goes over. Nobody bothers us there.

The next time we're at the Plaza, Isabel had just had karate and is quite flushed from all the exercise and, I suppose, happiness, for she really loves karate and she loves wearing the white suit. Oboe was harder than she expected. She's glad to do the work, but karate is just pure joy and I can see it in her face. Isabel, I swear, looks thirteen and talks twenty-five.

"I really think, Grandpa, I should get you a new tie. I think you ought to have one with more color in it. Red, pink, and orange," she said, "to go with your oboe." And she begins to count out her change and her carefully folded bills. All of a sudden that little blue purse just seems out of the question for such a big girl as Isabel appears to be. "I only have eleven dollars and forty-two cents," she says, "but I want to get you a really nice tie and I don't think that will do it, do you?"

"We'll see if we can find one on sale," I say. "You'll get me a tie and I'll get you a new purse."

I catch sight of myself in Lord & Taylor's windows later, as we're on our way in, and I have my hat at quite a rakish angle and Isabel, on my arm, looks like a teenager. I wonder how I could have come to put on my hat like that.

In more ways than one, time seems to fly. Isabel is growing practically before my eyes. Last week she was thirteen, this week I turn around and she's wearing lipstick and a wide-brimmed— very dashing, in fact—black hat and is, I swear, twenty . . . eighteen, at the least. And look at me. My clothes hang. My belt buckles two notches thinner. We stop and look at ourselves in the mirror wall at Fifth Avenue and Thirty-Sixth Street. I'm wearing my new "Arab" striped tie, my hat over one eye. I'm smiling. Isabel is smiling. Then she cuts another caper in sheer joy. This time she lifts a good five feet, kicking out in front of her and leaning forward into it, and then she comes drifting down as if my arm is the only thing keeping her from sailing right up to the top of the Empire State Building. We turn, then, and she's so tall she's looking at me, eye to eye and then we kiss. Not exactly a lover's kiss, but not exactly *not* a lover's kiss. A fun kiss. A happy kiss. "Marry me, Grandpa," she says. "Get a divorce and marry me." Then she goes along into a long tale about how it's all right because she's adopted and not my real grandchild at all, and I'm not believing a word she says because I remember when she was born and when she was one and two and three . . . I may walk around in a daze, as Margaret says, I may not see anything that's going on, but I do notice a few things.

"I'll never find anyone like you," Isabel says. "I'll never have this much fun with anybody. I'll never, never, never."

And I think that's true. I've lived a long time, and I certainly never had so much fun as I've had with Isabel. But I remember I was too young to have fun with Margaret. I was even more cautious than I am now and frightened. I still am. I wasn't afraid of Isabel because I'd, in a way, grown up with her. "That's not the point," I say.

"Let's run away before they come to take me back. Look," she says (we're still looking at each other in the mirror), "we make a great couple." (There's no doubt about that. I'm standing up straight for once and my pot belly's gone.) "I have to go home *next week!*"

But it turns out that doesn't happen quite so soon. It turns out (Margaret tells me) Isabel's mother and our son are fighting so much down there in Ipanema that things are worse than ever, so they will come home, but they don't feel they can cope with Isabel until things settle down a bit and, since they never fight in front of her and don't ever want to, could we keep her for another two weeks until they can get their lives straightened out. So, for one more of those two weeks, things are as they were before, and there is, I can see it, no doubt in the eyes of the Plaza doorman, nor in the eyes of the head waiter, nor in the eyes of the waiters, nor in the eyes of the man who brings the water, no doubt at all that Isabel is a desirable and nubile young lady.

And every day Isabel begs me to marry her, and every day I say, "No. Absolutely not. It's not for us." And I tell her that Margaret and I probably love each other more than we think we do, or might. I'm not sure. "And I made promises," I say. "And I haven't been the best husband. And every now and then I ought to have some courage to do or not do, and I'm your grandfather, for heaven's sake!"

But then Margaret finds the panties, and then all the rest of it. "Where did these come from?" she says, and then, "What are you doing to this child? Old lecher. Filthy man. Lipstick and nail polish. *Red* nail polish. Perfumes. What will her mother and father think? And that purse. Did you think I'd never notice? Did you think I was blind? A two-hundred-dollar lizard purse! How could you? And what about those clarinets? From now on," she says,

"*I'm* taking her to her lessons. And you," she says to Isabel, "are not allowed to say a word . . . not one word from now on. Thank God there's only four more days of it. I've a good mind to lock you both up in your rooms."

But she doesn't do that. She just locks me up . . . for a few afternoons. (She knows I like to get out and walk.) And Isabel goes home and I don't even have a chance to say good-bye. In fact I'm forbidden to see her. I don't know what happens to the karate suit and the oboes and the purse and panties.

Later on in mid-October, when Margaret and I have fallen back, more or less, into our old routine, we rent a car and go out on Long Island to see the fall leaves. I wear my tie. I still have that. It's exactly the colors—I realize it on the trip—exactly the colors of the leaves. Margaret says it's too bright, but I know that when I wore brown ties she didn't like those either. I tell her I want to wear it anyway, and she doesn't pursue it. It's as if she thinks to let me have this one small pleasure, and I'm grateful.

After we do the trees, we go down to take a walk on the beach. Several people are out all bundled up in sweaters. There's a man sitting on a piece of driftwood playing the flute. There's a dog fetching sticks. There are kids throwing things into the surf to watch them bob there and get washed back in. It all makes me think of Isabel even more than I already do think of her. I know I did the right thing. Everything right for a change, from popsicles, to oboes, to the Plaza . . . even those crazy panties, and to saying no. For once I did a whole series of right things. I feel sad, but I feel happy. Just thinking about those five and a half weeks, I feel my left shoulder hunch forward, hand back, then right hand up and out to steady me. I lift. About two inches so my toes still touch the sand. Nobody notices at first, least of all Margaret. Then I go up four . . . maybe five inches. It feels good even though I haven't practiced. I don't think I've even tried it for three or four years. Then I lift about a foot without any effort at all, and I begin to drift lazily toward the water. I feel the spray, cold on my ankles. Suddenly Margaret does notice. "What are you up to now?" she says. "What will I *do* with you?" And she reaches out to grab me, but I'm picking up speed. Then I think I hear another voice, "Look, look.

He's walking on the water!" I don't turn back to see who said it. Besides, I'm already much too high to seem to walk in the waves. I hear shouting. Dogs bark. Then I do look back, but the fog is drifting in. I can hardly see the beach anymore at all. Margaret is just a gesticulating dark smudge against the luminous white.

DRACULALUCARD
/ / /

"I'm a gamboling lamb. I'm a gambling man. I'm a rambler. I'm a riser and a doer," she says. "I'm a lucky buck. I'm a crazy stork." She *is* a crazy stork, or, more likely, some fatter, much smaller bird . . . a crazy chickadee, calling out in the snow, for there's snow and she's outside in it, jumping up and down, running around trying not to look lazy, saying I'm a this and I'm a that and the other, but she doesn't believe any of it. "I'm a lazy schmuck" is what she's really thinking. Maybe this is her way of turning over a whole new leaf just by saying so. Or maybe she's had too much coffee. She leers over her shoulder. Is she going back inside?

Just because she lost five pounds hasn't made her that different from before. She's got maybe twenty-five, thirty-five to go, and she's not tall . . . not tall enough to turn out tall and thin, ever, no matter how much she loses.

She has wanted to be called "the salt of the earth." She has wanted to be called Jane or Ann, salt-of-the-earth kind of names. One wonders what she wants to be called now, running around like this, and if she's changed her mind? She doesn't act like a Jane. Also she has married the chief inspector. (Long ago.) Does he want her to be the salt of the earth? Not likely.

Now she says, "I'm worth my salt," but it's just words. Nothing has changed that much except pretty soon she's going to freeze out there.

It *is* a nice snowstorm, no doubt about that. Snowflakes swirling around, going up as much as coming down. Tiny snow stars sit caught in her gray hair, not even wetting it. Midwinter. February something or other. Much too soon to hope for spring and not that good a time to go on out and be one's best self, though why *not* pick the hardest season? The darkest, longest nights? Except she's lain in bed lazy every morning, overeaten, hasn't paid attention, has a wart on her nose. Her breasts sag and she keeps writing tub for but and king for quit, Ashkenazie for Anasazi. Balboa might as well be Bilboa.

Now she has come back in because she doesn't have all that much on, but she gets bundled up and goes right on out again. Turns out she's going to get a new hat, a courageous new hat, kind of like a cowboy's. A hat—a whole new way of life comes with it. Maybe she'll get two hats.

Now smile. Now keep quiet. Wait. That's how she *used* to do. But courage can come quite suddenly when one least expects it. (And she's got a reason and a need.) It's salt-of-the-earth time now or never because not only is she past the menopause, but also the chief inspector has hinted that he might have found a younger woman, more beautiful than she ever was, even when she was sixteen. He's hinted that maybe he'll leave, but he's also hinted that maybe, on the other hand, he'll stay.

And she has just realized he doesn't call her anything, let alone not Jane. "Hey," he says, and, "Get me this or that." (Can she say about herself that she once was loved or ever will be, and, if she had been salt-of-the-earth, would that have made the difference?)

But she's back out now, standing on the corner wondering which way to turn and she's not wearing any hat at all. Her hair is already coming loose from its Psyche knot. Her scarf is flying up behind her. The snow is in her eyes. Had she listened to the radio, she might have known this was a real blizzard, and that it would last not only all day, but all night, too.

There's a man there, on the corner, looks at her with pale, close-set eyes so light she can't tell what color they are or if any color at all, though the pupils look extraordinarily black. He's waiting for the bus. (She had not thought about this being the bus stop until this very moment.) That man probably thinks she's waiting for the bus, too. He probably thinks she has a job just like everybody else. Maybe he even thinks she's happy. (She hums a tango just in case he doesn't.) He has a pale, cool face that shines out with some inner kind of light she thinks she's seen in deep, dark water.

It goes on snowing. She keeps on humming. It's so windy the man has to hold onto his hat, and his white silk scarf blows out and up just like her woolly one does. Finally he speaks, right in the middle of her humming. "I'm Mr. Snow," he says. "Alucard Snow."

"Jane," she answers, already lying, and not even sure yet if that's who she really wants to be, but then she does confess that she doesn't work—that she's only going downtown for a new hat. It's embarrassing to say it because it doesn't seem to be the sort of thing a salt-of-the-earth kind of person would do.

"Many curative possibilities in hats," Mr. Snow says. "One might do worse than seek out a good one. I, also," he says, "I was going to buy a pair of shoes specifically in hopes of beneficial results. But now I think the bus won't come." Is she mistaken, or hasn't he a slight accent and a funny kind of lisp?

Well, she'll not go home, that's one thing sure. Maybe she'll walk. She hadn't even thought to take the bus anyway until she saw Mr. Snow standing there, but "Cup of tea?" he is saying, and, "Corner deli?" Of course she says yes, thinking maybe something is happening now. Maybe something is well on the way to be happening. Perhaps even something a little bit dangerous.

Inside there's only the two of them and the man who serves them. Her bifocals get so fogged up that, for several minutes, she can hardly see where she is or who she's with, even so—or maybe *because*—she begins to tell him all about herself. The chief inspector sleeps alone. The chief inspector comes upon her suddenly when she least expects him. If she's reading, she forgets whole passages. If she's dozing, she can't sleep again for hours. If she's having just one little drink too many, she'll have two more. If she's sneaking into his room or if she's banging on his door thinking he's inside, he grabs her from behind and heads her toward the kitchen, where, if *he's* in there, she always drops her best china. He talks about precision versus passion. He talks about policies versus pleasures . . .

But now, when she can finally see through her glasses and get a really good look at Mr. Snow—here, so near, across the tiny table—she feels fat and awkward. Even her rather graceful (or so she'd always thought) hands look dumpy next to those of Mr. Snow, which are of extraordinary delicacy and finesse. All of him extraordinarily fine, the little hairs of his mustache like a silverpoint drawing . . . all of him like a silverpoint, and she, wishing she had not ordered a cupcake, which will surely make her even more the opposite of Mr. S. than she already is. If only she could sit in front of him every day, she might become like a sylph. An elderly sylph, if such there is, but sylphlike nonetheless.

But now it's as though he's asking, "Want to be a sylph?" though not in so many words. (Is there a choice between sylph and salt-of-the-earth? They might well be mutually exclusive.)

"You are caught"—he has just said it—"as, in the ultimate analysis, we are all caught, in the vagaries . . . in the swarms and eddies, and so forth, of time." (Had she not always known just such a thing though not had the wit to voice it?) "You are in a void," he has said, "a significant void." (*Significant* void! Had she not always known that also? Helpless, in a *significant* void!) "When, on the other hand, you'd rather be going forward with zest or something closely akin to zest."

"Yes, yes!"

"What's needed is a great metamorphosis." (Exactly what she's always wanted, and especially now. How had he come to know so much about her in such a short time?) "Transmogrification," he says, "and in one single season. The question is, how?"

And he leans very close across the table toward her. She'd like to pull back, but she doesn't dare. Now he seems to her as though his mother might have been a fox . . . a silver fox. But now he turns sideways and lifts his feet, both of them, to show her his shoes. (They're black and white wing tips.) "Look," he says, "see how they turn up at the toes like little hooks."

Mr. Snow. Mr. Fox. Like a bat is what he really is. Very like a bat. Not a fox, but a foxy bat, and his shoes, she's sure of it—well, not that sure, but it does occur to her—are for hanging upside down. Why is he bothering to show them to her?

She'll answer no. Whatever it is, she'll say no.

But he's reading no on her face, or so she thinks. Shows sharp eyeteeth. It's a nice smile, though, a nice V under his white mustache. "They don't squeak," he says.

How do you make love to a bat? Could she be that acrobatic at her age, and especially at her weight? And what about her acrophobia?

He has little pinpoint eyes. The pupils show so black in all that lightness, she thinks he must live in a house made of nice thick slices of snow with clear ice windows. Even inside you'd see your breath and even if everything weren't white, it would look white because of the light. Would she dare go there? She's never liked the cold, though today something has warmed her. Maybe it's her craziness that has kept her warm. The chief inspector would say so, but he calls her crazy every day anyway and then this morning he said, "That's it. This has gone far enough. That's it, now. What a to-do." That's what he said as he watched her out the window and then said it to her when she came in, so she knows that this *is* it, therefore what? Never come back? Therefore run off with Mr. Snow who hasn't even asked her? Say yes instead of no? And what about the two new hats she hasn't got yet? It could have been those hats that would have really changed her. Some hats take a lot of courage to wear, but she'd have done it. Even in front of Mr. Snow. And those hats . . . they would have been hats like she would never have worn before and yet each one the opposite of the other; one black and hard, one soft and yellow; or one gray and one red; one wool, one silk, as: one like her scarf, one like his.

But now, after another cup of tea and another cupcake, here she is creeping into her own house by the back door wearing Mr. Snow's black and white wing tips. (They pinch a little at the sides. His feet are, of course, narrow and long.) And here it is, or so it seems to her . . . here it is, the significant void. She could tell the minute she came in and stood in the dark back hallway, listening. Void. Even though she can hear him humming in the kitchen. She can hear the crunch of crackers or celery (it's way past supper time) and the rustle of papers. Munching and singing. The chief inspector's not so neat. He's not as neat as he says he is. Leastways when he thinks she's not around. And it's only right this minute that she realizes she doesn't want him to know she's back . . . doesn't want him ever to know that she came on back and not even with two new hats for him to complain about . . . though it's true she does have these shoes and, surely, "many curative possibilities" in them.

What a fuss the chief inspector would make if he saw them! And she's gone catatonic again with that fear he'll come upon her as he always does, jumping out at her from dark places though she is the one in the dark now . . . but he might jump out at her even as she stands here with the snow melting off the wing tips all over the back hall, thinking: no, please, no . . . and, for once, he does stay put and sings so she knows exactly where he is. And the shoes (they hurt, but not that much) soft and silent, white parts glistening in the dark—even the black parts shining out—let her pass through to the stairway and up it, undiscovered. Pinching more and more as they dry, they let her creep around her bedroom and then tiptoe across the hall and up the attic stairs and not a single board squeaks because she knows where all those boards are though, before, that never seemed to matter. He always found her out, anyway, not doing what he'd told her was essential, or reading some silly, romantic book or other. But now it's as though these flashy shoes make her invisible. And he had said it, Mr. Snow, that these two shoes were just as good as two new hats, only here she is, not having to do without the hats either.

Up here there are clothes from all over, and two hats, one salt-of-the-earth bonnet, blue cotton, and the other this pile of thin, gray-green stuff with feathers, rising up extravagantly on a purple platform. There's also an old, saggy bed and an encyclopedia from the 1930s . . . Almost everything she'd need up here, and Mr. S. (now wasn't that nice of him) had bought her, just at the last moment, a heart-shaped box of chocolates so, if she can make these last by taking tiny bites, not gobble them all up like she sometimes does, they'll do her, maybe, for a long time, especially after those cupcakes. She can suck on the chocolates very slowly and read that encyclopedia.

Maybe it's a "significant void" because there's so much to learn and she hasn't been learning it. It's as though the chief inspector, and she also, had closed off the world. Not closed it off as much as inspected it for flaws—as though the earth were too earthy; animals, too animal; women, too womanly; men, too mannish; dogs, too doggy (she's heard the chief inspector say that last many times); and she, also, no doubt about it, too much who she is . . . much too much herself, though now what a wonderful, great, empty void inside her. Like being a balloon.

And Mr. Snow had kissed her on the neck. Just once. That made her feel like floating away, too. Had the chief inspector ever done that, even in the beginning? Surely he must have, though, if he did, she's forgotten. But Mr. Snow. Alucard. His cool lips had brushed her cheek and then brushed on down and landed on her collarbone almost as though by mistake. For just a second . . . hardly a second. She wasn't even sure it had happened. Perhaps it hadn't. But there is a little red mark there. She looked and there was a mole beside a little pimple more or less in the same spot he'd touched. It still tickles.

No, she'll not eat the chocolates! For once not to do that. Or, at least wait a while. Just look at them and then go to bed on the saggy bed (with the shoes on—if she takes them off she'll never get them back on again), the wind and snow blowing about outside. There's so much white out there that, even though it's night and low clouds, the two little windows glow so she can almost see the whole attic and, instead of being dusty and dull, everything looks magic. She can't sleep for how magic it looks. Besides, her feet hurt too much, but she won't take those shoes off. Now salt-of-the-earth types probably would do that—would take off anything that hurts, but she needs this pain. It keeps reminding her that something's happening.

She can hear the chief inspector downstairs walking up and down. He doesn't know how cozy and warm she is up here and how bright everything is, how nice the wind sounds. She could sleep for a very long time . . .

But this is all wrong. Not sleep now. Something must be done, and, though not acrobatic, she must become so right away. Climb up, yes, like bats making love. Unless, that is, they do it as they fly.

Now these shoes have got to get up there in the eaves feet first. (If they were on Mr. S. they'd be there by now.) And must be quiet about it, though the chief inspector's already asleep. Now and then she can hear him below, faintly snoring.

Chair on bed. Feet up, as on monkey bars a long time ago. But that was before sciatica, and not such a klutz back then, or at least didn't know it. Nobody kept saying it, though maybe Mother did say it a little bit. Yes, Mother shaking her head, "You'll fall." So now she does fall. Thinks: naturally. Bed is there to catch her, though, and no harm done. When and if she does get up there, it will be just like Mr. Snow would do it.

Falls again. Tries again. Falls again. Tries again. Falls again. But finally feet at apex. Toes pointed and hooked up and in like little claws and hope not to fall again.

/ / /

Falls again. (Mother would have said, "What else is new?") But what's going on? Sound of birds and the brightness. Not snow and night, but spring and morning. Shoes still stuck up there. How come they let her go? What time is it? Looks like April. She tries to get to the window but trips over some gray silky stuff that's hanging about her shoulders. Has to crawl the last few yards. Yes, it *is* later. The apple tree's in bloom. And she's ravenous. Thank goodness she didn't eat the chocolates all up the night before . . . or whatever night that was. Her arms are so tangled in the gray stuff she can't open the box. She fumbles them free finally and, after all, the chocolates are gobbled up . . . (It's one thing about her not changed, though she'd hoped for that almost the most of all, but she can still eat a large box of chocolates at one sitting.) She tries to straighten that gray stuff out. It seems attached to her back. Finally she crosses the stuff in front, lets one side hang down almost to the floor and throws the other over her shoulder as you'd wear a large mantilla. It's nice stuff. She doesn't think she's ever had such nice silky gray stuff before. Like wearing a cloud. And it's elegant. Though it seems she's not changed at all in all this time between the third fall and the fourth, for she's still fat and no smarter for having spent all this time up here with the thirties encyclopedia . . . she may even have forgotten things. (What was his name? Has she forgotten that? Oh, it was beautiful! Alucard. Yes, Alucard Snow.) And still sciatica . . . still limping around and still bumping into things even with the gray stuff wrapped up around her and out of the way. But she does feel pretty good. Though she's hardly changed, maybe joy, or something very like it. She'll go right on out to the bus stop to find Alucard and tell him. She wants those shoes, though. She puts the chair on the bed again (it had fallen off) plus three volumes of the encyclopedia. Makes it to the rafters in just one try. (This time she's not trying to go up feet first.) Balances there, afraid, but doing it anyway. Thinks: Well, that's a change . . . one change, at least. Maybe really could do "it" with a bat. (Is one ever too fat for lovemaking? And what about having had too many chocolates? Already sated, that is, in a different way? Perhaps not eat so many next time so as to leave more room for love.)

I'm a gambling man, etc. Maybe those are not just words now. But salt-of-the-earth? Is that really the question? No, she'll not wear the salt-of-the-earth bonnet to come downstairs in. She'll wear that bird's nest hat that matches this gray shawl thing so perfectly. And she'll wear the shoes, tight as they are.

/ / /

"Where have you been?"

That's the first thing he says to her. Now that she's back, he's all of a sudden hungry for some of her cooking. "Where in the world? Attic all this time? Talk about crazy!"

She just smiles, wondering what she had seen in this odd old man who always says she's crazy?

"Take off that hat."

"No."

"That's my grandmother's hat. She was a great lady. She wasn't your kind of woman. That's her shawl, too."

"It isn't."

"I recognize it."

He snatches the hat, but she snatches it right back. A few feathers fly off, but no great harm done. She's really angry now, but, for a change, at him and not herself.

And then, slowly, the wings come out—as though angry air were being pumped into them. Good, clean, angry air. They grow . . . all that gray stuff fills and throbs until they touch the ceiling. One has to be bold with such as these stuck to one's back. Perhaps joy is necessary, too, though she has a moment of panic when she wonders if she'll be able to get outside with these things on. She has to curl herself around awkwardly, squat down and creep along the sill to get them out the front door after her and then, just as she straightens up, she falls down on the front steps for no reason at all. She never has had good balance, but perhaps the wings upset it even more.

Now she's jumping around as though she thought she could fly. Up and down, up and down, like a baby bird not yet fledged. At first a few more feathers bounce off the hat and then the hat bounces off. She puts it on more firmly so that it almost covers her eyes.

"I'm a bat. I'm an acrobat. I'm a fly. I'm a butterfly," she says, and now there's some truth to it. "My name is my name. My name isn't Jane." (She thinks Alucard will say he knew it all the time.)

(How does a bat make love to a butterfly?)

Now, she leers over her shoulder at the chief inspector watching from the window, and he's thinking his same old thoughts, that she looks really silly out there and is she ever coming back inside?

Jump, jump, jump, and still not off the ground. She doesn't even care, but the chief inspector doesn't know that jumping up and down is almost as good as flying sometimes, when you're in the mood for it . . . just exactly as good as flying—or hanging upside down. That was done, though she thought she couldn't, and who can tell, maybe flying will come later. There's this big, ballooning void inside her that might lift her up and keep her up.

(She's right to wonder, how *does* a bat make love to a big fat butterfly?)

Anyway, there's a black dot in the sky. (She can't possibly see it because her hat's too low over her eyes.) No, it's a white dot and rapidly getting larger as it nears. If she saw it, she'd know who it was right away. The sun is shining. April. But, even so, there are a few flakes of snow.

PELT

/ / /

She was a white dog with a wide face and eager eyes, and this was the planet Jaxa, in winter.

She trotted well ahead of the master, sometimes nose to ground, sometimes sniffing the air, and she didn't care if they were being watched or not. She knew that strange things skulked behind iced trees, but strangeness was her job. She had been trained for it, and crisp, glittering Jaxa was, she felt, exactly what she had been trained for, *born* for.

I love it, I love it . . . that was in her pointing ears, her waving tail . . . I *love* this place.

It was a world of ice, a world with the sound of breaking goblets. Each time the wind blew they came shattering down by the trayful, and each time one branch brushed against another it was, "Skoal," "Down the hatch," "The Queen" . . . tink, tink, tink. And the sun was reflected as if from a million cut-glass punch bowls under a million crystal chandeliers.

She wore four little black boots, and each step she took sounded like two or three more goblets gone, but the sound was lost in the other tinkling, snapping, cracklings of the silver, frozen forest about her.

She had figured out at last what that hovering scent was. It had been there from the beginning, the landing two days ago, mingling with Jaxa's bitter air and seeming to be just a part of the smell of the place; she found it in criss-crossing trails about the squatting ship, and hanging, heavy and recent, in hollows behind flat-branched, piney-smelling bushes. She thought of honey, and fat men, and dry fur when she smelled it.

There was something big out there, and more than one of them, more than two. She wasn't sure how many. She had a feeling this was something to tell the master, but what was the signal, the agreed-upon noise for: We are being watched? There was a whisper of sound, short and quick, for: Sighted close, come and shoot. And there was a noise for danger (all these through her throat mike to the receiver at the master's ear), a special, howly bark: Awful, awful—there is something awful going to happen. There was even a noise, a low rumble of sound for: Wonderful, wonderful fur—drop everything and come after *this* one. (And she knew a good fur when she saw one. She had been trained to know.) But there was no sign for: We are being watched.

She'd whined and barked when she was sure about it, but that had got her a pat on the head and a rumpling of the neck fur. "You're doing fine, Baby. This world is all ours. All we got to do is pick up the pearls. This is what we've been waiting for." And Jaxa was, so she did her work and didn't try to tell him any more, for what was one more strange thing in one more strange world?

She was on the trail of something now, and the master was behind her, out of sight. He'd better hurry. He'd better hurry or there'll be waiting to do, watching the thing, whatever it is, steady on until he comes, holding tight back, and that will be hard. Hurry, hurry.

She could hear the whispered whistle of a tune through the receiver at her ear and she knew he was not hurrying but just being happy. She ran on, eager, curious. She did not give the signal for hurry, but she made a hurry sound of her own, and she heard him stop whistling and whisper back into the mike, "So, so, Queen of Venus. The furs are waiting to be picked. No hurry, Baby." But morning was to her for hurry. There was time later to be tired and slow.

That fat-man honeyish smell was about, closer and strong. Her curiosity became two-pronged—this smell or that? What *is* the big thing that watches? She kept to the trail she was on, though. Better to be sure, and this thing was not so elusive, not twisting and doubling back, but up ahead and going where it was going.

She topped a rise and half slid, on thick furred rump, down the other side, splattering ice. She snuffled at the bottom to be sure of the smell again, and then, nose to ground, trotted past a thick and tangled hedgerow.

She was thinking through her nose, now. The world was all smell, crisp air, and sour ice, and turpentine pine . . . and this animal, a urine and brown grass thing . . . and then, strong in front of her, honey-furry-fat man.

She felt it looming before she raised her head to look, and there it was, the smell in person, some taller than the master and twice as wide. Counting his doubled suit and all, twice as wide.

This was a fur! Wonderful, wonderful. But she just stood, looking up, mouth open and lips pulled back, the fur on the back of her neck rising more from the suddenness than from fear.

It was silver and black, a tiger-striped thing, and the whitish parts glistened and caught the light as the ice of Jaxa did, and sparkled and dazzled in the same way. And there, in the center of the face, was a large and terrible orange eye, rimmed in black with black radiating lines crossing the forehead and rounding the head. That spot of orange dominated the whole figure, but it was a flat, blind eye, unreal, grown out of fur. At first she saw only that spot of color, but then she noticed under it two small, red glinting eyes and they were kind, not terrible.

This was the time for the call: Come, come and get the great fur, for the richest lady on earth to wear and be dazzling in and, most of all, to pay for. But there was something about the flat, black nose and the tender, bow-shaped lips, and those kind eyes that stopped her from calling. Something masterly. She was full of wondering and indecision and she made no sound at all.

The thing spoke to her then, and its voice was a deep lullaby sound of buzzing cellos. It gestured with a thick, fur-backed hand. It promised, offered, and asked; and she listened, knowing and not knowing.

The words came slowly.

This . . . is . . . world.

Here is the sky, the earth, the ice. The heavy arms moved. The hands pointed.

We have watched you, little slave. What have you done that is free today? Take the liberty. Here is the earth for your four-shoed feet, the sky of stars, the ice to drink. Do something free today. Do, do.

Nice voice, she thought, nice thing. It gives and gives. . . something.

Her ears pointed forward, then to the side, one and then the other, and then forward again. She cocked her head, but the real meaning would not come clear. She poked at the air with her nose.

Say that again, her whole body said. I almost have it. I *feel* it. Say it once more and maybe then the sense of it will come.

But the creature turned and started away quickly, very quickly for such a big thing. It seemed to shimmer itself away until the glitter was only the glitter of the ice and the black was only the thick, flat branches.

The master was close. She could hear his crackling steps coming up behind her.

She whined softly, more to herself than to him.

"Ho, Queenie. Have you lost it?" She sniffed the ground again. The honey-furry smell was strong. She sniffed beyond, zigzagging. The trail was there. "Go to it, Baby." She loped off to a sound like Chinese wind chimes, businesslike again. Her tail hung guiltily, though, and she kept her head low. She had missed an important signal. She'd waited until it was too late. But was the thing a master? Or a fur? She wanted to do the right thing. She always tried and tried for that, but now she was confused.

She was getting close to whatever it was she trailed, but the hovering smell was still there too, though not close. She thought of gifts. She knew that much from the slow, lullaby words, and gifts made her think of bones and meat, not the dry fishy biscuit she always got on trips like this. A trickle of drool flowed from the side of her mouth and froze in a silver thread across her shoulder.

She slowed. The thing she trailed must be *there*, just behind the next row of trees. She made a sound in her throat . . . ready, steady . . . and she advanced until she was sure. She sensed the shape. She didn't really see it . . . mostly it was the smell and something more in the tinkling glassware noises. She gave the signal and stood still, a furry, square imitation of a pointer. Come, hurry. This waiting is the hardest part.

He followed, beamed to her radio. "Steady, Baby. Hold that pose. Good girl, good girl!" There was only the slightest twitch of her tail as she wagged it, answering him in her mind.

He came up behind her and then passed, crouched, holding the rifle-rod before him, elbows bent. He knelt then, and waited as if at a point of his own, rod to shoulder. Slowly he turned with the moving shadow of the beast, and shot, twice in quick succession.

They ran forward then, together, and it was what she had expected—a deerlike thing, dainty hoofs, proud head, and spotted in three colors, large gray-green rounds on tawny yellow, with tufts of that same glittering silver scattered over.

The master took out a flat-bladed knife. He began to whistle out loud as he cut off the handsome head. His face was flushed.

She sat down nearby, mouth open in a kind of smile, and she watched his face as he worked. The warm smell made the drool come at the sides of her mouth and drip out to freeze on the ice and on her paws, but she sat quietly, only watching.

Between the whistlings he grunted, and swore, and talked to himself, and finally he had the skin and the head in a tight inside-out bundle.

Then he came to her and patted her sides with a flat, slap sound, and he scratched behind her ears and held a biscuit for her on his thick-gloved palm. She swallowed it whole and then watched him as he squatted on his heels and ate one almost like it.

Then he got up and slung the bundle of skin and head across his back. "I'll take this one, Baby. Come on, let's get one more something before lunch." He waved her to the right. "We'll make a big circle," he said.

She trotted out, glad she was not carrying anything. She found a strong smell at a patch of discolored ice and urinated on it. She sniffed and growled at a furry, mammal-smelling bird that landed in the trees above her and sent a shower of ice slivers down on her head. She zigzagged and then turned and bit, lips drawn back in mock rage, at a branch that scraped her side.

She followed for a while the chattery sound of water streaming along under the ice, and left it where an oily, lambish smell crossed. Almost immediately she came upon them—six small, greenish balls of wool with floppy, woolly feet. The honey-fat man smell was strong here too, but she signaled for the lambs, the "Come and shoot" sound, and she stood again waiting for the master.

"*Good* girl!" His voice has special praise. "By God, this place is a gold mine. Hold it, Queen of Venus. Whatever it is, don't let go."

There was a fifty-yard clear view here and she stood in plain sight of the little creatures, but they didn't notice. The master came slowly and cautiously, and knelt beside her. Just as he did, there appeared at the far end of the clearing a glittering silver and black tiger-striped creature.

She heard the sharp inward breath of the master and she felt the tenseness come to him. There was a new, faint whiff of sour sweat, and a special way of breathing. What she felt from him made the fur rise along her back with a mixture of excitement and fear.

The tiger thing held a small packet in one hand and was peering into it and pulling at the opening in it with a blunt finger. Suddenly there was a sweep of motion beside her and five fast, frantic pops sounded sharp in her ear. Two came after the honey-fat man had already fallen and lay like a huge, decorated sack.

The master ran forward and she came at his heels. They both stopped, not too close, and she watched the master looking at the big, dead, tiger head with the terrible eye. The master was breathing hard. His face was red and puffy. He didn't whistle or talk. After a time he took out his knife. He tested the blade, making a small, bloody thread of a mark on his left thumb. Then he walked closer, and she stood, and watched him, and whispered a questioning whine.

He stooped by the honey-fat master and it was that small, partly opened packet that he cut viciously through the center. Small round chunks fell out, bite-sized chunks of dried meat, and a cheesy substance, and some broken bits of clear, bluish ice.

The master kicked at them. His face was not red anymore, but pale. His mouth was open in a grin that was not a grin.

He went about the skinning then.

He did not keep the flat-faced, heavy head nor the blunt-fingered hands.

/ / /

The master had to make a sliding thing of two of the widest kind of flat branches to carry the new heavy fur, as well as the head and the skin of the deer. Then he started directly for the ship.

It was past eating time but she looked at his restless eyes and did not ask about it. She walked in front of him, staying close. She looked back often, watching him pull the sled by the string across his shoulder and she knew, by the way he held the rod before him in both hands, that she should be wary.

Sometimes the damp-looking, inside-out bundle hooked on things, and the master would curse in a whisper and pull at it. She could see the bundle made him tired, and she wished he would stop for a rest and food as they usually did long before this time.

They went slowly, and the smell of honey-fat master hovered as it had from the beginning. They crossed the trails of many animals. They even saw another deer run off, but she knew that it was not a time for chasing.

Then another big silver and black tiger stood exactly before them. It appeared suddenly, as if actually it had been standing there all the time, and they had not been near enough to pick it out from its glistening background.

It just stood and looked and dared, and the master held his rifle rod with both hands and looked too, and she stood between them glancing from one face to the other. She knew, after a moment, that the master would not shoot, and it seemed the tiger thing knew too, for it turned to look at her and it raised its arms and spread its fingers as if grasping at the forest on each side. It swayed a bit, like bigness off balance, and then it spoke in its tight-strung, cello tones. The words and the tone seemed the same as before.

Little slave, what have you done that is free today? Remember this is world. Do something free today. Do, do.

She knew that what it said was important to it, something she should understand, a giving and a taking away. It watched her, and she looked back with wide eyes, wanting to do the right thing, but not knowing what.

The tiger-fat master turned then, this time slowly, and left a wide back for the master and her to see, and then it half turned, throwing a quick glance at the two of them over the heavy humped shoulder. Then it moved slowly away into the trees and ice, and the master still held the rifle rod with two hands and did not move.

The evening wind began to blow, and there sounded about them that sound of a million chandeliers tinkling like gigantic wind chimes. A furry bird, the size of a shrew and as fast, flew by between them with a miniature shriek.

She watched the master's face and, when he was ready, she went along beside him. The soft sounds the honey-fat master had made echoed in her mind but had no meaning.

/ / /

That night the master stretched the big skin on a frame and afterward he watched the dazzle of it. He didn't talk to her. She watched him a while and then she turned around three times on her rug and lay down.

The next morning the master was slow, reluctant to go out. He studied charts of other places, round or hourglass-shaped maps with yellow dots and labels, and he drank his coffee standing up looking at them. But finally they did go out, squinting into the ringing air.

It was her world. More each day, right feel, right temperature, lovely smells. She darted on ahead as usual, yet not too far today, and sometimes she stopped and waited and looked at the master's face as he came up. And sometimes she would whine a question before she went on . . . Why don't you walk brisk, brisk, and call me Queen of Venus, or Bitch of Betelgeuse? Why don't you sniff like I do? Sniff, and you will be happy . . . And she would run on again.

Trails were easy to find, and once more she found the oily lamb smell, and once more came upon them quickly. The master strode up beside her and raised his rifle rod . . . but a moment later he turned, carelessly, letting himself make a loud noise, and the lambs ran. He made a face, and spat upon the ice. "Come on Queenie. Let's get out of here. I'm sick of this place."

He turned and made the signal to go back, pointing with his thumb above his head in two jerks of motion.

But why, why? This is morning now and our world. She wagged her tail and gave a short bark, and looked at him, dancing a little on her back paws, begging with her whole body.

"Come on," he said.

She turned then, and took her place at his heel, head low, but eyes looking up at him, wondering if she had done something wrong, and wanting to be right, and noticed, and loved because he was troubled and preoccupied.

They'd gone only a few minutes on the way back when he stopped suddenly in the middle of a step, slowly put both feet flat upon the ground and stood like a soldier at a stiff, off-balance attention. There, lying in the way before them, was the huge, orange-eyed head and in front of it, as if at the end of outstretched arms, lay two leathery hands, the hairless palms up.

She made a growl deep in her throat and the master made a noise almost exactly like hers. She waited for him, standing as he stood, not moving, feeling his tenseness coming in to her. Yet it was just a head and two hands of no value, old ones they had had before and thrown away.

He turned and she saw a wild look in his eyes. He walked with deliberate steps, and she followed, in a wide circle about the spot. When they had skirted the place, he began to walk very fast.

They were not far from the ship. She could see its flat blackness as they drew nearer to the clearing, the burned, iceless pit of spewed and blackened earth. And then she saw that the silver tiger masters were there, nine of them in a wide circle, each with the honey-damp fur smell, but each with a separate particular sweetness.

The master was still walking very fast, eyes down to watch his footing, and he did not see them until he was in the circle before them all, as they stood there like nine upright bears in tiger suits.

He stopped and made a whisper of a groan, and he let the rifle rod fall low in one hand so that it hung loose with the end almost touching the ground. He looked from one to the other and she looked at him, watching his pale eyes move along the circle.

"Stay," he said, and then he began to go toward the ship at an awkward limp, running and walking at the same time, banging the rifle rod handle against the air lock as he entered.

He had said, "Stay." She sat watching the ship door and moving her front paws up and down because she wanted to be walking after him. He was gone only a minute, though, and when he came back it was without the rod and he was holding the great fur with cut pieces of thongs dangling like ribbons along its edges where it had been tied to the stretching frame. He went at that same run-walk, unbalanced by the heavy bundle, to one of them along the circle. Three gathered together before him and refused to take it back. They pushed it, bunched loosely, back across his arms and to it they added another large and heavy package in a parchment bag, and the master stood, with his legs wide to hold it all.

Then one honey-fat master motioned with a fur-backed hand to the ship and the bundles, and then to the ship and the master, and then to the sky. He made two sharp sounds once, and then again. And another made two different sounds, and she felt the feeling of them . . . Take your things and go home. Take them, these and these, and go.

They turned to her then and one spoke and made a wide gesture. *This is world. The sky, the earth, the ice.*

They wanted her to stay. They gave her . . . was it their world? But what good was a world?

She wagged her tail hesitantly, lowered her head, and looked up at them . . . I do want to do right, to please everybody, everybody, but . . . Then she followed the master into the ship.

The locks rumbled shut. She took her place, flat on her side, take-off position. The master snapped the flat plastic sheet over her, covering head and all and, in a few minutes, they roared off.

/ / /

Afterward he opened the parchment bag. She knew what was in it. She knew he knew too, but she knew by the smell. He opened it and dumped out the head and the hands.

She saw him almost put the big head out the waste chute, but he didn't. He took it into the place where he kept good heads and some odd paws or hoofs, and he put it by the others there.

Even she knew this head was different. The others were slantbrowed like she was and most had jutting snouts. This one was bigger even than the big ones, with its heavy, ruffed fur and huge eye staring, and more grand than any of them, more terrible . . . and yet a flat face, with a delicate black nose and tender lips. The tenderest lips of all.

WOMAN
WAITING

/ / /

There goes the plane for Chicago. They're up safely. In here you can't hear any of their racket.

There they go, engines screaming, but we can't hear it.

For us, they're silent as birds.

For them, we here below are diminishing in size. We are becoming doll-like and soon we will be like ants, soon no more than scurrying gnats and, later still, bacteria perhaps and fungi. I, too, nothing but a microbic creature. I might be the size of a camel or a mouse, it's all the same to them up there. Even if I were to stand in the center of the landing field they couldn't see me at all.

There they go, swelling toward the sun. Only the sky will have room enough for them now. This landing field will seem infinitesimal. There will be no place on this whole planet, not a bit of land anywhere, unless some gigantic desert, that will seem to them large enough to land on. There, they have already swelled themselves up out of sight.

But now I see they have begun to board the plane for Rome. In a moment they will fly up as the others did, a great expanding bird, starting out at our size, but growing too big for us. Behind this thick glass I hardly hear those Rome-bound engines begin, one by one, to scream out their expanding powers.

How nice it must be for all those people to enlarge themselves so. How condescendingly they must look down upon us here.

I have a ticket.

I am not unlike those others boarding their planes for Chicago, Rome, Miami, and so soon to be transformed. And I am not unlike these who sit here waiting too. I am, in fact, quite a bit like them, for I have noticed that within my view there are actually three other coats of almost exactly the same brown as mine and I see two other little black hats. I have noticed myself in the ladies' room mirror, though not so that anyone knew I was watching myself. I only allowed myself to look as I combed my hair and put on lipstick, but I did see how like everybody else I am in my new clothes and from a certain distance. If I could just keep this in mind, for my looks, when I can remember them, influence my actions, and I am sure if I could see myself in some mirror behind the clerks, I would feel quite comfortable approaching them. But then there will be no more need of that.

But I know rest room mirrors are not quite trustworthy. They have a pinkish cast that flatters and, for all I know, a lengthening effect to make us all think of ourselves as closer to some long-legged ideal. I must remember that and be careful. I mustn't fantasize about myself. I must remember I am not quite what the mirrors show me. They are, in a way, like subway windows where one sees oneself flashing by along the dark walls and one looks quite dashing and luminously handsome, needing, one thinks, only red earrings or a modish hat to be a quite extraordinary person, even standing out from the others.

There go those Rome people. Soon I will be off up there too. The thought is enough to make me feel dashingly handsome again, as handsome as all these clean-cut people so comfortable in themselves, so accustomed to their clothes and their bodies, and I feel young, almost too young, like a little girl on her first voyage alone (and it has been a long time since I went anywhere so it does seem like a first voyage).

That Rome plane looks slow from here, but I know how fast they're really going, and then, the larger you are, the slower you seem. I think they are already noticing how huge they are getting now. Once up, they may not be able to come down at all. They may sit looking out the windows, circling forever, dizzy at their own size compared to down here, unable to risk a landing.

I'm going back. (I don't call it home anymore since I've been here so long.) I'm going back, but once I get up in that plane I don't think anything will matter. I'll see the world as it really is then and I won't mind never coming down at all.

I have a seat here by this wall of glass and I don't think anyone is noticing me. I have been here quite some time, but others come and go. They don't keep track of how long I've been sitting here. And, as I glance down at myself, I think again that I look quite as ordinary as anyone else. Why should they notice me with either criticism or admiration? I don't think it is at all evident that all my clothes are new.

I have a little black satchel on the floor beside me. In it I have my glasses, my newspaper, a cantaloupe, and a little bag of peanuts. The cantaloupe is certainly very ripe. I think I can smell it now and then, a sweet, good smell.

Just now I noticed a woman who came near me and then moved away to take a seat farther on. I think I know why that was. It could have been the cantaloupe—that strange (to her) pungent sweetness—but I think not. In my haste to come here in time (it's true I arrived unnecessarily early) I put on all my new clothes without washing myself. I might say that washing in my apartment was never easy, and I may not really have washed very well for quite some time. I might as well have feet like a fat man, a very fat man, I should say. My feet are not fat, I mean, but they have a certain fat quality. That woman has found me out, and that is why she is sitting over across the way. So I am not really at all like the others under all my nice clothes. Yet is it a crime to be dirty? I can see very well that it is in a place like this, though I never noticed back in my own room. Here it is certainly a crime, or certainly outstanding in one way or another, different, eccentric, extraordinary, and, I do think, a crime. Well, there's nothing to be done about it now, though it makes me feel quite shrunken, new clothes or not. How will it be in the plane, how will it be to be shrunken and expanded at the same time, for surely in the plane someone will have to sit next to me whether they like it or not. Perhaps the cantaloupe will help. Perhaps I will keep my satchel on my lap.

Think if I should drop it somehow up there and this elephantine cantaloupe, swollen with altitude, should squash down on some tiny building, covering it with its cantaloupe-colored pulp, spreading its rich, sweet smell over everything, a cantaloupe large as the moon, ripe and ready, squashing them all in too much sweetness and too much juice.

Flight 350, Flight 321, Flight 235, Flight 216. I wonder if my feet together with my cantaloupe are capable of permeating the air of this whole interior as that voice does. Perhaps they already have and I am completely unaware of it. Wondering, I almost do not hear my own flight number, 216, even though I have memorized it, rechecked and memorized it a dozen times. Flight 216 has been, the voice tells everyone in the whole airport without a tremble or change of quality, everyone, it tells, not seeking us, the passengers, out, to impart its private information . . . Flight 216 has been (I should have guessed) postponed.

Well, so that is the way it is, and now, immediately after, I'm not sure if the voice said just postponed or postponed indefinitely. I wonder if there's any sense in asking why or when. I wonder if there's any sense in waiting.

There goes another plane, I have not noticed where to this time. All the other people's planes are coming and going but I don't know why I ever thought mine would, even with my new clothes and my ticket.

Senseless or not, I am going to wait exactly as I waited before I knew my flight was postponed, but already I see there is a difference in my feelings as I watch the other planes rise. I am quite shrunken. I am shrinking as they rise up. I am growing too small for my new clothes. They will hang upon me in a most noticeable way, I am sure. I will be a spectacle. I will make a spectacle of myself just walking from here to the door. Everyone will notice.

But why am I disappointed in Flight 216? I have not even been sure I wanted to go back at all. In truth, I do not want to go back, not really. What did I want then? And the three hundred dollars? If I can get that back will it make up for what I wanted, whatever that was? I wonder if I *can* get it back, for it certainly would be something to have. I wonder should I try now? But the flight was just postponed, not cancelled.

I see a man at the desk who seems to be asking something. He is quite out of place there. He is wearing a homemade coat made out of an Army blanket, and he has a tangled, olive-drab beard. If he is asking about Flight 216, and he certainly must be, then I don't believe that I should. I don't believe that I should put myself in the company of such people. They might even think we were together, going off to the same destination. Still, I would like to have that money. Perhaps if I wait a half hour or so and ask then, they will not connect me with him.

So, here I am, a woman waiting. I wish I had some greater meaning at this time of disappointment. Were I a man, I could even be humanity waiting, all humanity, whose flight is indefinitely postponed, but I am woman waiting. Women always wait. Rather a cliché. It doesn't matter. Let her wait.

If I sit very still I feel a tiny sliding movement, a tiny, snaky motion of withdrawal inward. My feet just barely touch the ground. Away goes another plane and I feel my heart lurch.

But the three hundred dollars. Has it been a half hour yet? I forgot to check the clock at the start. I will have to wait for another half hour to go by before approaching the desk. My feet dangle. I am like a girl in woman's clothes. Anyone glancing this way will wonder who has dressed me in these woman-sized things and why. Has she lost her own clothes somewhere, they wonder. Was she in some sort of accident? Did she soil herself? Was she sick and had to wear her mother's grown-up things? I do not think, if I went to the desk in my present condition, that they would give me the three hundred dollars at all. And even if I did have the money, would they serve me in the coffee shop? If I wait much longer I will have difficulty climbing up on their stools and it would be quite embarrassing for everyone if I continued to shrink right before their eyes as I sat there with my coffee and my sandwich. They would all know I wasn't a bit like them then. Just as we suspected when we first saw her sitting down and watching the planes, they would all say. Just as we suspected all along.

By now I don't even mean woman anymore. I am midget, waiting. I represent all midgets (there can't be so very many) waiting for their midget life to turn into real life, which is, of course, indefinitely postponed. (I am becoming quite sure that they did say "indefinitely" now.)

This slithering sensation, minute as it is, makes me itch, but, here in this huge, public place (there is room for quite a few airplanes in here, should they ever wish to pull away the glass walls and wheel them in upon these polished floors), here, I do not believe I should scratch myself.

My feet no longer dangle. I must slide off this chair before the drop becomes too steep. This I can manage easily within my clothes. By now people must think someone has left a new brown coat on the chair. I squat, wrapped in a stocking, under the overhanging edge of it, and in a few minutes more I am small enough to step into my satchel. There it is comfortable and dark. I curl up next to the cantaloupe and newspaper and nibble on a peanut. I had not realized it, but I am quite exhausted. I roll my stocking into a pillow and lean back upon it. Smallness, I am thinking, must be quite as comfortable as largeness. They each have their advantages. Here, snug as . . . as anyone might be in a soft and dark, black satchel, I fall asleep quickly.

How long I sleep, I have absolutely no idea, it may have been but a few minutes or the full clock around (and at my size time may seem different); at any rate, I wake, still within my satchel, to the movement of being carried, smoothly and with a rhythmic, wavy motion. I put my eye to the hole in the center of one of the grommets that hold the handles on. I see a sign, *Lost Articles Department.* Inside this large, shelved hallway, I am filed beside other satchels and suitcases of similar size and color. Well, I have my cantaloupe, my peanuts, and my newspaper. But I do see that the man here already wrinkles his nose as he comes by my shelf.

No one will be coming for me. That I am sure of. How long will they keep me here? Not long, for I see he has wrinkled his nose again. You don't suppose my feet, my tiny feet can still . . . ? What is that smell? he is thinking. I will have to search it out. Something is spoiling here in one of the packages, something just recently brought in. People just aren't careful, he thinks. They put perishables in their suitcases and then forget them for other people to clean up. Disgusting messes. They don't care. He thinks, perhaps I'll just throw it out without the disagreeable task of examining it. No one could want something spoiled anyway. I won't wait the allotted time (is it a week? a month?). Well, I just won't wait, he thinks. Out it will go by tomorrow, sure.

Perhaps, just at the last moment, I will call out to him and he will discover me here.

How will it be, finding a not very attractive, one-foot high, completely naked woman in the lost and found department? Not so young anymore, either. (But *he* is not so young and quite completely bald.) How will it be finding a woman who was, to say the least, peculiar . . . different, even when she was of normal height?

Will he blush, seeing me? Would he take me home with him secretly, hidden in the satchel? Keep me, perhaps, in a comfortable corner of his room with a little box for my bed and a cushion for my mattress? Of course sex will be impossible between us . . .

But this is ludicrous.

No. No. I will not call out. I will not . . . I will never reveal myself. If I have to perish at the bottom of a garbage heap, I will never call out.

CHICKEN
ICARUS
/ / /

I keep thinking there must be some place for me somewhere. I keep thinking of some kind of gelatin land, some puddingy spot all viscous, muculent, where the air is thick and wet as water. I wouldn't even ask to be able to fly around in it. I'd be happy just to ooze along the bottom as long as it was nothing like floors, or mattresses, or pillows. But the way it is around here you can get pretty bored with gravity.

I keep thinking about this sticky-slippery kind of land but I think about legs, too, a lot more than I think about arms. I don't know why. Maybe because I always hear walking sounds. Around the house I hear the floors creak and thump, accepting feet. Outside, the ladies' heels tick-tock, tick-tock, measuring out time in distance covered. Steps per minute about sixty-five, breaths twenty, heartbeats seventy-two. It takes me ten heartbeats to cross my mattress. Rolling. Well, more like five heartbeats or four. Four little bird heartbeats. (I exaggerate myself, but sometimes I feel pretty exaggerated.)

Doorknobs, on/off switches, buttons, zippers, drawer pulls, toenail scissors, the little thumbscrews that hold my reading stand, the handles on the sides of my mattress, the armholes of my shirt, even birds . . . When they sit along the wires they remind me of feet, robin-red-breasted feet cut off just above the ankle; flying, they remind me of feather-fingered hands flip-flopping themselves into the sky, palms down. For them the air is thick enough.

But I have one thing.

When I was young I felt the world two ways, by mouth and by that one impetuous finger (I cannot say between my legs) that would rise up in curiosity at any interesting texture or temperature. Now it seems not so inquisitive. But then it has already tested cotton, wool, wood, paper, the wall, the floor, the reading stand, and so forth. It has ventured—omnivorous, can one say?—into holes in the sheet. It has examined the interior of a velvet purse (silk-lined). It has pushed a toy car. It has entered a shoe. All this in its younger days.

There is, in my world, also—well, it isn't really *my* world. As I said, mine would have to be a lot slushier. Anyway, I've got balance, rolling, flopping, and the arching of the back. Balance I have never completely mastered. I suppose I should mention other small diversions such as defecating, urinating, the blinking of eyes, the wiggling of ears, and watching TV.

And I've got drama, too. Down the hall at five o'clock or so comes Mrs. Number One all dressed up like a nurse. I think I must, at some time, have been bought outright, else why does she keep me on like this? She doesn't get paid anymore. Who would pay her? And what do I give in exchange for the emptying of bedpans or a lift into the bathroom, for food so considerately cut up so I can feed myself? Why, only what I *can* give. She likes it with brute force. "Rape, rape," she says, but not loud enough to attract attention outside of my little room.

I bounce her on the point of my one and only (or she makes me believe I do). Actually I couldn't rape an old glove. At the time I think I would not trade this one for any other protuberance, but afterward I think two legs are well worth one of these. However, the price is too high. If I had three of them it might be possible to come to some terms, but one, even as well functioning as this one . . . No sale!

Rape, rape, to me was Run, run.

That day (the day she locked the door and said, "If you ever tell . . ." But there wasn't anybody *to* tell. I think I was forgotten the moment I was born.) that day I thought I knew what running felt like. This was skimming over the earth, rampant, halfway to the ceiling with only the soles of the feet touching bottom. This was one foot lightly, before the other, the swing of the leg underneath, the body riding smoothly on top of it all (amazing!), the counter-balancing arms, back and forth, the toes giving a last pushoff, the knee raised, bent, the foot circling upward, pivoting out, falling ahead to catch the ground, then pushing off again, and so on. Hundreds of takeoffs, and that's what this was, too, a hundred takeoffs until I flew into the air, but I came to rest again, flat upon the mattress.

I suppose she was grateful. One of us was.

She has been my nurse since God knows when, since before I knew what a calendar was or that time was anything but fresh sheets now and then. I must have been about ten, a backward, slobbery ten, when she came, squashing about on her nursing shoes. She squeaks when she turns. She bites into the floor, sawtoothed, as if she felt as I do about the surfaces of things. Maybe she wanted me to have a better view of those aqueous soles of hers because the first thing she did was to have my mattress put upon the floor. I admit I gained in freedom and that my distances could then be measured. I learned that the wearing down at the heel was a long time.

But Mrs. Number One isn't the only person in my life. There is a Miss Number Two, oh, yes, and quite beautiful. Miss Spanish Eyes, Miss (I wonder if it would make any difference if Mrs. Number One were beautiful) Miss White Gloves (the white gloves just in case she might, by some mistake, touch me). She came to me fresh from racing cars, mountaintops, airplanes, at least it seemed so to me, but I see things from a floorish point of view. Everything may look like that from here.

What she brought first were the ABC's, then *Run, Tom, Run,* then *The Easy to Read Book of Far Away Places,* and all the way up to books-of-the-month and Shakespeare.

I think that Miss Number Two is, most probably, my sister. Not that there's ever been anything sisterly-brotherly between us, but I have a hundred clues. The most obvious, that she's always been around, one way or another, in a sneaky way even before she came to me with her books and that Nefertiti tip of her head. I remember a breezy kid not much younger than myself in a tree outside my window, blue jeans, red shirt, sticking out her tongue at me, and I, happy that the gesture was one I could return. Now and again I remember a furious voice from some other part of the house screeching for her to "Get down, my God, get down." I remember an eye, brown, lustrous, like a little mouse nose waiting at the crack in the door, sometimes during my bath. I even remember the knob turning and the door opening to make that crack. Later a decision was made, out of a sense of obligation or out of resentment, and she, or someone else, decided and she came to me. I cannot say with happiness. I think I was happier before. What with five o'clock drama, everything seemed complete to me. No, it wasn't happiness and she knew it.

And yet I count on her for my salvation. If anyone is going to rescue me I know it will have to be bold Miss Number Two, and even though I first approached Mrs. Number One, it is Number Two I had in mind all the time. I was afraid. I was in such a cold sweat of hope that I didn't dare to go to Number Two and I didn't even mention to Number One what I really had in mind.

What a vision I had then . . . I still have. I see myself in a bright and revealing costume, all Harlequin colors and diamond shapes. I am in a stall with streamers, festoons, and flags, American flags . . . no, flags of all nations. I belong to the world. Loudspeakers on the roof send out fanfares interspersed with Handel's "Fireworks" music and I, highlighted with a pinkish spotlight, perform upon my mattress such movements as I can perform (and many of these require the utmost skill and concentration). After the day's work, and I do think I can call it work, I see myself in a close and comfortable association with the rubber man, the fat lady, the human pincushion, and the half- man/half-woman.

Though I have this grand vision in mind, and really even grander than this, for I see myself as a champion of champions— though I have this vision, I decided that I would ask only that Mrs. Number One should borrow a camera and should take a dozen pictures of me from various angles and in various poses. I thought I could not only use these in some way as an advertisement of myself, but also to get some real idea of myself since I had, so far, never seen myself in any way at all. It was from the pictures that I thought I could make my further decisions about my future. It's true that it's hard to be really self-evaluating but I thought I might judge well enough if I subtracted a certain percentage for too much self-love and another equal percentage for self-hate. The good thing about photographs would be that any initial shock I might have at my first real view of myself could be gotten over by getting used to the pictures. I felt I might get enlargements made and I would have Mrs. Number One tack some along the walls and I promised myself I would make no decisions whatsoever for at least two weeks of living with them. Then I hoped to be able to look at myself with a truly cold eye.

She agreed. No arguments. Not a blink or shiver. No ambiguous glances, irresolute phrases or imponderable sighs, and yet days passed and nothing happened. Finally I approached her firmly, my eyes my only weapon though they couldn't even stop her bustling about, swishing away nonexistent spots on the dresser front, picking little black threads off the rug. Yes, even at my five o'clock drama she is all business, that busy business of getting herself "raped" by me. Maybe she thinks it's part of her job, and yet now she keeps me all on her own as if I am something she dressed up to amuse herself with, nothing but her back-room dildo.

Maybe this sex is *my* job.

But suppose I was inherited after my mother's death. Did I come with the house? A condition of its ownership? And I wonder if my mother, herself, could have paid for that first time. Or Miss Number Two. Did Mrs. Number One really say not to tell?

Impossible to know whose obligation this drama is, mine or Mrs. Number One's. No use wondering. I'll keep on doing my duty, or she hers, and I don't think that I, at least, will ever be able to find out. (But if I had anything more than just this one thing, then I could. One dactylic protuberance more to pit against the other in some way, one threat, one appeasement, one offering, one retreat, one decline, one weapon other than this one, then I could find out who is the willing one and who the slave.)

However . . .

At this time I said to her that I believed she had no intention of going through with this photography business at all.

What I lacked, she told me then—"probably due to your environment . . . you can't be expected . . . so naive . . . not like the rest of us . . ." and so on and on—what I lacked, it all came down to, was Good Taste, capital G, capital T, otherwise I would have known that a picture of myself would be an oh-so-gross violation of propriety and could certainly serve no good purpose either to others or to me, so, she said, she had decided from the beginning not to do it for my own good (as well as for everyone's) but I had been so forceful, so firm, she hadn't known how to argue with me . . . at that time, at least. She was, of course, terribly sorry about the whole thing. Besides, what would the man who printed the pictures say? Chances were he wouldn't return them. Society sees to such things, she said. There are censors at work, even on photos, whether I knew it or not. (Can I, somehow, be lewd simply existing like this? Do I lie here on my sheets, pornographic every day? But hasn't everyone got his pornographic parts?)

At times like these, grasping at distracting details, I watch her nose point out her line of sight. Look ahead, it tells me, but life surely cannot be as earnest as most noses would have it be. Yet it is from this eager nose that I got the idea of asking to see my mother. I thought I might have more courage to speak out to someone I didn't know as well.

"Your mother," Number One said, "leads a comfortable life. She has surrounded herself with loveliness." (This I understand now much more than I did then, for it was to me that Mother willed many of her nice things. A handsome Louis XV table is now against my far wall, above it hangs a print of Madame Vigée-Lebrun and her daughter [all arms], upon it is a small statue of Hermes that used to be a salt and pepper holder.)

At this time, however, my room was more simply furnished. The mattress on the floor, the books lined up beside it, each with a little leather pull so I can grab it with my teeth—a slow process, finding one's page—book holder, chest of drawers, eating stand, not a single ornament unless you can call decorative a pinkish little creature Miss Number Two had brought me. She often brings things, all sorts, once a covered glass with three grasshoppers, once a white mouse, once a wounded bird. I suppose for my education, yet they give me great pleasure. This time she had been to the beach and had thought of me and brought back a jar of sea water with a starfish in it. (Even though there is no friendship or love between us, I am well aware that she constantly thinks of me. What must it be like to have me curled up at the back of your mind? Seeing everything as though through my eyes? Thinking that I have not walked upon this sand nor felt the edges of these grasses grate against my ankles? That I have not smelled the dried foam on the rocks? And never will? And so she brings these creatures to give me a realization that she herself has already. But I have always wondered, does she do it to torment me, as she may have brought the *Book of Far Away Places?* Does she do it for the torments of understanding so that I will come, finally, to really know the extent of my losses?) The starfish gave me the most pleasure of all.

When I finally did convince Number One to arrange for a visit with my mother (during which Number One would be present, of course, since she feels herself a guardian of Good Taste—but I was ready to be the essence of propriety), this jar lay on the far corner of my eating stand. I would move my smallest pillow to the near edge of the stand and rest my chin there and watch the starfish feel its preposterously slow way along the glass. Note the suckers along the undersides of starfish fingers. You might say they are the starfish's tiny army. Commands move across them like a wind, a very slow wind, that is, over grass. Move, suck, release, and each starts a little after the one next to it.

This was not my first starfish, though the largest, and I have come to know them intimately. I have learned to love them in a way that I have not loved any other creature. I have thought: What if I had this army for my own? If this were my hand? My little suckers all along the palm? I have thought I might button a button, blow my nose, answer a telephone, turn out the light. I have thought I might feel my way across the floor, this star on the end of some long radius and ulna. I might risk the stairs, letting myself down, reaching lower and letting myself down again. I could run away and, even if it took all night, moving at a starfish pace, to get as far as the next house, I might find a hiding place to spend the day and set out farther the next night, each day finding a hovel or a thicket to rest in, never discovered, ever onward by silver moonlight.

Later, this same starfish was dried and it is still here upon my low shelf. I once felt it with my tongue and now I know the sea tastes of sauerkraut.

I insisted that I be dressed up for the interview in my best shirt and even a tie, though I never wore one; also, I never had the top button of my shirt buttoned, for you can imagine to what uses I have to put my neck. I wished, then, I had a jacket and a pair of real pants for the occasion. I thought they might be stretched out beyond me and a pair of shoes stuck into the pants legs. After all, so much of what we do is for show; why not, out of deference, do a little something extra? But Number One thought not. Still, she arranged a quilt very prettily up around my waist, made tea, brought out a box of pastries, combed my hair, wiped the sweat off my forehead. A pity I had no toes to tap, no knuckles to suck nervously, hardly anything to fidget until Mother came, but I chewed on my upper lip and posed myself as calmly and as aesthetically as I could manage, twisting slightly in a sort of reclining contraposto.

And so Mother came in. She was wearing one of those basic blacks with a silver necklace and one could see at a glance that she was chock-full of cultivated charm. Sedate, nothing flashy or overdone. She crossed her legs and her little skirt snuggled up around her thighs, bonneting her stockinged knees, which leaned together like two nuns, a bit of white slip peeping out beside their cheeks. (Could she really be all this and pious, too?) I felt quite untidy beside them even in my best expression.

"Tea . . . a cake? . . . Disturbing news of Cuba . . . Yes, South America is so revolutionary . . . Cold for fall . . . an early frost . . . I was wondering . . ."

I remember best her feet (this is not unusual, considering my low position here upon my mattress) in little black pumps reflecting the squares of the window and reminding me of Number One's nose . . . something classical about them both. I would have liked to press my tongue across the shine of the shoes . . . well, yes, and the nose, too. (I still wonder what their flavors might have been, the nose certainly vanilla or apple, the shoes a red-winy taste soured by the sidewalks.)

(I do often wonder if they can appreciate flavors as I do, if they even know the real pleasures of eating. Certainly they have too many diversions and, though as babies they tested things as I test them, I am sure that, by now, they have forgotten the joys and understandings of tongue and lip.)

Mother, pressing her dactyls into lady fingers in a useless proliferation, had just said the view from my window was the best in the house and I had just said that I had been thinking about my future and would like to have her help, at least for some of the details, until I could get started on my own. "Future," Mother said, just at that moment glancing down, and then she saw it. She forgot the studied beauty of the classical smile, the corners of the mouth faintly Ionic but not yet Corinthian, and she forgot to watch out for those knees under that tight skirt of hers. Her eyes saw a wound . . . some horrible wound of the genitals, lustrous, blistered, purple. (And yet I suppose exposed genitals, pure and simple, healthily blooming and blushing, would be enough to cause her stunned and outraged look.) And my starfish was firm-bodied, beautifully turgid, and a rosy, tan-pink color.

"What is that thing?" The way she said "thing," to flush it down the toilet was too good for it, though she would certainly want to dispose of it as quickly as one would dispose of a particularly hairy spider . . . Still, nothing hairy here.

The starfish reclined (one might say) near the top of the jar, one finger hidden by the punctured lid, one stretched languidly sideways along the ridge where the glass curved, and three almost straight down. Infinitesimally, one of the lower fingers was edging upward. I don't believe Mother could have noticed this movement and certainly she couldn't have had time to examine or understand the waving suckers, yet gall touched her tongue and even her knees paled. I saw she saw the world in that jar, caught in that abyss, sour sea water all over it, and she, without wanting to, drinking its juices . . . or me. Was it me she thought she looked at? Opposites reflecting each other, he all digits and he of none? Whichever it was, I saw, in the shape of her lips, that the taste of death (or life) was on them and I held my breath.

That's the last I ever saw of her; isn't that strange? Those rejecting lips and then the shoes departing in uneven clicks, for though she was hardly half as old as Number One (but I must admit Number One keeps up her strength extraordinarily well, rinses it in, I suppose, with the henna of her hair, or sucks it from me with that avid other mouth. I do age fast)—for though she was hardly half, as I said—Mother, who refused, ever after that, to come into my room, died a year later. One could say that she faced her moment of truth with a starfish.

And so, after all, I have been forced into approaching Miss Number Two, whom, as I've already mentioned, I really felt to be my only salvation from the beginning, but instead of photographs (I had started with Number Two in exactly the same way I started with Number One in spite of the mention of a censor)—not understanding what I had in mind at all—instead of photographs, Number Two brought me a mirror, a rather large hand mirror, round and with a blue cast to the glass.

I was surprised to find that I had a handsome, rather noble head. No reactions, no expressions on any of the faces of those that had appeared before me had ever led me to believe that this might be. In fact, I was sure of the opposite and I had only hoped I might be passable. Also I found that I did resemble, to a surprising degree, Miss Number Two, and was, in my own masculine way, quite as attractive as she was, my hair the same matt black, my eyes mysterious, my cheeks with an aristocratic pallor, my nose stark. I had a thick, muscular neck not exactly in keeping with my fine-featured face and, as she held the mirror farther from me, I saw a barrel-chested manatee-thing, certainly ichthyoid, with little wing shapes lumping under my clothes at hips and shoulders as though I could actually, as I've dreamed, swim into the air, and I saw the eyes of Number Two leaning to get the same view as I had of myself. I could see her thoughts reflecting my own: What a curious shape, and is it beautiful or ugly? Has it a meaning of its own? Is it a symbol of sloth or courage or of sex? Or is it a symbol at all?

"I had thought," I said to her eye as it floated languidly at the edge of the mirror—I could scarcely tell mine from hers, three haughty eyes there, moving slightly eastward about a foot under the watery surface. I decided to speak to all three. "I had thought," I said, "that I might go on display." Two eyes remained immobile while the other contracted its lid a quarter of an inch. I could see I wasn't getting sympathy from any of them.

One of them closed for a moment, as though an eye could take a deep breath. Was it exasperated with me? Have you any concept at all, it seemed to be asking, of what you really are? Does the fat lady, monstrous as she is, have anything to do with you? And the half-man/half-woman?

Ah, but *I* am certainly all male and perhaps nothing *but* male.

I see. Here, in other words, is the flying phallus at last, a truncated Hermes. Are you going on display for that? A little chicken Icarus (cut down, but winged, it is true) doing five o'clock drama in a different sort of back room?

But none of those eyes can know about that drama. They swim smugly in little back and forth motions, contracting their corners rhythmically in order to maintain their equilibrium. I see I have gone beyond the eyes. I'll tell them that fashions in freaks change; that, just as with sex, what was unacceptable last year is accepted this year. People always accept more as they become sophisticated, don't they? And isn't this equally desirable in freaks as in sex? Liberalize them, I say, and let me be one who struggles for this cause, this great opening out of understanding, this acceptance without censure. The presentation will make such a difference, too. We'll do it with finesse and delicacy. To start, I will take the name Désiré. And certainly with my so unforeseen personal beauty . . . But the eyes won't think so. I can see that. The two, led by the one most energetic and most opinionated, will agree with each other. They will certainly feel that the mirror is too small a place for any arguments.

Let me approach them, instead, from the point of view of love. I might ask them: Shouldn't people be taught to love? People don't realize, I will say, how hard it is to love and that it must be practised daily with some difficult exercise. And *I* might provide that exercise.

But I'm sure I won't be that hard to love. Everyone loves a winner and I'll be the freak of freaks. They'll come to think of me as beautiful. The details of my body might even be, eventually, exposed on TV. My life story might be written, and surely, if I did have such a life, there would be something to write about, such as how I first decided to join the carnival and the difficulties I had, in the beginning, in doing so; how they all doubted that I would be accepted by the public, for I was, after all, a new concept in freaks. I had, it was felt, carried freakishness to its ultimate degree. I was wholly and utterly the freak, whereas people were used to half-freaks. It was felt I might be too startling. I might upset people. They might be more than just disgusted, but shaken to their very bones. But, at last, in some small circus sideshow, someone had had the courage to take me on. At first reactions were mixed. There were letters of protest: This was going too far . . . an insult to the public . . . poor taste that I should be where others could see me at all, let alone be on public view. I was even banned in a few cities, but of course this helped in the long run. Still, it was an uphill fight. Other freaks were jealous of my purity, my authenticity. No rubber, no makeup, no mutilation necessary. Yet I had my champions, including the circus owners who had invested in me, and also some freaks who were generously able to appreciate someone who was far beyond them. Still it will have taken me, let us suppose, about ten years to achieve any real acceptance. In any field one must certainly count on at least this much time, and I am not asking for a quick and easy success. And so, by then, people would have become used to me. Some would say I had a fishlike beauty, some that my movements were graceful and well adapted to my shape and to my needs. Some would argue that my achievements in rolling and flopping about had taken at least as much practice and concentration as would be needed by a concert pianist. Films would then be made to preserve my movements for posterity. Perhaps I might have had my body, by this time, tattooed with flowers and the faces of pretty girls. A book on my life would be written, and in it, also, would be a description of how I came to be married and how I manage in my household with a little electric cart steered with my teeth, my children normal (there is no need for my sort of mistake twice), and there would be something about my beautiful sister who helped me from the very beginning, at the first mention that I might be put on display.

"I had thought," I said, "that I might go on display. Yes, the carnival, the circus, no matter how small . . . "

But the fish eye had already given its answer.

"I suppose," said Number Two, "that you would like me to see that a proper suit is made, the beginnings of tights and a brocade . . . vest, shall we call it? Pink or blue? No, let's make it gold or silver with touches of red. I can sew it up myself out of silk and satin and, if you like, with little white wings to give the feeling of lightness to it all. Would you like them on the shoulder blades or buttocks?"

And she'll do it. I know she will and it will be better than I could possibly have conceived it myself, luminous as a peacock, gay as Santa Claus. I know Miss Number Two. Somehow, instinctively, she will touch the seed of my inner dream and make it grow into something greater than itself. Such work she will put into it! A month of hours. She'll hang it on my wall and, with great joy, I'll dream of myself wearing it. I will grow old, leaning at my reading stand and dreaming. I know I will.

Then one day I will ask Mrs. Number One to put the suit on me. I will try (at least try, but she does have ways . . . warm water and such) to withhold all else until she does, and then I'll know if it really fits or only seems to.

SEX AND/OR
MR. MORRISON

/ / /

I can set my clock by Mr. Morrison's step upon the stairs, not that
he is that accurate, but accurate enough for me. Eight-thirty,
thereabout. (My clock runs fast, anyway.) Each day he comes
clumping down and I set it back ten minutes, or eight minutes or
seven. I suppose I could just as well do it without him but it seems
a shame to waste all that heavy treading and those puffs and sighs
of expending energy on only getting downstairs, so I have timed
my life to this morning beat. Funereal tempo, one might call it,
but it is funereal only because Mr. Morrison is fat and therefore
slow. Actually, he is a very nice man as men go. He always smiles.

I wait downstairs, sometimes looking up and sometimes hold-
ing my alarm clock. I smile a smile I hope is not as wistful as his.
Mr. Morrison's moon face has something of the Mona Lisa to it.
Certainly he must have secrets.

"I'm setting my clock by you, Mr. M."

"Heh, hey . . . my, my," grunt, breathe. "Well," heave the
stomach to the right, "I hope . . ."

"Oh, you're on time enough for *me*."

"Heh, heh. Oh. Oh yes."

The weight of the world is surely upon him or perhaps he's
crushed and flattened by a hundred miles of air. How many
pounds per square inch weighing him down? He hasn't the inner
energy to push back. All his muscles spread like jelly under his
skin.

"No time to talk," he says. (He never has time.) Off he goes. I like him and his clipped little Boston accent, but I know he's too proud ever to be friendly. Proud is the wrong word (so is shy) but I'll leave it at that.

He turns back, pouting, then winks at me as a kind of softening of it. Perhaps it's just a twitch. He thinks, if he thinks of me at all: What can she say and what can I say to her? What can she possibly know that I don't know already? And so he duckwalks, knock-kneed, out the door.

And now the day begins.

There are really quite a number of things that I can do. I often spend time in the park. Sometimes I rent a boat there and row myself about and feed the ducks. I love museums and there are all those free art galleries and there's window-shopping, and if I'm very careful with my budget, now and then I can squeeze in a matinee. But I don't like to be out after Mr. Morrison comes back. I wonder if he keeps his room locked while he's off at work.

His room is directly over mine and he's too big to be a quiet man. The house groans with him and settles when he steps out of bed. The floor creaks under his feet. Even the side walls rustle and the wallpaper clicks its dried paste. But don't think I'm complaining of the noise. I keep track of him this way. Sometimes, here underneath, I ape his movements, bed to dresser, step, clump, dresser to closet, and back again. I imagine him there, flat-footed. Imagine him. Just imagine those great legs sliding into pants, their godlike width (for no mere man could have legs like that), those Thor legs into pant holes wide as caves. Imagine those two landscapes, sparsely fuzzed in a faint, wheat-colored brush, finding their way blindly into the waist-wide skirt-things of brown wool that are still damp from yesterday. Ooo. Ugh. Up go the suspenders. I think I can hear him breathe from here.

I can comb my hair three times to his once and I can be out and waiting at the bottom step by the time he opens his door.

"I'm setting my clock by you, Mr. M."

"No time. No time. I'm off. Well . . ." and he shuts the front door so gently one would think he is afraid of his own fat hands.

And so, as I said, the day begins.

The question is (and perhaps it is the question for today): Who is he really, one of the Normals or one of the Others? It's not going to be so easy to find out with someone so fat. I wonder if I'm up to it. Still, I'm willing to go to certain lengths and I'm nimble yet. All that rowing and all that walking up and down and then, recently, I've spent all night huddled under a bush in Central Park and twice I've crawled out on the fire escape and climbed to the roof and back again (but I haven't seen much and I can't be sure of the Others yet).

I don't think the closet will do as a hiding place because there's no keyhole, though I could open the door a crack and maybe wedge my shoe there. (It's double A. He might not notice it.) Or there's the bed to get under. While it's true that I am thin and small, almost child-sized, one might say, still it will not be so easy, but then neither has it been easy to look for lovers on the roof.

Sometimes I wish I were a little, fast-moving lizard, dull green or a yellowish brown. I could scamper in under his stomach when he opened the door and he'd never see me though his eyes are as quick as his feet are clumsy. Still I would be quicker. I would skitter off behind the bookcase or back of his desk or maybe even just lie very still in a corner, for surely he does not see the floor so much. His room is no larger than mine and his presence must fill it, or rather his stomach fills it and his giant legs. He sees the ceiling and the pictures on the wall, the surfaces of night table, desk, and bureau, but the floor and the lower halves of everything would be safe for me. No, I won't even have to regret not being a lizard, except for getting in. But if he doesn't lock his room it will be no problem and I can spend all day scouting out my hiding places. I'd best take a snack with me, too. No crackers and no nuts, but noiseless things like cheese and fig newtons.

It seems to me, now that I think about it, that I was rather saving Mr. Morrison for last, as a child saves the frosting of the cake to eat after the cake part is finished. But I see that I have been foolish. As he is really one of the most likely prospects, he should have been first.

And so today the day begins with a gathering of supplies and an exploratory trip upstairs.

The room is cluttered. There is no bookcase but there are books and magazines by the hundreds. I check behind the piles. I check the closet, full of drooping, giant suit coats I can easily hide in. Just see how the shoulders extend over the ordinary hangers. I check under the bed and the kneehole of the desk. I squat under the night table. I nestle among the dirty shirts and socks tossed in the corner. Oh, it's better than Central Park for hiding places. I decide to use them all.

There's something very nice about being here for I do like Mr. Morrison. Even just his size is comforting for he's big enough to be everybody's father. His room reassures with all his father-sized things in it. I feel lazy and young here.

I eat a few fig newtons while I sit on his shoes in the closet, soft, wide shoes with their edges all collapsed and all of them shaped more like cushions than shoes. Then I take a nap in the dirty shirts. It looks like fifteen or so but there are only seven and some socks. After that I hunch down in the kneehole of the desk, hugging my knees, and I wait and I begin to have doubts. That pendulous stomach, I can already tell, will be larger than all my expectations. There will certainly be nothing it cannot over-shadow or conceal, so why do I crouch here clicking my finger-nails against the desk leg when I might be out feeding pigeons? "Leave now," I tell myself. "Are you actually going to spend the whole day, and maybe night, too, cramped and confined in here?" Yet haven't I done it plenty of times lately and always for nothing, too? Why not one more try? For Mr. Morrison is surely the most promising of all. His eyes, the way the fat pushes up his cheeks under them, look almost Chinese. His nose is Roman and in an ordinary face it would be overpowering, but here it is dwarfed. "Save me," cries the nose. "I'm sinking." I would try, but I will have other, more important duties, after Mr. Morrison comes back, than to save his nose. Duty it is, too, for the good of all and I do mean all. Do not think that I am the least bit prejudiced in this.

You see, I *did* go to a matinee a few weeks ago. I saw the Royal Ballet dance *The Rite of Spring* and it occurred to me then . . . Well, what would you think if you saw them wearing their suits that were supposed to be bare skin? Naked suits, I called them.

And all those well-dressed, cultured people clapping at them, accepting even though they knew perfectly well . . . like a sort of Emperor's New Clothes in reverse. Now just think, there are only two sexes and every one of us is one of those and certainly, presumably that is, knows something of the other. But then that may be where I have been making my mistake. You'd think . . . why, just what I did start thinking, that there must be Others among us.

But it is not out of fear or disgust that I am looking for them. I am open and unprejudiced. You can see that I am when I say that I've never seen (and doesn't this seem strange?) the very organs of my own conception, neither my father's nor my mother's. Goodness knows what they were and what this might make me.

So I wait here, tapping my toes inside my slippers and chewing hangnails off my fingers. I contemplate the unvarnished underside of the desk top. I ridge it with my thumbnail. I eat more cookies and think whether I should make his bed for him or not but decide not to. I suck my arm until it is red in the soft crook opposite the elbow. Time jerks ahead as slowly as a school clock, and I crawl across the floor and stretch out behind the books and magazines. I read first paragraphs of dozens of them. What with the dust back here and lying in the shirts and socks before, I'm getting a certain smell and a sort of gray, animal fuzz that makes me feel safer, as though I really did belong in this room and could actually creep around and not be noticed by Mr. Morrison at all except perhaps for a pat on the head as I pass him.

Thump . . . pause. Clump . . . pause. One can't miss his step.

The house shouts his presence. The floors wake up squeaking and lean toward the stairway. The banister slides away from his slippery ham-hands. The wallpaper seems suddenly full of bugs. He thinks (if he thinks of me at all): Well, this time she isn't peeking out of her doorway at me. A relief. I can concentrate completely on climbing up. Lift the legs against the pressure. Ooo. Ump. Pause and seem to be looking at the picture on the wall.

I skitter back under the desk.

It's strange that the first thing he does is to put his newspaper on the desk and sit down with his knees next to my nose, regular walls, furnaces of knees, exuding heat and dampness, throwing off a miasma, delicately scented, of wet wool and sweat. What a wide roundness they have to them, those knees. Mother's breasts pressing toward me. Probably as soft. Why can't I put my cheek against them? Observe how he can sit so still with no toe-tapping, no rhythmic tensing of the thigh. He's not like the rest of us, but could a man like this do *little* things?

How the circumstantial evidence piles up, but that is all I've had so far and it is time for something concrete. One thing, just one fact is all I need.

He reads and adjusts the clothing at his crotch and reads again.

He breathes out winds of sausages and garlic and I remember that it's after supper and I take out my cheese and eat it as slowly as possible in little rabbit bites. I make a little piece last half an hour.

At last he goes down the hall to the bathroom and I shift back under the shirts and socks and stretch my legs. What if he undresses like my mother did, under a nightgown? Under, for him, some giant, double-bed-sized thing?

But he doesn't. He hangs his coat on the little hanger and his tie on the closet doorknob. I receive his shirt and have to make myself another spy hole. Then off with the tortured shoes, then socks. Off come the huge pants with slow, unseeing effort (he stares out the window). He begins on his yellowed undershorts, scratching himself first behind and starting earthquakes across his buttocks.

Where could he have bought those elephantine undershorts? In what store were they once folded on the shelf? In what factory did women sit at sewing machines and put out one after another after another of those other-worldly items? Mars? Venus? Saturn more likely. Or perhaps, instead, a tiny place, some moon of Jupiter with less air per square inch upon the skin and less gravity, where Mr. Morrison can take the stairs three at a time and jump the fences (for surely he's not particularly old) and dance all night with girls his own size.

He squints his Oriental eyes toward the ceiling light and takes off the shorts, lets them fall loosely to the floor. I see Alleghenies of thigh and buttock. How does a man like that stand naked before even a small-sized mirror? I lose myself, hypnotized. Impossible to tell the color of his skin, just as it is with blue-gray eyes or the ocean. How tan, pink, olive, and red and sometimes a bruised elephant gray. His eyes must be used to multiplicities like this and to plethoras, conglomerations, to an opulence of self, to an intemperate exuberance, to the universal, the astronomical.

I find myself completely tamed. I lie in my cocoon of shirts not even shivering. My eyes do not take in what they see. He is beyond my comprehension. Can you imagine how thin my wrists must seem to him? He is thinking (if he thinks of me at all), he thinks: She might be from another world. How alien her ankles and leg bones. How her eyes do stand out. How green her complexion in the shadows at the edges of her face (for I must admit that perhaps I may be as far along the scale at my end of "humanity" as he is at his).

Suddenly I feel like singing. My breath purrs in my throat in hymns as slow as Mr. Morrison himself would sing. Can this be love? I wonder. My first *real* love? But haven't I always been passionately interested in people? Or rather in those who caught my fancy? But isn't this feeling entirely different? Can love really have come to me this late in life? (La, la, lee la, from whom all blessings flow . . .) I shut my eyes and duck my head into the shirts. I grin into the dirty socks. Can you imagine *him* making love to *me!*

Well below his abstracted, ceilingward gaze, I crawl on elbows and knees back behind the old books. A safer place to shake out the silliness. Why, I'm old enough for him to be (had I ever married) my youngest son of all. Yet if he were a son of mine, how he would have grown beyond me. I see that I cannot ever follow him (as with all sons). I must love him as a mouse might love the hand that cleans the cage, and as uncomprehendingly, too, for surely I see only a part of him here. I sense more. I sense deeper largenesses. I sense excesses of bulk I cannot yet imagine. Rounded afterimages linger on my eyeballs. There seems to be a mysterious darkness in the corners of the room and his shadow covers, at the same time, the window on one wall and the mirror on the other. Certainly, he is like an iceberg, seven-eighths submerged.

But now he has turned toward me. I peep from the books, holding a magazine over my head as one does when it rains. I do so more to shield myself from too much of him all at once than to hide.

And there we are, confronting each other eye to eye. We stare and he cannot seem to comprehend me any more than I can comprehend him, and yet usually his mind is ahead of mine, jumping away in unfinished phrases. His eyes are not even wistful and not yet surprised. But his belly button . . . here is the eye of God at last. It nestles in a vast, bland sky like a sun on the curve of the universe flashing me a wink of heat, a benign, fat wink. The stomach eye accepts and understands. The stomach eye recognizes me and looks at me as I've always wished to be looked at. (Yea, though I walk through the valley of the shadow of death.) I see you now.

But I see him now. The skin hangs in loose, plastic folds just there, and there is a little copper-colored circle like a quarter made out of pennies. There's a hole in the center and it is corroded green at the edges. This must be a kind of "naked suit" and whatever the sex organs may be, they are hidden behind this hot, pocked, and pitted imitation skin.

I look into those girlish eyes of his and there is a big nothing, as blank as though the eyeballs are all whites . . . as blank as having no sex at all . . . like being built like a boy doll with a round hole for the water to empty out (something to frighten little-boy three-year-olds).

God, I think. I am not religious but I think: My God, and then I stand up and somehow, in a limping run, I get out of there and down the stairs as though I fly. I slam the door of my room and slide in under my bed. The most obvious of hiding places, but after I am there I can't bear to move out. I lie and listen for his thunder on the stairs, the roar of his feet splintering the steps, his hand tossing away the banister as he comes like an engulfing wave.

I know what I'll say. "We accept. We accept," I'll say. "We will love" (I love already) "whatever you are."

I lie listening, watching the hanging edges of my bedspread in the absolute silence of the house. Can there be anyone here at all in such a strange quietness? Must I doubt even my own existence?

"Goodness knows," I'll say, "if I'm a Normal myself." (How is one to know such things when everything is hidden?) "Tell all of them that we accept. Tell them it's the naked suits that are ugly. Tell them the truth is beautiful. Your dingles, your dangles, wrinkles, ruts, bumps, and humps, we accept. (We will love.) Your loops, strings, worms, buttons, figs, cherries, flower petals, your soft little toad shapes, warty and greenish, your cats' tongues and rats' tails, your oysters one-eyed between your legs, garter snakes, snails, we accept." (Isn't the truth always more lovable?)

But what a long silence this is. Where is he? For he must (mustn't he?) come after me for what I saw. If there has been all this hiding and if he must wear that cache-sexe thing across his front, then he must silence me somehow, destroy me even. But where is he? Perhaps he thinks I've locked my door. But I haven't. I haven't.

Why doesn't he come?

GLORY, GLORY
/ / /

I was walking down the Bogashtha Stah with my husband when
suddenly a well-dressed old man (in our kind of suit and tie)
bowed down to me and touched his forehead to my left shoe. "Oh
my God, my living God," he said in quite good English. "You are
my one and only." My husband started laughing even before I'd
realized what had happened.

"Ooo, ooo," my husband said, "I married a goddess and didn't
even know it."

Then a young girl came running out of a corner flower shop—
flower hovel is more like what it was—with a bouquet that she laid
at my feet, and she also bowed down. She even kissed my shoe,
and this is not a very good city for kissing shoes in. "No, no," I
said, trying to lift each of the people at the same time. "No need
for that." What I said, I don't know why, sent my husband into
another fit of laughing.

"Need!" he said, "need!"

The old man had quite a hard time getting back up even though
squatting down is a common position in this culture, and even
with me and the girl helping. My husband was, all this time,
leaning against the wall (one of their ancient walls of huge stones
which everybody wonders how they brought here and from
where) still laughing. "I'd help," he said, "but I can't right now.
Hoo, ooo, there must be something about you I haven't noticed.
Let me take a good look," which he didn't do. He just kept

laughing and pounding the wall with his fist, though not so hard as to hurt himself.

We hadn't been in this country more than half a day and we were suffering from the altitude and were exhausted though we'd had a little nap. Nothing in the guide book had said anything about something like this. And I'm not an imposing person. At barely five feet, how imposing can you be? Though here the people are generally as short as or shorter than me. My husband, on the other hand, is quite tall even in our own land and, of course, towers over everyone here. I was wondering why they hadn't picked him to bow down to. He seemed a much more logical choice and he is an important man.

I tried to give the bouquet back to the girl but she wouldn't let me. (She spoke no English.) "Take it," the old man said. "It's of no use to her now that it is given in your name."

What name? I wondered, for they couldn't possibly know my name, but I took it. My husband still leaned against the wall weak from laughing.

"And why not?" I said. "What's so funny?"

I knew I should be laughing at myself, too. Not take myself so seriously, and I wouldn't have if my husband hadn't kept on and on and not even looked at me to see if there really was anything special about me, though I knew there wasn't. As we continued, only (as we'd said to each other before), "only a little bit lost"—for behind us, on that same Bogashtha Stah, was our hotel—as we kept walking other passersby didn't even look at me. Perhaps I had my face buried in the bouquet. I did keep sniffing it. It wasn't as if I was used to getting flowers anymore. It had been a long time since I'd had some. I kept saying how nice they were, partly just for spite, and they really were nice. The flowers here are spectacular and strange . . . sexy flowers with long, fuzzy stigmas, branched stamens, pendulous styles. I'd never seen the like before.

But then it did happen again. This time a boy—a ragged little thing sitting on the curb—looked at me and his face lit up with such delight that I was delighted myself, especially to see such a look on the face of this forlorn little creature, and then he, also, fell to his knees, forehead on sidewalk. Then a young couple just behind him did the same and then a woman my own age, rather plump, as I am, though she was very short and, of course, brown-skinned and had those lovely almond eyes. She bowed down as the others did and then raised herself to kiss my dress. And then the people brought more flowers, four, five bouquets, big ones, and spread them out in front of me as though I was to walk on them, and more people came. They smiled and I smiled back, rather tentatively because I didn't have any idea what was going on. But suddenly I felt my arm grabbed from behind just above my elbow and in a grip that hurt. For a moment I panicked and tried to twist away, but I couldn't, and then I saw it was my husband. He hurried me through the crowd at a trot, scattering the flowers, trampling them, bumping into people and making me do it, too. When we got to the corner he jumped on an already moving bus and pulled me up with him.

"That was a dangerous thing to do," I said when I had caught my breath. "I'm too old for that." Really, I was put out at having been pulled away from those flowers and smiling faces, and so roughly that my arm still hurt. Also he had laughed at me for something I thought rather nice.

"Too old for *this*," he said, "*this!*" And then he turned his back on me and when there was a vacant seat he took it for himself, though that's not his usual way. He has always kept a certain decorum in our relationship even when we're alone. It helps make things go smoothly between us, and I appreciate that.

We rode without speaking for what must have been a half an hour. I knew he needed to cool off so I kept silent. The bus was now circling a slum. I was worried, but I thought all we'd have to do to get back would be to cross the street and take the same numbered bus back, though there wasn't a number on it, but a symbol. I looked it up in my phrase and symbol book. It meant big tree and big, big tree. The bus crossed a long rather rickety bridge and my husband began to look a bit worried, too. He stood up and, at the other side of the river, we got off, crossed the street and waited for a bus going back.

This was the edge of the city. Huts were all along the banks of the river, but behind them were fields of what looked to me like red amaranth though I wasn't sure. Several dirt roads converged at the bridge. One road was so small, little more than ruts, it looked as though it hardly mattered at all.

We'd both cooled down by then and we were both worried, which brought us closer to each other. I felt like reaching out and holding hands, but I didn't, especially since I knew the whole thing was my fault. When things happen like that on the street, I should do as I've been taught all my life, look straight ahead, pay no attention, above all no eye contact, and keep walking. I know that. "I'm sorry," I said. "I shouldn't have let it happen. I should have known better. I *do* know better."

He grunted that he'd heard. It wasn't much of an answer, but I felt better for having apologized anyway, and that's the important thing, or so they say.

We waited. A few buses came but so full of people and goats and turkeys that we hesitated to get on, though my husband went to the doorway of each and asked "Bogashtha?" but the drivers all said, no, or what we took as no, so we waited and waited, sitting on a marker stone. Finally my husband said, "Next bus that comes we take, no matter what."

By now the sun was as though sitting in a notch between two of the mountains, and about to go down. As soon as it did, the wind began to blow and it got colder. Many people began to cross the bridges on foot now, most carrying big, raggedy bundles. They all seemed tired and hardly noticed us at first, but then it happened again. Two women saw me and there was that same look of joy as before. I felt my own spirits lift as theirs did. Other people looked at me then, too, and they stopped being tired and bowed down, some, again, putting their foreheads on the ground. I said, as I'd said before, "Please. No need for that."

This time my husband was too tired to laugh, but gave a disgusted "Humph." And then they began to lay things at my feet . . . odd things that they happened to have with them, a star fruit, a cashew fruit, a purple melon, a little bag of strange, round seeds . . .

"We can't eat any of this," my husband said, but I was so hungry I thought I would in spite of the dangers we'd been warned about and I nibbled a star fruit without even trying to wipe it off, which probably wouldn't have done much good against all the things they'd told us we might catch.

Then some of the women saw that I was shivering and gave me their shawls, old and ragged shawls, but they had that special beauty that these people weave into everything they wear, those reds and pinks and honey yellows. I suppose the shawls looked funny over my packable nylon print dress and with my pearls, but I felt better as soon as I wrapped them about me. The people laughed and nodded when I did it, but I hated, anyway, to take anything of theirs. They had so little, but it did seem as if it was a pleasure for them to give things to me. My husband said the shawls probably had fleas on them, but by then I cared less about fleas than I did about keeping warm. After all, I only had on my light dress while he had his suit jacket.

I had very little money with me as I always depended on my husband for that, but I decided to hand it all out to them—they hadn't asked me for any, but I wanted to. My husband said it was like overtipping and would ruin their whole economy . . . make them discontented, but I did it anyway. After all, I didn't have that much.

"You're enjoying yourself, aren't you?" my husband said. "You love all this attention." I realized he was right. I *was* enjoying myself. Nothing at all like this had ever happened to me and I liked it.

Then a man came up to us who spoke some English and asked me to say a few words to the people. "Please, Mrs.," he said, "speak of this unexpected meeting. Just a few words," and he said he would translate.

"Good Lord!" my husband said. Of course he knew I'd never spoken in public in my life and he was right to worry that I'd make a fool of myself, but I did want to thank the people. I felt so much warmer wrapped up in their shawls and I was happy with the reds and oranges and the soft wool of them. Softer than most. Odd, here they were with almost nothing of material wealth and yet their clothes were the softest and warmest I'd ever felt.

I thought, then, how hardly any of them could speak English anyway, so I did speak. "All these nice things," I said. "You are so kind." I was trying to speak clearly and simply so if they knew any English at all they could understand. "We were cold and hungry, but now we'll be fine because of you. Thank you. Thank you."

Then the translator began to talk and he went on and on, his voice rising and falling with emotion. It wasn't possible that he was translating what I'd said unless he was repeating it ten or twelve times with different words and inflexions. It's the usual thing, I thought. Nobody ever pays any attention. I've often said I might as well be talking to the wall.

My husband tried several times to interrupt and even became quite harsh with him, but the man wouldn't stop. Then my husband tried to pull me away as he had before, but the translator grabbed my other arm so that I was jostled back and forth between them even as the translator talked. They were both strong men, though the translator was small, and, though my husband gave several hard jerks, the translator managed to keep hold of me. My shoulder hasn't been the same since and I had bruises—five little black and blue spots for each of their fingers—on each of my arms.

When the translator finally stopped talking, the people cheered and surged toward us. There must have been a hundred or more by now and, though they were all smiling, it was frightening. Then two small but stolid men lifted me to their shoulders before I or my husband knew what they were doing and began to trot down the road with me—down that tiny road that led away from the bridge and toward the mountains, and all the people followed and began to sing.

The translator trotted by my side and said their song was about how, "Mountains will rise yet higher." I wanted to ask him what that meant, but I wasn't sure I could trust him to give any right answers anyway. "A known song," he said, "a very, very, very known song. 'Uphold us with your own right hand.' You," he said, pointing at me. "Birds will be fed. As a child, birds."

I could see my husband also in the crowd, towering over all the others, but he was having a hard time staying near me. The translator had been having a hard time, too, but now he was holding on to my ankle so as not to be swept away from me. I wondered that my husband hadn't thought to do it, but perhaps he hadn't had the chance. I could see he was struggling, though, and I felt warmed that he would work so hard for my sake. The translator saw me looking back and said not to worry, that he would take care of me, which did not reassure me.

We went on and on, the ground rising sharply now that we had passed the fields so that I worried about those who carried me— these small men hardly as tall as I, and I'm not thin . . . not at all thin. I wondered how they had the strength. I saw my husband far behind now, looking red and out of breath even though he had no one to carry, though of course there was the unaccustomed altitude.

Then the road became a mere trail. Hardly room for one person.

I was carried sideways and the crowd thinned out to a long, long line. I was frightened when I looked at the steep drop to the right of us, but the men were like mountain goats.

Whenever the trail allowed it, the translator held on to my foot and talked to me. "For you," he said. "This is all for you and in your name." I asked him what name, but he would only answer, "Yours, Mrs."

It was almost dark when we rounded a curve and before us was a hanging valley, steep, but not too steep to stop there for the night. Fires were already being started, but everyone came and called out to me. "They're asking you to speak," the translator said. "Open your arms. Point out the moon and its star."

"You'll just tell them anything you please. Why should I speak at all?"

He squeezed my foot until it hurt. "You must. It doesn't matter what you say. These are your lucky days. The moon shines in your eyes and in your white hair. Moon is the name of the mole on your chin. You have a star on your cheek."

Yes, I do have a star—one of those blood vessel bunches. I forget what you call them. I was going to have it fixed. I didn't think it would ever be important.

Then here was my husband, climbing up toward us. I thought maybe he'd given up. He could have turned around and walked the easy way, down and over the bridge and gotten help in town. That probably would have been the logical thing to do, but here he was, for once not logical, pale and panting, and I felt that warmth for him again. Perhaps this would be a whole new beginning for us. He might rescue me, though it was hard to tell if I needed rescuing or not and, actually, I wasn't sure I wanted to be rescued even if I needed to be. At least not yet. Things were happening. I'd always wanted things to happen and nothing much ever had. For a long time I'd been feeling that I was trying to play the part of myself as though I were a character in a drama that wasn't even about me.

"Speak," the translator said. "They won't put you down until you do." I saw that that was true, and that, for their sakes, I should speak and so I did. I said how the thing on my chin was a mole and the thing on my cheek was just a bunch of blood vessels that I'd forgotten the word for, and that I was an ordinary person. Then the translator spoke. He was too tired to go on very long this time, but I was sure what he said had nothing to do with what I'd said. Once the people even cheered.

Then they put me down on a pile of blankets that had been prepared for me. My husband came up and collapsed beside me. Women brought us soup, just one bowl for us to share. (I tried, surreptitiously, to give the most to him while I could see that he tried, surreptitiously, to give the most to me.) My husband said that the translator had told him not to worry, that help would be on its way soon, that he, the translator, would see to it, and my husband had given him a hundred-dollar bill. I thought about what he'd said about their economy and how I'd hardly given out ten dollars worth of coins, but I didn't mention it. Perhaps it was different giving it all to one person. We were too tired to talk much. Again I said I was sorry and curled up close to him. I felt guilty that I'd somehow gotten us out here cold and dirty and in even more altitude than before, wrapped up in ragged blankets that smelled of hay.

/ / /

In the morning we both felt better. How could we not? Wisps of clouds hung over each mountain top and mist streamed up our hanging valley from below. I hadn't seen anything so mysterious in a long time, if ever. I felt like a child, everything new and so much yet to know and see. Women came then and gave me a big skirt so I could urinate in privacy under it as they do, and we all went off—all us women, to the far side of the valley . . . they, laughing and talking. Then I had the idea that I would bow down to them as they had done to me, so I did that, and it made everybody happy. They taught me the words for sun, sky, mountain, cloud . . . I'm pretty good with languages and I'd already picked up other words. I was trying hard because of not trusting the translator. I knew their words for secret or sacred and non-secret or non-sacred. The translator's accent was so bad I couldn't be sure which was which.

"Women," the women said, laughing, "women, yes, yes," and I knew what they were saying, both their words and what they meant by it. "Men," they said, and pointed with their thumbs to the opposite side of the valley, turning toward it but covering their eyes at the same time. I also covered my eyes and laughed.

Then we women and the men came back together in the center of the valley and everybody had a bowl of grains of some sort. The translator sat beside me as we ate. "That is not the language of the city," he told me. "That is only ordinary mountain language. It is not worth learning. I can speak all the languages," he said, "from the lowest, which they speak here, to the highest, as the proof is this English I am speaking."

I was disliking the translator more and more. I couldn't stand him near me. I preferred the women even if I didn't understand them. "Go away," I said, which was quite unlike me. I even told him he was spoiling my breakfast, but then I realized how irritated I was sounding and tried to soften it. "You've been a great help," I said, "but I really would rather try to manage as best I can by myself."

"Mrs., I am still helping," he said. "Believe me, this language is no good."

Then the two little men lifted me again and this time my husband grabbed my leg and held on. "Speak," the translator said.

I didn't hesitate. I knew what to say. First I gave their greeting words—the ones I'd heard so often that morning. They were delighted. Then I pointed with my thumb—not like hitch-hiking, but straight out as I'd seen them do—pointing at the translator. "No," I said and waved him away. (I knew about the dangers of wrong gestures. I'd seen programs about that on TV, but I took the chance anyway.) Then I closed my mouth and covered it with my left hand, still pointing at the translator and would not speak until the women pushed him away. "You'll be sorry," he said. "Without my help, it is forever." After that I said all my new words with my arms raised and out. I said, sky, and sun, and mist. Then I said that word that meant either secret or sacred, and I pointed to myself and said, non-secret, or non-sacred, and they laughed again. I nodded and smiled back at them and everyone thought it was all very funny and so did I. Then we were on our way, again at a trot—my husband beside me this time—up, up, and over the mountain pass, and rounding down, and the view was like nothing I'd ever even imagined I would be privileged to see. Beyond and beyond, always more mountains, and far below another hanging valley, sister to the one we'd camped in the night before except for huge old trees scattered about it, and houses there, and things that glittered and lots of red, and you could hear a sound as of several piccolos a little out of tune. Faint. You could almost think it was the ringing in your ears.

The translator hovered, always a few yards behind us, and my husband, still holding my ankle, kept saying, "I don't know how we're going to get out of this mess without that man." I didn't answer. Besides, all I really cared about right then was how beautiful everything was.

Then we rounded a switchback and met five women coming up from below shaking wind-chime kind of things and playing little tin flutes that looked to be from the five-and-ten. When they got to me they kissed my hands and feet and they all said, "Thank

you," in English but only one could really speak it, though not very well. "It's you," she kept saying. "It's really you."

"Who?" I said. "Tell me who?"

"Mountains will rise yet higher," she said. "Birds will be fed. As a child, birds."

The five women played us down the mountain and soon we were at the entrance proper to the valley where carved wooden gates crossed the walkway from the rising cliff on one side to the drop-off on the other.

"If we go through these gates," my husband said, "we'll be prisoners. I'm going to give that translator another hundred dollars." At that moment I didn't care. Besides, feeling like a prisoner was nothing new to me. My husband must have seen something of this on my face. "If I were you," he said, "I'd not make that translator angry. He's the only one who can help us. I know he's utterly without conscience but he's sensible."

"Sensible," I said, and I was wondering of what use hundred-dollar bills were way out here.

"You've let this go to your head. You're thinking very well of yourself, that's easy to see, but you know you never even finished college." He was always reminding me of this, but this time in particular it didn't seem right, neither college nor hundred-dollar bills.

We went through the gates and entered the valley. Blue jays were everywhere and so tame that they sat on people's heads. And then those old, old, old trees . . . Ribbons and mirrors hung about them and beyond was the village, low, long, red houses, some quite large.

They brought me to what seemed the very oldest tree of all and sat me down facing it. The woman who could speak a little English said, "We want your forehead on the ground in front of her." So I did that, as they had done for me. I liked doing it, smelling the earth, touching it with my forehead. I even rested my cheek on a circle of lichen on a nearby stone. It was certainly a tree worthy of worship: rather short, but the widest I'd ever seen, and one whole side of it was dead. Still, here in front, one part struggled on, alive.

Then they tried to get my husband to do the same but he wouldn't. I told him I thought it might be best to do it, "under the circumstances," I said, "and it's nice to do—you'd be surprised." But he said he wouldn't bow down to any tree no matter what the circumstances. He was looking quite unlike my husband by now (and I suppose I was looking even less like myself than he looked like himself, for I had that big striped skirt on and several shawls). He was dirty and his suit was wrinkled and had sweat marks on the back and under the arms. He no longer had his tie. His left breast pocket looked funny now with its three little pens.

They all lined up and began a ceremony, singing and dancing, patting trees as if they were friends. Even the children came and danced with them. Some so small they must have only just learned to walk. I went to the old, old tree and put my arms around the part that was still alive and kissed it. I did it without thinking. I had the idea that, if I ever did get back home, what a nice thought it would be to know that my kiss was thousands of miles away and maybe three miles high. They noticed, of course, though they said nothing, but I didn't care who saw, I just wanted my kiss there: Hello and/or Good-bye. Whichever.

Then a bundle was brought out by the woman who could speak a little English. "A little bird," she said. "A flying snake," and she unwrapped it so I could see.

It lay so still at first I thought it was the statue of a child, painted utterly lifelike, brown with shiny black Chinese hair, and with those almond Indian eyes. He was naked and on his head was a crown of brilliant jay feathers. But then he blinked and made a soft sound. "He is in your name," the woman said, and, "He is secret and sacred." (She used both words in English.)

"My God!" That was my husband who had come up beside me. "My God, now what!" And then the child smiled and reached out to me and I to him, but the woman held him back. "No," she said, "you serve him in other ways. May you live long enough so that many small things should not suffer."

They brought me a bouquet of poison oak mixed with prickly teasels. They brought me buffalo burrs and Spanish dagger fronds. They brought me bitter fruit. I took everything. I didn't mind.

"You will enter a cave. There will be a long, steep tunnel. At the end of it you will be born into the place where a priest will already be dancing death. There will be many other things never seen in the light of day, but there will be women on each side of you and women front and back. Every new moon you will be asked if you accept what it is you must do. You will say yes though there will be times you'll want to say no. But most of the time you will live as we do and be looked up to, as we are all looked up to here. If you don't agree to this, you are free to go now, but it must be now."

It's odd that just when the woman said we were free to go and go now, my husband suddenly got very angry. He lashed out, punching men and even women, and yelling, saying everybody was insane. It took the small men several minutes to throw him down and tie his arms behind his back. They were brutal, but they had to be. He was like a crazy person though he was calling everybody else crazy. (Of course it wasn't the first time he'd called *me* crazy.)

Even when he was somewhat calmer, he still shouted out. He said I wasn't capable of answering for myself because I was as far from reality as they were. I'd even, all on my own, kissed a tree. I was escaping from the truth. He said my answer was no, and that I didn't have the sense to say it. He shouted no, then. "No, no, and no!" All this didn't make me angry anymore. I knew I had to decide, calmly, for myself.

"Reality" and "escaping." Those were the words that stuck with me. I have never thought my life to be particularly real, and it occurred to me that I didn't relish it much either, and I liked this whole adventure, including, or especially, the hardships. I do know pain and hardship aren't reality any more than joy is, but this place had both, and I'd not had either one. And it was full of beauty, and rituals, and the great, old trees, and mist, and earthquakes, and laughter. And I was to have a part to play. I'd never had a real part in anything before. I said yes.

"Crazy," my husband said, still panting from the exertion in this altitude. "You've no concept. No concept at all."

I said I knew I had no concept, but that I was willing to accept whatever this would turn out to be.

"You'll regret it."

"I'm sure there'll be times I will," I said, "but my life is already full of regrets."

So then a group left to take my husband back. There were just six of them including my husband and the translator. "We come back and get the Mrs.," the translator kept saying. "The police will come if you pay for it, Mr." But I'd never let anyone take me from my new real life.

CAROL EMSHWILLER
/ / /

I wrote these stories because I'm a writer, and I like to write, and I'm always sitting down at the typewriter. I hardly ever start out with a preconceived idea of what I'm going to write about. I write to find out what I want to write. I like to surprise myself. I'd never write if I knew too much about what I was going to do. These stories (mostly) turned up as I was improvising. They grew out of first sentences and first paragraphs that looked promising. They seemed to come out of my fingers, not my mind. My mind, it has always seemed to me, isn't very clever — is too pedestrian. My fingers and my typewriter seem much smarter.

This doesn't mean that things don't come out formed. I believe in structure, though not always the standard plot structure (though I believe in that, too). I think up my structures and plots as I go along. I throw out all sorts of clues and foreshadowings. In my more plotted stories I have tried to get my characters into difficult situations I'm not sure I can get them out of. I like

to look down at what I've written and think: "Oh my God, how will my hero or heroine get out of this?" and I like it when I think my protagonist has solved the problem but that turns out not to be true. Take "Looking Down." I thought my bird-man was going to escape and fly away and maybe have a different problem of surviving the winter, but he got recaptured and chained up more securely than ever. I knew that was right for the story and that I had to find a different pathway for the story from the one I'd expected. And in "The Start of the End of It All," when I found myself writing that all those cats had washed up on shore, I thought, "How am I going to solve this?" But I knew it was right. And I knew that, if I couldn't solve it, I'd have to back up and take the cats out, but I hoped I wouldn't have to, and I didn't.